UNLEASHED

Dark Moon Shifters One

BELLA JACOBS

D1568501

UNLEASHED

Dark Moon Shifters Book One

By Bella Jacobs

To all the brave women who inspire me daily. Thank you for your big, beautiful, fearless hearts.

ABOUT THE BOOK

One woman on the run. Four dangerously sexy body-guards. And a war brewing that will change the shifter world forever...

I'm living on borrowed time, fighting for survival against a deadly new virus that has no cure and a cult doing its best to brainwash me.

But when a mysterious note shows up on my windowsill one night, its chilling message--*Run, Wren*--launches me out of the frying pan and into the fire.

Within hours, everything I thought I knew about my life, my family, and my origins is obliterated, and I'm racking up enemies at an alarming rate.

Between the cult I've just escaped, a violent shifter faction out for my blood, and an ancient evil who eats "chosen ones" like me for breakfast, my last hope is to join forces with four dangerous-looking men who claim they were sent to guard my life.

Luke, a werewolf with a rap sheet.

Creedence, a lynx shifter who never met a mark he couldn't con.

Kite, a bear kin with a mean right hook and heart of gold.

And Dust, my childhood best friend and dude voted least likely to be a secret shape-shifting griffin.

But are these men really what they seem?

Or are my alpha guardians hiding a secret agenda of their own?

I'm not sure, but one thing is for certain—choosing the right allies will mean the difference between life and death. For me, and everyone I love.

UNLEASHED is book one in the Dark Moon Shifter's series. It is a true reverse harem featuring one woman and her four mates.

CHAPTER 1

WREN

I don't believe in ghosts. I don't believe in ghosts. I don't—
Believe.
In ghosts.

Palms sweating and a sour taste rising in my throat, I stand tall, forcing a smile to my face for the next girl in the cafeteria serving line.

She has red hair and moon-glow skin just like Scarlett. But she isn't Scarlett.

She isn't, she isn't, she isn't...

This is just my virus-addled brain playing tricks on me.

I refuse to get my hopes up. I know better. After eight years and a dozen cases of mistaken identity—racing after a woman boarding a train or taking a stranger's hand at the farmer's market—I know my sister is never coming back to me.

Scarlett is gone. Forever.

Scarlett is dead, and I don't believe in ghosts. Only the kooky extremists and the old hippies in our church actually believe in things that go bump in the night and exorcisms and all the rest of the crazy. The rest of the Church of Humanity movement is firmly grounded in reality and helping people come together to make a better world.

Which means not scaring away newbies to the movement by rushing up to hug them like they're your long-lost best friend.

As the girl slides her tray closer, her blurred features come into sharper focus, revealing a forehead that's too wide, a nose that's too sharp, and blue eyes instead of brilliant, glittering green. She isn't Scarlett, but the sadness dragging at her delicate features reminds me of my sister, and my throat goes tight as I ask her, "Beef stew or veggie?"

"Um...either one is fine, thanks," she whispers, ducking her head to hide behind a shock of dirty auburn hair. "Whatever."

"Well, I can't get enough of the veggie. The tofu has great flavor," I say gently, "but I'd love for *you* to choose. I want to make sure you get what you'd like best. Your opinion matters."

The girl looks up sharply, suspicion blooming in her tired eyes. I smile in response, silently assuring her this isn't a prank and I'm not being a smartass B-word. I truly care about her opinion and her preferences. I care about *her* and every teen who comes into the Rainier Beach C of H shelter.

After three years as an assistant coordinator, this is

my shelter now. And in my shelter, every soul is precious and valued. Any staff members who thought differently were relocated when I took the reins last August. And I intend to hold on tight to those reins through this relapse and all the pain, dizziness, and exhaustion that goes with it.

I may only be able to work part-time, but the hours that I am here, I'm all in.

When Lance, one of our regulars, sighs heavily behind the new girl and grumbles, "Just pick something already," I shoot him a gentle, but firm, look and say, "It's fine, Lance. We're not in any rush." I glance back at the girl. "What's your name, honey?" I just got here an hour ago and haven't had time to look over the new intake forms.

"Ariel," she mumbles, glancing nervously between Lance and me.

"Like the mermaid." I grin. "That was my favorite cartoon when I was little. My sister has pretty red hair like yours, and she would let me brush it while we watched and sang along with all the songs."

Ariel's lips curve shyly. "That's my sister's favorite princess, too." She blinks, her smile vanishing as quickly as it appeared. "Or, at least it was. I haven't seen her in a couple of years. Not since my stepdad kicked me out."

I want to hurry around the counter, pull her into my arms, and promise her things are going to be better for her from now on. She's at a Church of Humanity Shelter, not one of the poorly funded nightmares on the east side of town. No one will hurt her here. No one will judge her. It's finally safe for her to grieve and grow and begin to heal from all the horrible things she's no doubt been through as a beautiful young girl living on the streets of post-Meltdown Seattle.

But I've learned to keep my heart off my sleeve and my touchy-feely hugging instincts in check.

A lot of the kids in my care have yet to learn the difference between touch that offers comfort and touch that makes demands—sometimes ugly demands. Until they make it clear a hug is welcome, I keep my hands to myself.

Instead I lean in and whisper confidentially, "I bet Ariel is still her favorite. Once you go mermaid, you never go back. I still have mermaid pictures on my wall and I'm a grown woman." I cast a glance at Lance as I add with mock seriousness. "But keep that just between us, okay? Gotta keep my street cred."

"What street cred?" Lance snorts. "It's too late, Miss Frame. We all know you're a hopeless cheese case by now. The secret's out. Now give the girl some stew before she passes out." He nudges Ariel's arm gently with his elbow. "You're starving, right?"

Ariel laughs softly and nods. "Yeah. I am." She grins across the counter at me, hope cautiously creeping into her eyes. "I'll have the beef stew, please. I'm a meat eater in a big way."

"A girl after my own heart," Lance booms, making Ariel laugh again as she scoots her tray down toward the dessert station. "Two servings of beef for me, please, Miss F. I'm starving after all that nature exploration shit today."

"Language," I admonish, but my heart isn't in it.

Lance came to us an angry street kid with two misdemeanors for drug possession and a history of taking out his frustration with life on smaller teens. After six months, he's become a kind young man who enjoys helping the newbies at the shelter fit into our rhythms and who volunteers for campus clean up and laundry duty without being asked.

All it took to unlock his heart was for someone to show him how to turn the key. He just needed someone to care about him first, to show him he was worth it, so he could start learning how to love himself and others. It's simultaneously so simple and so hard, and I'm so, so proud of him.

"You're doing great, Lance." I mound his tray with as much stew as I can fit into the main compartment on his plate. "I appreciate the light you shine around here."

Lance's cheeks go pink beneath his golden-brown skin as he rolls his eyes. "Yeah, yeah, Miss F, don't get sappy on me. Trying to play it cool in front of the new girls."

"You know the policy on inter-shelter dating, Lance," I remind him, arching a brow.

"Yeah, yeah." He flashes a bright-white smile over his shoulder as he slides his tray away. "But a guy can dream. I won't be here forever, you know."

The words make my chest ache. It's true. He won't be here forever. That's the hardest part of my job— falling in love with these kids and then seeing them go off to foster families, most often never to return.

I don't blame them for wanting to leave the past in the past and move on with their lives, but that doesn't keep me from missing them. From wondering where they are and wishing we could stay one big extended family.

But that's part of my own set of mental glitches—I hate for people to leave. Too many people have left me already. First the biological mother and father I can't remember, then my best friend, Dust, and finally my sister, the person who meant the most to me in the world. She was my hero, my protector, my playmate, and my confidante. She was everything I wanted to grow up to be, even though she never made it past the age of nineteen.

I've been thinking of her more than ever recently.

For a time, years after the fire, I was able to put her out of my mind for days, sometimes even weeks, and go about my life.

But now...

Now my health is failing the same ways hers failed.

Now there are days when I can't get out of bed, the agony burning through my bones is so bad.

There are moments—flashes of despair—in which I consider taking a few too many steps at the edge of the train platform. I don't want to die, but I don't know how much longer I can live with the pain, the weakness, the uncertainty of whether I will ever go back into remission.

The virus my drug-addict bio-mom caught from a dirty needle and passed on to both of her daughters is a Meltdown disease, one of the many exotic new autoimmune viruses that oozed out of the polar ice caps as they melted to near nothingness in the years before I was born. Researchers and scientists are working as fast as they can to find cures for the Devour virus and the other diseases plaguing humanity, but a cure is still decades away.

I won't live to see it. Not unless there's a miracle.

There are days when that's okay with me, when I'm grateful that there will soon be a day when I won't have to drag my body out of bed, stuff my mouth full of ten different kinds of meds, and fight to pass as a normal, functional adult anymore.

And then there are days like today, when I look out at a cafeteria filled with once hopeless kids, now laughing and chatting and eating with the gusto of healthy people who need fuel for all the big things they're going to do with their lives, and I pray for another year.

Two.

Three or more—if somehow my body can be convinced to stop attacking itself.

"We good to close the line, boss?" a voice rumbles softly from beside me, making my cheeks heat.

That's what he does to me, this man who is another reason I would like to stick around a little longer. Long enough to see what having a steady boyfriend might be like, maybe...

Or at least long enough to see if Kite's kisses are as lovely as the hugs he gives me every evening as we say goodbye and head for our separate train stops.

"Yeah, let's close up." I turn, smiling up at him as whips off his hairnet with a relieved sigh, setting his long, glossy black hair free to stream around his broad shoulders. "Aw, poor Kite," I tease. "I'm telling you, you're pulling off the hairnet. It's a solid look for you. You should take a selfie."

His rich brown eyes narrow on mine. "Very funny, Bird Girl," he says, the nickname making me grin even wider. "Are we saving the peach cobbler, or can I pack up what's left for the staff?"

I glance over at the warming pan to see only a few inches of untouched cobbler. "Go ahead and wrap it up for the staff. You're going to make Carrie Ann's day. She lives for an excuse to have dessert for breakfast."

"Amen!" Carrie Ann, my right-hand woman, cruises by with an arm full of dirty salad bar dishes bound for the kitchen. Her blond bob is still safely secured under her hairnet and her face is makeup free, but she looks as adorable, a real-life pixie with a mischievous grin that always lifts my spirits. She flashes it now as she says, "Make mine a big one, Kite. My legs are jelly from that hike around the bay. I need sugar to restore me. Lots of it."

I keep my grin in place, refusing to feel envious of my friend or the others who were able to make the hike around the new beach line today, exploring the places where the rising ocean has intruded and where Seattle's manmade barriers to the overflow are holding strong.

Yes, I would have loved to spend hours out in nature with Kite, absorbing his teachings on native flora and fauna, interspersed with the always fascinating stories passed down from his grandfather—former chief of the Samish Indian Nation—but I learned a long time ago not to waste energy feeling sorry for myself.

Besides, Kite will fill me in on our way to the train. He always does. My newest hire is not only a gentle giant with a heart of gold and a knack for winning over even the surliest street kid, he's also patient, generous, and thoughtful.

And gorgeous, a wayward voice whispers in my head.

I avert my gaze, pretending great interest in the chafing dishes as Carrie swoops in to grab the empty green bean container near my elbow. I'm not ready to let Kite see how much appreciation I have for his sculpted features, silky hair, and big, burly, and completely snuggle-perfect body. I have as many fantasies about curling up in Kite's arms and going to sleep with my head on his chest as I do about other, racier things. Maybe it's a side effect of being so tired all the time—nap fantasies are totally a thing for sicklies like me—but I don't think so.

I think it's a side effect of him being absolutely adorable.

"You need vegetables," Kite calls after Carrie as she scoffs and continues about her business. "For a grown woman, you're eating habits are shameful."

"Good thing I'm not done growing yet," Carrie Ann shoots back as the kitchen door swings closed behind her.

Kite turns to me with a sigh. "Someone needs to teach that girl the basics of good nutrition."

"I've tried," I say, turning off the warmers beneath the stew. "But she's set in her ways. Sugar, caffeine, and sliced deli meat are her three basic food groups. Maybe she'll rethink things when she's older. She's only twenty; she has time." I reach for the edges of the chafing dish, engaging my abs as I prepare to lift the metal container. It's half empty and can't weigh more than ten pounds, but I still struggle to work it free, sweat breaking out in the valley of my spine as I slide it to the edge of the counter.

"Here, let me." Before I can protest, Kite claims the meat dish in one hand and lifts the leftover tofu stew free with the other, making it all look as effortless as plucking a couple of summer cherries out of a bowl.

"I could have done it," I say, but Kite is already headed toward the kitchen.

"Just wipe down the serving line, boss," he calls back. "Let your minions take care of the heavy lifting."

He's clearly trying to dismiss my struggle with a joke, but it isn't funny. It's demoralizing, and the way my arms are trembling as I finish cleaning the serving line is enough to make me want to grind my teeth in frustration.

By the time Carrie Ann sidles up beside me, clutching her Tupperware container of cobbler, I'm fighting tears.

Like the sweetheart she is, she puts a hand on my back and reminds me, "You don't have to do any of this, you know. Kite, the others, and I are happy to do the grunt work."

I shake my head. "But I hate that. I feel like such a diva."

"Oh, please." Carrie laughs her bright, musical laugh, making a few of the kids seated nearby glance our way with smiles instinctively curving their lips.

That's what Carrie's laugh does to people, and one of the many reasons she's the best choice for my replacement when the time comes. Other people have more education and fancier degrees, but Carrie is an upbeat force of nature who lifts the spirits of everyone she meets.

And she knows exactly where these kids are coming from. Just four years ago, Carrie was one of them, one of the shattered souls that ended up on our doorstep after the rough streets of Seattle chewed her up and spit her out. But, lucky me, this time one of the new friends I'd made stuck around to join our crew on a more permanent basis.

"You're the farthest thing in the world from a diva," Carrie continues, gazing up at me. "You're the hardest working woman I know. And we need your brain and your heart more than we need your muscles. Seriously, when you come in tomorrow, sit your ass down in your office and give your energy to your counseling sessions. That's where you work the magic. Anyone can man the serving line, Wren—even Kite, though he clearly was never taught how to properly clean up after himself."

"I heard that," Kite calls from the bowels of the kitchen. "It's not my fault I have six older sisters who never let me in the kitchen."

Carrie rolls her eyes as she leans in to whisper, "Six older sisters. Can you imagine? I bet they used him as a dress-up doll when he was little."

"I heard that, too," Kite says, proving his hearing really is something extraordinary. "And no, they didn't, but I did have to wear their clothes until I was too big to fit into them." He emerges from the kitchen, two containers of cobbler held lightly in one hand. "My mother couldn't see the point in wasting good money on boy clothes since I was the last baby on the docket."

Carrie giggles, and I smile as I say, "Aw. I would pay good money to see those baby pictures. You in ruffles."

"Stay on my good side, and I'll show them to you for free someday," he says with a wink that sends warmth flooding through my chest. He turns to Carrie with a mock glare and adds, "But not you, Trouble. I'd never hear the end of it from you."

"Correct," Carrie cheerfully agrees, pressing up onto tiptoe to peck my cheek. "See you tomorrow, Sunshine. Text me if you want to chat later. I'm just hanging at home tonight, hiding from my miserable roommates and the cockroaches. No money to go catch a band until next payday."

"Will do. Get home safe," I say, sweet anticipation dumping into my bloodstream as she departs, leaving me alone with Kite.

It's my favorite time of the day, the fifteen minutes it takes to walk to the place where our paths diverge on the way to our separate train stations. I look forward to it from the moment my eyes creak open in the morning.

There are days, when I wake up aching and feverish in a nest of sweaty covers and roll over to be sick in the bucket by my nightstand, when this walk is the only thing that gets me out of bed. This walk is the lifeline I cling to as I force my throbbing joints into the shower to sit on the stool Mom bought for me a few months ago when she realized I no longer had the strength to stand under the stream until my meds had kicked in.

Unless something changes, there will come a day—a day not far from this one—when I will no longer have the strength to make this walk, either. But it isn't today. Today I am still alive and upright, and my meds are holding the pain at bay enough for me to enjoy the way my blood pumps faster as Kite rests a warm hand on my shoulder and asks, "You ready, boss lady?"

I nod, beaming up at him. "I am. Just let me grab my jacket and I'll meet you out front."

I make my way slowly to my office, conserving my energy, wanting to save it all for the walk through the misty spring afternoon with Kite.

I may not have many afternoons like these left, but that isn't a reason for sadness. It's a reason to savor, to treasure, to soak up every minute of sweetness and pack it away for a day when I'll need good memories more than ever.

CHAPTER 2

WREN

Outside the air smells like cedar and the salty, fish-and-earthworm scent of the bay. I know a lot of people find the smell offensive, but I don't mind it. It reminds me of home. My parents' house was once three miles inland—back when it belonged to Grandma Frame—but after the Meltdown, they ended up with beachfront property.

Pops jokes that someday I'll inherit a houseboat, but Mom doesn't find that funny. Sea rise, even the slightly slower creep of the past decade, scares her.

"So how did the hike go today?" I ask Kite as we step onto the sidewalk outside the shelter gates. "Lance and Carrie seemed to enjoy it, but I know you had some of our problem children along. Were Tawny and Gage respectful?"

Kite shrugs, the dimple in his right cheek popping as he says, "Define respectful…"

A soft huff of laughter escapes my lips. "This isn't

funny, Kite. I have to get those two on board. I can't protect them forever. If they don't at least pretend to try, the head of the shelter network is going to make me free up those beds."

Kite's grin fades as his chin dips closer to his chest. "I hear you. It's just hard… I know what it's like to get stuck in bad habits. It can take a long time to change."

"I still can't believe you used to beat people up for a living." I take the arm he offers at the curb, holding on to his elbow as we cross the deserted street. There isn't much traffic around here anymore. Since the schools and government buildings shut down due to flooding concerns, and half the local population relocated farther inland, there isn't much reason to be in Rainier Beach.

Not unless you're a fisherman or part of the shelter system taking advantage of cheap real estate.

"I did," Kite says, his voice somber. "I can't say I ever truly enjoyed it, but it gave me a sense of control. Being able to beat the hell out of anyone who threatened me or the people I cared about made me feel safe. And when you grow up like these kids, scared out of your mind, abused by the people who are supposed to be protecting you, safety is important. Safety is life. You know?"

I nod, brow furrowing. "I know. I mean, I don't *know*, but I can imagine."

"I know you can." Kite's free hand covers mine, holding my fingers in the crook of his arm as we step onto the curb on the other side of the street, making my heart soar a little higher.

He's touched me like this before, but even little signs

that he likes being with me as much as I love being with him make me giddy with hope.

"So maybe you can talk to Bill," Kite continues, "encourage him to give Tawny and Gage a little more time. Yeah, their behavior isn't great, but violence is what kept them alive to find a place where they get three square meals and a clean bed to sleep in. It's going to be hard for them to let that go. Even if they decide they want to."

"That's the part that worries me," I confess. "That they might not decide they want to in time. I can definitely appeal to Bill's better nature regarding the fights and bullying, but if Tawny and Gage are still openly hostile to the Church of Humanity movement, it's going to be an uphill battle to convince him to keep them around."

Kite grunts softly but doesn't respond.

He's quiet all the way up Potter street, past the black cottonwoods bursting with new leaves and the smoky, green, balsamic smell of bud break, past the creepy abandoned Bowman mansion where we usually take a moment to stop and stare, just to give ourselves a delicious case of the chills.

Soon we're nearly halfway to our separation point, and there's no longer any denying that the silence has become uncomfortable.

I pause at the end of the block, sliding my hand from his arm as I turn to face him beneath the trees of heaven, twin goliaths that reach splayed fingers toward the sky above a bungalow still sporting high-water marks from the last time the bay flooded two years ago. "Did I say something wrong?" I ask.

Kite sighs, meeting my gaze briefly before his falls to the sidewalk. "No, of course not."

I stuff my hands into my jacket pockets. "Well, that was convincing."

He grins again as he glances up, sending another jolt of electricity through me as our eyes connect. "Sorry. I just…" He shakes his head as his smile dims. "Never mind. It's not a big deal."

"No, please," I insist. "I want to know what's on your mind. I like your mind. It's a smart, interesting mind, and it often gives very good advice."

Kite's gaze warms. "I like your mind, too. I like how open it is to people who don't think the way you do or believe the things you believe."

I nod, slowly, then picking up speed at the pieces fall into place. "I see."

"Do you?" His dark brows climb higher. "I'm not saying the beliefs of your movement shouldn't be presented to the kids as an option. Faith is important, and it was one of the things that got me out of hell when I was going through it, but there are lots of different things in the world worth believing in. And making a safe place to sleep contingent on signing a pledge to join the C of H seems pretty harsh. And manipulative. And not what church is supposed to be about."

I curl my hands into fists in my jacket, hunching my shoulders against the cool wind picking up off the bay. "I know. And I agree with you. I mean, our beliefs have always made sense to me—humanity coming together beyond religious and cultural differences to put each other first seems like a no-brainer if we ever want to have peace on this planet—but I was raised in the C of H since I was a toddler. I don't know how I'd feel if I were coming to it as a teen who's been living on the streets, or as someone with strong religious beliefs they feel compelled to put ahead of the movement's teachings."

I glance back the way we came, skin prickling as I share something I know I shouldn't with someone outside the movement. "Honestly, a lot of the elders are on board with waiving the pledge. They say it makes our church look like the cult some people say we are, and that's bad for PR. But the motion hasn't passed committee, and I'm not sure what to do about that. I wrote a letter, but I'm too young to run for a place on the elder council, and even if I weren't…"

Kite lifts one big hand, gently smoothing my hair behind my ear, securing it against the breeze. "It's okay. You do the best you can. That's all any of us can do."

"I just wish I had more energy," I say, the words out before I can stop them. I never talk about my condition with Kite. I don't want to remind him that I'm not the shiniest apple in the barrel. Fair to him or not, I want him to pick me.

At least for a little while.

His jaw tightens and something that looks a lot like rage flickers across his features before the expression is gone, but it still leaves me speechless. I'm so shocked by that glimpse of something other than the gentleness I've always seen in Kite that I flinch as he cups my face in his hands and says, "Things can change, and they *will* change, Wren. I promise you. As long as there's breath in my body, you're not going to die. You've just got to be ready when the time comes."

I tip my head back, bringing my lips terrifying, thrillingly close to Kite's as my eyes go wide. I swallow hard, thoughts swarming in a mixture of confusion and longing. "What are you talking about? Ready for what?"

His brow furrows as he searches my face with an intensity that makes my stomach flip. "I've already said things I shouldn't. Just promise me you'll keep that beautiful mind of yours open, okay?"

"Kite, I don't—"

"Do you trust me, Wren?" he asks, using my given name for a second time in just a few minutes, making me realize how rarely he uses it and how rarely I've seen him with this kind of fire in his eyes.

"I…" I hold his gaze, but no matter how deep I look, I only see concern. Caring. Maybe something even stronger than caring. Maybe something close to the way I feel when I'm in his arms and the world suddenly makes more sense than it did before.

I exhale, heart slowing as I say, "Yes, I do. I trust you."

His shoulders sag with a relief that makes me feel like I've done something much more important than answer a question. "Good. Keep trusting me, Bird Girl, and I'm going to show you a whole new world. A world where you can be the powerhouse you are on the inside."

The backs of my eyes begin to sting, but I'm smiling when I say, "There's no cure, Kite. I might never go back into remission, let alone get better."

He pauses, seeming to debate something silently before he whispers, "But then again, you might." Before I can assure him that hope is a lost cause in this case, he leans down and presses his lips to mine, and I'm the thing that's lost.

My eyes slide closed as my heart lights up, each warm, sweet brush of his lips against mine filling my body with magic. Electricity floods my nerve endings, and my pulse races so fast I know I would fall over if Kite let me go.

But he doesn't let me go. He wraps me up in his strong arms, hugging me close as he lifts me off my feet, bringing our lips onto a level playing field as he takes charge of holding us both steady. With a soft sob of gratitude for this kiss, this miracle, this moment of feeling like the luckiest girl in Seattle, I wrap my arms around his neck and kiss him with everything in me, not caring if I use up all the energy I'll need to get home.

I'm always so careful—I've had to be in order to keep working long after most people with my condition would have taken to their beds for good—but I don't want to be careful right now. I want to be alive and wanted and on fire. I want to burn with this man who makes me feel things I never have before.

In just a few moments, Kite banishes every teenage kiss and every lukewarm make-out session from my memory, leaving nothing but his smoky, sexy, earthy taste in my mouth and his campfire and almond scent swirling through my head.

Finally, I have to pull away, coming up for air with a gasp that makes Kite rumble a soft, "Sorry. Didn't mean to suffocate you."

Biting my lip as I point the toes still dangling off the sidewalk, I tighten my grip on his shoulders. "I don't mind. Air is overrated."

He grins, his dark eyes alight with the same fire that's smoldering inside me. "You like me more than air?"

"I definitely like you more than air." A nervous laugh escapes my lips as I add, "I've liked you more than air for a while."

"I've liked you more than air for a while, too." His tongue sweeps across his bottom lip, making me long for another taste of him as he warns, "Don't look at me like that, Bird Girl."

"Like what?"

"Like you're hungry," he whispers, sending heat and a thick, achy feeling spreading between my hips, down to tingle across my thighs.

Before I can respond, the hollow notes of a wooden flute echo through the afternoon, and Kite curses. "Sorry," he says, setting me back on my feet. "I have to take this."

"That's fine." I sway but recover my balance fairly quickly considering how dizzy with lust I was a moment ago.

That's what that feeling was—*lust*. It's not something

I've experienced before, at least not with someone else present.

Back when I was in remission, there were nights when I would lie awake in the dark, fantasizing about the men in the books I read. I would fall into imaginary trysts with heroes from fantastical foreign worlds who would do anything to protect the women they love— slay dragons, battle armies of the undead, quest to the ends of the earth and back again to retrieve a cursed treasure—but none of the boys I casually dated in real life ever made me feel like this.

As Kite turns away, his broad shoulders hunched against the wind as he mutters softly into the phone, I realize with a zip of shock that I would very much like to climb him like a tree. I would like to climb him, wrap my legs around his waist, and devour him from the mouth down. I want his hands all over me, my hands all over him, and his mouth everywhere.

Absolutely everywhere...

For the first time in my life, I'm dying to be skin to skin, breath to breath, heart to heart, with a real live person. It's so dizzying that I miss the first several moments of Kite's conversation. It isn't until he softly hisses, "Yes, I understand, relax," and abruptly ends the call without signing off that I start making sense of words again.

"What's wrong?" I ask as he shoves his cell into his back pocket.

Kite shakes his head hard enough to send his silky hair sliding across his shoulders. "Nothing. Just work stuff."

My brows lift. "From the shelter?"

"No, my other work." He shoots me what looks like a forced smile. "I do some part-time stuff for a family business. That was my uncle, wondering why I'm not in the office yet."

"Tell him I'm sorry. I walk slowly. It's my fault."

Kite's lips soften into a genuine grin. "I think it was the kissing, not the walking, that slowed us down."

I blush as I return his smile. "Hmm…could be. But I'm not sorry about that. Not even a little bit."

"Me, either," Kite says, taking my hand. His palm is twice as large as mine, and his fingers far longer and thicker, but as we twine our hands together, it feels like they were meant to fit. It's so perfect I can barely keep myself from breaking out into a Snoopy Dance of happiness right there in the middle of the sidewalk.

I tell myself to relax—it was just a kiss, something most twenty-four-year-olds do all the time without having a coronary about it—but my heart keeps pounding so hard and fast it feels like it's going to punch a hole in my ribs. Finally, I lose the battle against a goofy little giggle.

"Come on, let's get you on the train." Kite laughs with me, clearly not concerned about playing it cool. "Uncle D has waited this long. He can wait a little longer."

"Are you sure? I'm fine to walk alone if you need to go," I say, hoping he can tell I don't mean a single word of that nonsense.

Kite's nose wrinkles. "Nah, screw that asshole." He

freezes, his lips pulling to the sides as he winces. "Sorry. I forgot about the language ban."

"It's fine," I assure him. "We're not at work, and I won't tell."

"I appreciate that."

"Anytime, motherfuckah," I say in my best impression of Eli, our resident gangster, making Kite throw back his head and laugh so hard I can feel the vibrations in my chest.

I bite my lip and bounce lightly on my toes, ridiculously pleased that my joke is going over so well. I rarely let the raunchier side of my humor out to play with anyone but Carrie, and that's usually only after she's let me have a puff of her joint in an attempt to spur my appetite into action. My parents are firmly anti-marijuana therapy—they say pills from a doctor are the only drugs their generation can get behind—but pot helps me feel hungry on days when the mere thought of putting food in my mouth turns my stomach.

And I figure what they don't know won't hurt them.

Speaking of things they don't know...

I weigh the fun of telling Mom and Pops that I met an amazing man against the backlash that will follow when they realize Kite works at the C of H, but isn't a card-carrying member of our movement, and decide to keep this afternoon's developments to myself.

I can tell Carrie, however, and I will...soon.

But for now I want to keep that kiss and this incredible laugh of his—how have I known him for four months and never heard this big, booming belly laugh?—to myself.

"You're funny, Bird Girl," he says as we start toward the station hand in hand, the fondness in the words making me happier than I have felt in ages.

"Thanks. But don't tell the board. They think I'm a very serious person."

"It'll be our secret," he assures me. "So you've never slipped up and let a curse fly at the shelter? Even when you walk into the dorms and realize Lance hasn't washed his socks in three weeks again?"

I shake my head. "Not yet. I got close the time I dropped a giant pot of chili on my foot, but so far, so good. At least at work. I do occasionally horrify my parents with a salty phrase during my monthly transfusion therapy. The meds they add to the donor blood burn so badly going in," I add, finding it so easier to talk about this stuff now that I know being sick isn't a dating deal-breaker for Kite. "But I think they're more worried about me horrifying the nurse than anything else. She's Church of Humanity, too, and her parents are both elders, so…"

Kite squeezes my hand. "That sucks."

"Tell me about it. Having one elder parent is bad enough. Poor Tricia, I'm sure she can't blow her nose without one of her parents telling her she isn't doing it right. Makes me glad my mom and dad are just normal followers and pretty laid back about all the covenants."

"Yeah. That's not what I meant, but…good for them." His tone clearly communicates contempt, but I can't quite tell who it's for.

Tricia? The elders? The movement in general?

Surely not my parents…

Just in case, I say, "Mom and Pops are definitely keepers. Since the day they adopted me, they've stood by me. No matter what. No matter how sick I got or how much my treatments cost or how long it's taking me to finish growing up and fly out of the nest. Hank and Abby are my rocks. I don't know what I'd do without them."

Kite can have contempt for my movement or the elders all he wants—there are days when I get punch-the-wall frustrated with the bureaucracy of it all—but if he goes after Hank and Abby, we're going to have a problem. Hank and Abby aren't just my adoptive parents; they're my friends and people I love with all my heart.

Thankfully, Kite squeezes my hand with a smile and says, "Hopefully you'll never have to find out," making it clear he gets where I'm coming from. And then he says, "And I hope you can meet my mom someday soon. She's the coolest, and she makes the most kick-ass sticky cinnamon bread. You'll love her," and my heart is so busy soaring I forget all about the uncomfortable moment that came before.

Kite wants to introduce me to his mom!

His mom, who he adores beyond all reason and who is the most important person in his life. He wants me to meet his most important person! Which means he must think I'm fairly important, too.

Again, I'm struck by the certainty that most women my age aren't as easily elated by something as minor as meeting the folks, but my illness kept me well behind the curve when it comes to dating.

And falling in love.

And all the rest of it…

Sex, Wren. If you can't even say the word to yourself, you're a lost cause, girl.

But I'm *not* a lost cause. That kiss proved it. I can experience desire as deeply and profoundly as any of the heroines in my favorite epic novels, and from here on out, who knows what's possible? I swear, the kiss even made me *feel* better. As Kite and I climb the stairs to the train platform, my legs are strong and steady, and by the time we reach the top, I'm only a little out of breath.

"See you tomorrow?" I pause in front of the turnstile, taking my time pulling out my train pass, secretly hoping for a repeat performance of that kiss.

"Not if I see you first." He leans down, pressing his lips gently to my forehead before he whispers against my flushed skin, "Get home safe, beautiful. And hang in there."

"I will," I promise, butterflies launching in my chest as he steps back, winking at me before he turns and jogs down the stairs, moving with that easy grace of his, so different than most of the big men I've known in my life.

But Kite isn't like any of the men or boys I've known. He's special, and he thinks I'm beautiful, and he kissed me like a real girl, not a person made of glass.

No, he kissed me like a *woman*.

As I claim my seat on the train, I gaze at the reflection staring back at me in the smeared train window. Same long, rather limp black hair, same pale blue eyes, same too-thin face, but there's something different about that chick...

That lady looks like she has a secret, a flame smoldering deep inside her, and a few tricks up her sleeve.

She looks like a woman with a reason to feel hopeful about the future.

A woman who's finally been thoroughly, properly kissed.

CHAPTER 3

WREN

I walk the last few blocks of my evening commute through pink sunset light, arriving at my front door just as the sun is slipping beneath the waves, that familiar musty sea scent welcoming me home.

At the end of our street, at the bottom of the last hill standing between civilization and the relentless encroachment of the sea, a massive concrete structure holds back the tide. But it will only stand firm for so long. At some point in the next fifty to sixty years, the ocean will overflow our puny mortal dams and levees and take possession of more of our coastlines, devouring more of the world's famous cities and landmarks.

On most days, the wall is a sobering reminder of how feeble human beings are beside the immortal forces of time and tide. But today, the sight of all that endless, churning sea unfurling to the horizon makes me giddy with possibilities.

There is an entire wild world out there to explore; there are mysteries waiting to be discovered and treasures waiting to be hunted, and I have been Kissed with a capital K, and suddenly the tight square frame hemming in my life has widened to a sweeping panorama.

I know I'm still living in the same condemned skin I left home in this morning, but logic is no match for the love bug, and I've been bitten hard.

It's probably just a crush and will most likely proceed the way my previous crushes have proceeded— a few rapidly cooling dates as my dude realizes how early I have to go to bed, a couple of lukewarm follow-up phone calls, and a terse breakup via text—but even as I try to talk myself back to earth, I can feel my heart soaring higher, riding giant fluffy eagle wings of anticipation.

Pushing through our weather-ravaged front gate, with the peeling paint Pops finally stopped fixing as it became clear the sea air was going to keep winning that battle, I tiptoe across the paving stones to our front door, careful not to step on any of the spring veggies filling every inch of the front yard. The garden used to be a backyard affair, but in the past few years, since Pops retired from the plumbing company he ran for nearly forty years, the garden has spread like a rash.

A delicious, oh-so-tasty rash...

My dad has a green thumb like nothing I've ever seen, and soon our spring and summer dinners will be overflowing with healthy treats. It's barely the first week of May, but already the asparagus are shooting elegant stalks from the dark earth next to baby spring lettuce with leaves like tiny fairy wings. The vegetables are as lovely to admire as they are to eat—arranged in paisley-shaped beds that form a quilt of green in front of our white bungalow—but today, I don't stop to soak in the botanical art.

For the first time in weeks, I'm actually eager to get to the dinner table. Mom's a killer cook, but the meds that help me get out of bed usually have the nasty side effect of turning my stomach to acid by five o'clock. By the time I get home from serving the kids dinner at the shelter, it's always after six and I'm sporting a bilious lava pit where my belly should be.

But today I'm ravenous, starving for food as well as for new and fantastical experiences with irresistible men.

Maybe I'll call him after dinner, I think as I push through the door, calling, "I'm home," as I hang my jacket on the hook by the door.

After all, I'm a grown woman, and I have Kite's phone number. Why not call him and tell him how much I enjoyed our walk home? Why not ask him if he wants to meet up for lunch this weekend or maybe a walk around downtown? Kite doesn't seem like the kind of guy who would care if a girl makes the first move, and I prefer not to waste time I could be getting to know him better, staring at my cell, waiting for *him* to call me.

One of the good things about living on borrowed time is that it makes you brave.

Ballsy, even.

I grin as I head into the kitchen, anticipating the smell of veggie lasagna or roasted chicken, one of Mom's Thursday night staples, but the sunny kitchen is empty and the stove still and cool.

Nose wrinkling in disappointment, I turn, searching the backyard, figuring that's where my parents must be whiling away this lovely evening. Sure enough, I spot them by the far end of the fence, but instead of up to their elbows in potting soil, they're both huddled around Mom's phone, anxious expressions tightening their features. The worry creasing Mom's pale brow reminds me they aren't getting any younger.

The Frames adopted my sister and I late in life, after they realized they couldn't have children of their own. Now, Pops is pushing seventy, and Mom's not far behind at sixty-five. Her blond bob is now more gray than gold, and all the fretting she's done in the past twenty years—first over my sister and then over me—is starting to show on her face.

Sadness worms through me, banishing the giddiness that followed me home. I know Mom and Pops chose Scarlett and me with their eyes wide open—they knew we were both sick when they signed the adoption papers—but I can't help feeling guilty sometimes. Knowing a child is ill is one thing; standing by a kid you've come to love while they fight a losing battle for life is another.

I know it's been hard on my parents. Especially when Scarlett started lashing out, and then later, after the addiction treatment facility where they'd sent her to get help burned to the ground.

If only the police had been able to recover her body, maybe it would have been easier on all of us. Maybe we would have been able to grieve and move on instead of turning to search a crowd every time a woman with Scarlett's particular autumn-leaves shade of red hair walks by. But Scarlett's dorm was right above the blast. When the furnace exploded, it obliterated the first floor, sending the entire Greater Good treatment center sagging into its foundation.

The police said it was deliberate—a makeshift bomb likely fashioned by one of the troubled kids housed at the facility—and that whoever had detonated the device was no doubt dead, as well.

They shared the news in a way that inferred we should find that comforting.

But another kid dead didn't make anything better. It didn't bring Scarlett back, it didn't assuage my parents' guilt for sending her away in the first place, and it didn't give any of us closure. We grieved for a long, long time, and we're still not the people we were before we lost my sister.

Still, I haven't seen Mom look this worried in years. Even after Pops ends the call and their conversation becomes something private, her brow remains furrowed and her lips turned down hard at the sides.

The realization sends a shiver across my skin, lifting the hairs on my arms and at the back of my neck. Before the goody-two-shoes voice in my head can talk me out of eavesdropping, I slip to the back door and creak it slowly open, straining to catch part of the conversation outside.

"It could work. It could change everything…" Pops's voice is deep, solid, but tinged with doubt.

Mom takes his hand, giving it a firm squeeze as she assures him, "It's going to work. She's going to get well, and the future will be wide open for our baby. She's going to have a real life and real hope and maybe, some-day, precious babies of her own. Can't you imagine? That beautiful life for her?"

The words send tears springing to my eyes. I know how much my parents want me to get well, but I've never heard either of them sound so desperate. That, more than anything else—my exhaustion or the rest of my symptoms—makes me realize how close I am to the end, how quickly my time is running out.

I move away from the back door, pressing a fist to my lips as my throat works, willing the wave of emotion to pass. I have no idea what my parents are talking about or what's given them hope this time—hopefully not another quack doctor wanting to pump me full of pomegranate juice mixed with flax seed oil or some-thing equally pointless—but I have to pull myself together before they come in, or they'll realize I've been listening to things I shouldn't.

Sucking in a breath, I close my eyes and try to relax, but all I see in the darkness is Scarlett's face, gone fuzzy around the edges because my weary brain has started to forget what she looked like.

CHAPTER 4

WREN

I'm about to retreat to my room to find my center, but before I can make it out of the kitchen, the door bursts open and my mom calls, "Wren, baby! There you are! Oh honey, I'm so glad you're home!"

A moment later, her arms are around me from behind, hugging me tight before turning me gently around and lifting her shaking hands to my face. She's barely five feet and a smidge tall, a good seven inches shorter than my five eight, but Abby Frame has a presence that fills a room.

I'm immediately enveloped in her warm energy and the glow of her smile as she says, "It's happening, sweetheart, the day we've been praying for."

"What's happening?" I glance up at Pops, who's still standing by the door, his muddy boots on the mat.

He smiles tentatively in response, hope and caution warring in his brown eyes as he waves Mom's way. "Let

Abby tell it. She's the one who found the doctor. She should get to share the good news."

I shift my focus back to Mom, forehead furrowing. "Another doctor? Mom, you know I'm happy to go see anyone you want me to see, but I've already been to—"

"Not just a doctor," Mom breaks in, practically prancing in place as she grips both of my hands tightly in hers. "A research scientist and doctor on the cutting edge of Meltdown virus research, who's just put four children into permanent remission with his new procedure. Six months out, and there are no signs of the virus returning. And we got word this afternoon that the doctor has room for you on his schedule! You're next on the list!"

"Seriously?" My pulse picks up even as my brain fights to keep my blood pressure steady. The brain realized hope is dangerous a long time ago, but the heart never learns. "When? How? What are the success rates? The risks?" The questions spill out of me, but I don't really care about those things. I'm ready for anything, no matter what the risk vs. reward ratio. If there's even the ghost of a chance that I can get better, I want that.

I want to live, to dream big instead of editing every ambition. I want to look into my future and see endless possibilities and love and maybe those children Mom was wishing for.

My head spins with excitement, making it hard to concentrate on her words as she begins to lay out the details of the procedure.

But by the time she gets to the risks, I've regained my focus.

"There have been some fatalities. About two percent for children, closer to thirty percent for teens." Worry creeps into her pale-blue eyes, such a close match to my own that people have always assumed she's my birth mom, even though that's where the resemblance between us ends. "You'll be Dr. Highborn's oldest patient so far, and that likely means an even higher risk of complications. But when I explained your situation, how..." She swallows. "How hard things have been lately, well..."

How *hard*...

When she explained that I'm dying. That's what she means. We've all been dancing around it for months, looking the other way, "Tra-la-la nothing to see here, folks," while my organs slowly began to fail.

But here it is, laid out in the cool, mint-and-earth scented air.

Pops must have been working in the herb garden, one part of me observes as another solemnly acknowledges, *There goes any doubt about that. You really are dying. You haven't been being a big melodramatic baby, after all.*

"I'm dying." A sinkhole opens in my chest that widens to encompass the kitchen and then the house and then the entire neighborhood. I feel like I'm in free fall—panicked and helpless as I tumble through an endless black void—but strangely peaceful at the same time.

There's a power in labeling things.

In facing them.

In looking a monster right in the eye and calling it by its name.

Death, I see you there. I know you're watching, but I've got my eye on you, too, motherfuckah...

"No, you're not," Mom says, the words as fierce as she is, my tough little mama who has always refused to give up on me, no matter what. "You're going to be Dr. Highborn's first adult success story. You've got a good chance, Wren. You're not that far out of adolescence. I mean, as far as I can see, you look the same as you did the day you turned eighteen."

"Never could put any meat on your bones." Pops comes to stand behind Mom, leaving muddy footprints on the tile. His tone is calm and easy, but those footprints make it clear how upset he is.

Pops doesn't track in dirt. He lives to get dirt under his fingernails, but he's too proud of our home to muck it up. He doesn't own the bungalow, not even after thirty years of on-time disbursements to pay off the second mortgage, but he loves it.

It's hard to pay off a house when you're shelling out thousands of dollars a month for experimental medicine our insurance won't cover. Even with the help of the Church of Humanity Compassion House scholarship fund, my sickness has brought our family to the brink of financial ruin more than once.

"How much is it going to cost?" I ask, my voice small, guilt pressing down on my shoulders again.

I want to live, God knows I do, but I don't want to ruin my parents in the process. Especially since it sounds like this is a long shot for me, as the first adult guinea pig of this new procedure.

Mom's eyes fill, but I know immediately it's her

angry cry, not her sad one. Her gaze is on fire behind the shimmer, and I half expect her to send me to my room for a time out until I learn to control my temper, the way she did when I first came to live with her as a feral four-year-old determined to tear off my clothes and run wild through the neighborhood every chance I got.

"Don't you dare, Wren Frame." She sniffs, and her lips pucker into a crooked bow at the center of her face. "Don't you dare talk money at a time like this. Your life doesn't have a price. We've already talked to the bank about a third mortgage, and the lender promised we'd be approved."

"But then you'll never pay off the house," I say, some twisted part of me driven to make the argument for letting me die, for avoiding the risk when there's a very real chance there will be no reward.

"Wren, I swear—"

"Screw the house." Pops's uncharacteristic curse is so firm and loud that Mom and I both turn his way, our eyes going wide. "I don't care if we lose the house. It's worth it. Even if there are no guarantees..." He trails off, his throat working as he swallows. "Even a chance is worth it to me. Anything to help my baby girl."

And that does it. Those two sweet words from the sweetest man I know break me. My face crumples as I lean into my parents, tears making my voice thick as they wrap me up in their arms. "I love you, Pops. Mom. I love you both so much."

"And we love you, miracle girl." Mom uses the old

nickname, the one she and Pops stopped using months ago when my health started to fail like all the others.

Most people with my condition don't make it out of their teens, and only a precious few see thirty. If I'm the luckiest of the lucky, I could have six more years.

I literally have nothing to lose.

Nothing, except the chance to know what it would be like to be more than friends with the man who, just this afternoon, splashed color all over my black-and-white world, showing me brilliant new things I wasn't sure existed before.

But if I don't have the procedure and I don't go into remission soon, it's all over. At this rate, I could have three months, maybe six if my doctors can find a better drug cocktail before one of my major organs fails.

But if I risk the procedure, I could have even less time than that.

Almost nothing at all.

A 30 percent chance of fatal complications is nothing to take lightly, and as an adult my risk is probably higher, Mom said. If I put myself in this doctor's care, I'm flipping a coin for my life. No matter how much I want that permanent remission, I don't know if I'm ready to make that call.

"How long do I have to decide?" I sniff as I pull back from my parents' embrace, swiping tears from my cheeks with the backs of my hands.

Mom's forehead furrows. "I told you, sweetie. We have to go in the morning. First thing. They're holding the seven a.m. surgery slot for you."

"Oh," I say, blinking fast. "I'm sorry. I must have been

zoning out during that part. Tomorrow. Wow." I exhale sharply. "That's so fast."

"I know." Mom shakes her head. "But if we miss it, we might not get another chance. People from all over the world are fighting for a place on Dr. Highborn's schedule. But he's based right outside Seattle, so we're one of the few families who can take advantage of this last-minute cancelation."

I pace a few steps away, one hand propped on my hip as my free fingers tug on my earlobe, fighting to see my way through to a clear decision. But my thoughts are racing too fast to be corralled. My mind is a swarm of sounds and smells and faces—Carrie and Kite and the kids at the shelter and Mom and Dad.

What if I go to sleep on the operating table tomorrow and never get to tell them all goodbye?

What if you say no and miss your one shot at a real life?

"I have to go call Carrie," I say softly, decision made. It lands hard inside me, making my stomach knot and my blood pressure drop with a suddenness that makes me dizzy, but I know it's the right choice. "Tell her how much she means to me. Just in case."

Mom and Dad let out a breath in unison, and Mom reaches first for Dad's hand and then mine. Glancing between the two of us, she says, "But there won't be any 'just in case.' We've got this. We're leaving here as a family tomorrow morning and coming back as a family."

After promising them I'll get packed for the surgery trip while I'm calling Carrie, I slip down the hall to my room. It used to be Scarlett's room, this dark, cool space shaded by the cherry tree outside the window, but I moved in a few years ago, freeing up my childhood bedroom for Mom's crafting and sewing supplies. By then, we were finally ready to take down Scarlett's band posters and paintings, to tuck away her vibrant sheet set and the brightly colored tapestries she hung in front of the windows.

But I kept one of my sister's pieces, one she painted when she was just nine years old, of a fox at the edge of a field. The fox appears to be dancing, its luxurious tail rippling in the sunset light as it lifts paws to the faint moon visible in the sky above.

It's one of my favorite works of art—ever.

I know it's kid art and far from museum quality, but it speaks to me. Something about the fox, the field, the certain slant of light makes me breathless with longing. If I stare at the painting long enough, I can imagine that I've been to this place, danced with that magical creature, lifted my hands to the moon, and known that I was loved.

Loved by the moon and the stars, loved by the earth and the trees, loved by the wind whispering through the tall grass and the light warming my skin, all of them assuring me that I am part of an endless dance.

I walk to the painting now, but when I bring my fingers to hover above the fox's tail a sharp flash of pain ignites behind my eyes.

I wince, squeezing them closed as my vision goes white and then blue, and then a pudgy hand swims into focus over my head, fingers spread wide as if to reach up and touch the tree limbs waving above.

I'm struck by the sudden certainty that the hand is mine—my toddler hand from long ago, from somewhere in the lost years I can't remember.

It doesn't make sense, though, all the sunshine and trees. I was rescued from a drug den in an industrial part of Seattle, where my mother was living with other junkies, selling her body for her next fix. It's been inferred through the years—though never said outright by anyone, not even the therapist I saw for a year after Scarlett died—that there was a chance my sister and I were sold, too. That people did unspeakable things to us that are better off forgotten.

But the feeling that floods my chest as I watch my starfish fingers spread against a pale blue sky isn't terror. It's bliss. Innocent happiness. Certainty that I belong and I am deeply, profoundly loved.

And safe.

And...home.

Smells rush in, cedar and the same smoky-sour nut scent of black cottonwood from earlier today. Also raspberries and spring grass, sunshine-warmed skin mixed with the musky scent of fur and earth. Another flash of memory—a bed in a cool room where I sleep snuggled with half a dozen other children, all of us cozy in a puppy pile of contentment—and then I'm back in that field, reaching for the sky, certain I can touch the treetops if I wanted to. I could grow wings and fly, even though Mama says it isn't safe for me to fly so young.

Mama...

Another scent—turpentine and vanilla sugar—slams into me so hard I flinch, followed by images and sensations flickering so fast inside I can barely grab hold of one before it's replaced by another—full lips, big smile, green dress, blue water, peace, golden grass, fox tail, sharp teeth, safety, my hand, red hair, red fur, softness, love, full moon, fireworks, belonging and belonging and belonging until the fireworks are replaced with gunshots and then—

My phone vibrates in my hand, and I emerge from the rush of memory with a gasp.

I press my fist to my chest, where my heart is doing its best to crash through my sternum, and glance down at the screen to see an unfamiliar number. I answer without a second thought—some of the kids at the shelter have secret cell phones, even though they're supposed to turn them over when they check-in, and I've been on the receiving end of more than one panicked after-hours call from a kid in need of a friendly ear.

"Hello?" I say, my voice breathy and weak from the hallucination.

That had to be what it was. I was two months shy of four years old when I was adopted, and I've never been able to access any of my earliest childhood memories, not even when my therapist attempted to guide me into the past under hypnosis.

There is nothing back there but static and blur.

Static…

A faint hum on the end of the line…

"Hello?" I say again. "This is Wren, can I help you?"

"You can help yourself," a distorted voice garbles from the other end of the line, making my brows snap together. "Go to the window. Open it. Wait for a message."

"What? Who is this? How did you get this number?" A *click-click-click* sound as the line goes dead is the only response.

With a shudder, I toss my phone onto my flowered bedspread, where it lies there contaminating the field of poppies. Heart racing, I start toward the door to call out to Mom and Pops, but pause at the last second, something deep inside me telling me to wait.

To think.

To remember...

My fingers dive into the front pocket of my jeans, closing around the lucky coin I carry with me everywhere I go. The gold warms immediately against my skin, sending a pulse of calm threading through my fear.

There was a phone call like that once before, wasn't there?

A long time ago...

I bite my lip, tugging the coin out of my jeans and flipping it over the tops of my knuckles the way my friend Dust taught me when we were kids, fighting to resurrect the recollection from my graveyard of forgotten memories.

One of the side effects of being exhausted all the time is that the brain tends to prioritize certain functions over others. My body is focused on preserving the energy to keep waking up and walking around and processing food into energy from one day to the next. Archiving memories is way down the list on my biological to-do list, which means many entries in my personal history book are murky at best, blank pages at worst.

But that call...

The garbled voice...

Lifting the coin to hover in front of me, I stare into the eyes of the lion on the smoother side before flipping over to study the eagle with gnarled talons on the other. Sometimes watching the coin twirl in slow circles helps me focus, another trick Dust taught me before he moved away.

Or before he died. I'm not sure which story is true.

My parents told me Dust and his parents moved back to England to be closer to family. George, a fellow seventh grader who lived next door to Dust back in the day, swore he saw a body being wheeled out of his house on a stretcher in the middle of the night, just days before the family allegedly returned to the UK.

A small body, about the size of Dust at thirteen...

We were all sick, all of the kids at the Church of Humanity Chosen Charter School, and becoming increasingly familiar with death. We'd lost Grace over the summer between my fourth and fifth grade year, Vince before Halloween the following year, and both of the twins—Regina and Rafe—during the Christmas holidays mere months before Dust vanished without a trace.

But Dust...

The thought of him gone, vanished along with his fantastic stories and his magical way of turning every silly schoolyard game into an adventure, hit me hard. Even though he was two years ahead of me in school,

Dust was my best friend, and the only person I could talk to about Scarlett's increasingly wild behavior and how terrifying it felt for my sister to pull away from me. Dust listened with his entire self and set about solving problems like it was his mission on earth. Even at thirteen, it was clear that he was going to grow up to be an incredible person, one that fights to keep the lights on in an increasingly dark world.

So I told George to keep his lies to himself and chose to believe that Dust was out there somewhere, hiding treasures in his pockets and making up wild stories and being the same old Dust I'd known.

Years later, when I was in college and I received a waiver for the Church of Humanity's ban on online activity so I could pursue my degree in social work, I tried looking for him. I hoped to find a social media page with his grinning face, or some sign that he was out there, alive and happy. But there was nothing. No birth certificate, no death certificate, no adoption forms filed in the state of Washington, not even an entry in the movement's annual member registration database.

His parents' names were still there, but he'd been scrubbed out.

Erased.

He must have left the movement as a Hostile Faction. Only those in open opposition to the Church of Humanity, those determined to undermine our mission to unite all people, are erased when they leave. Once I'd realized that, I'd stopped looking for Dust.

No matter where he was or what he was doing, he was a H.F. and forever beyond my reach.

But I kept this coin, the one he promised me would keep me safe.

My gaze softens as I spin the coin faster and the locked doors in my mind begin to creak open. I catch flashes of Scarlett at nineteen, at seventeen, and then Scarlett on the last day of her sophomore year of high school.

We're having a party to celebrate. Mom and Pops and all our friends are out in the backyard. Scarlett and I are inside, preparing to bring out the box of cupcakes we bought for dessert—I'm insisting I get the only red velvet—when the phone on the wall rings. Scarlett picks it up, and there's a voice on the other end, a deep, distorted voice telling her to take her sister's hand and run to the front door.

Run. Now, the voice says, so loud I can hear it from by the refrigerator halfway across the room. I start toward Scarlett, watching her face pale and her eyes go wide. *This may be our only chance to get you out. The Frames aren't who you think they are. You aren't safe. If you stay, you and your sister will both die. Go. Now.*

The phone falls from Scarlett's hand, and I run to hug her, but I don't remember what comes next...

I don't remember...

A scratching sound on the other side of the room snaps me out of my trance, sending my heart jerking back into panic mode. Squeezing the coin in my fist, I spin to face the window.

Immediately, my gaze locks on the fat, fluffy raccoon perched on the sill outside, it's onyx eyes sparkling in its brown mask. It's an enormous creature with steel-gray fur shot through with white highlights and a damp black nose that wiggles up and down as it presses one eerily human hand to the window.

I shake my head, not knowing what to make of this night animal out at dusk and looking me dead in the eye with an intelligence that makes my skin crawl. But I'm glad I didn't open the window the way the voice on the phone told me to do. If I had, that massive beastie and its teeth would be in my room.

That's clearly what it wants.

The raccoon scratches plaintively at the glass, flinching when my Mom shouts from the kitchen, "Wren, are you okay with red sauce on your pasta? Or do you want your noodles plain with a little butter and pepper?"

"Red sauce is fine, Mom," I call back, pulse throbbing faster in my throat as the raccoon shakes its head like it understands what we've said and is against red sauce.

Or against dinner.

Or against me sticking around to eat it

"Definitely option three," I note in a trembling voice as the raccoon lifts his—her?—other hand and presses a small, square sheet of paper to the window.

Even from ten feet away I can read the bright red words on it loud and clear. There are only two of them, scrawled in thick capital letters—*Run Wren.*

Before I can get across the room, the raccoon
has dropped the paper and leaped from the
windowsill. Forcing my trembling arms to
function, I shove the old glass up and lean out, peering
into the yard as the raccoon scurries through the
vegetable garden and vanishes into what looks like a
tunnel dug under the fence.

A part of me wants to call out to the creature—to
demand that it come back and tell me what the hell is
going on—but the logical voice in my head fights back,
reminding me that animals don't talk.

But they don't usually deliver ominous warnings
either.

Lunging forward, I grab the piece of paper before
the wind can blow it away, wondering what happened
to the screen that usually covers the window. It was
there yesterday, I'm sure of it. But now it's gone, and
there's nothing in my way as I draw the note inside,

fingers probing at the edges of the tightly folded paper as I realize there's more to this than two words.

Freeing a sharply creased edge, I spread the creamy stationary open on the ledge to read—*Don't take your medication after dinner, watch this window, and be ready to run when you see the sign. Let us help you, Wren. Before it's too late. You can trust us. We'll explain everything as soon as you're free. On the chance that this note is discovered, we can't say more, but be assured that luck is on your side—and in your pocket—tonight.*

Eyes going wide, I turn my right hand over and uncurl my fingers, revealing the coin sitting in my sweating palm.

Only a few people know about my lucky coin. When we were kids, Dust made me swear never to tell anyone. It was something he'd brought with him from England, a relic from his life before the Parsons adopted him. He knew if his parents found it or any of his other secret treasures, they would be taken away.

It's real gold, lucky, and it will help me find you if you get lost, he'd promised me, pressing it into my hand one afternoon beneath the bleachers, when we'd snuck away to play pretend instead of baking in the sun at the annual Church of Humanity Portland vs. Seattle softball tournament.

For years after, I never said a word to anyone about it.

After Dust disappeared, I finally confessed my secret to Scarlett, knowing it would help her understand why I was so sad that Dust had gone away. And then, just last year, the coin fell out of my pocket while Carrie and I were on our hands and knees dragging contraband beer cans out from under the bed of one of our residents. She'd picked it up and passed it over to me, asking what it was.

"Just my good luck charm," I said with a shrug, popping it back into my pocket without further explanation.

If anyone would understand toting around a coin your best friend gave you when you were eight, it would be Carrie—she still has a charm bracelet her grand-mother gave her when she was five and wears it every day to remind her of the one loving parental figure in her life—but I still hadn't wanted to say more.

The coin is one of the most deeply personal, private things I own.

But now maybe Carrie and I should have a talk about good luck charms.

Shoving the window closed, I hurry over to my bed, grabbing my cell. But when I pull up my text thread with Carrie, I hesitate, thumbs hovering above the screen.

How to ask your best friend if she's part of a secret society trying to liberate young adults from the movement?

That must be what this is, some sort of "cult rescue" operation.

But I don't need to be rescued. The movement isn't a cult, and we're not involved in weird exorcism rituals or human trafficking or selling children to billionaires overseas or anything else we've been accused of over the years. All of that noise is just reporters looking for a sensational story and finding an easy target in a relatively new church.

Our particular beliefs and practices—based on spiritual teachings from all over the world and promoting love for our fellow humans above all else—were only organized into a recognized religion in the 1980s. The mere fact that we're a modern creation makes some people freak out about our customs in a way they never would an older, more established tradition.

So we have a ban on online activity for younger members? So what?

That doesn't mean our elders are trying to keep us ignorant while they plot to sell us on the dark web. It means they're trying to keep us safe and healthy in a digital world that's been scientifically proven to have negative effects on the minds and social development of young people. And they're happy to waive the ban when it's necessary for study or a member's job.

I mean, the Catholics drink wine and break bread they believe are the blood and flesh of Christ. I'm not one to judge anyone's religious practices, but objectively that sounds way creepier than staying off the web until you're thirty...

And Carrie seems like she's truly committed to the movement, even more than I am. Being part of the C of H is about community for me. I love the people I grew up with in the church, and I work for a movement charity. I also happen to truly believe loving my fellow humans and making cooperation not war is an excellent idea. Therefore, I remain a member, even though, the older I get, the more I find some of the movement's policies counterproductive to the mission they say they're trying to accomplish.

But from the day Carrie showed up at the shelter—half starved, with an infected dog bite on her leg and tiny, moon-shaped scars from years of her abusive father putting his cigarettes out on her arms and legs—she's embraced the movement with fervor. She's been transformed by her faith, healed physically, mentally, and spiritually by the soul work she's done. Her strength and her happiness truly seem to be grounded in her commitment to the movement and the causes we champion.

The longer I think on it, the harder it is to fathom that she could be an undercover Hostile Force.

But who else could it possibly be?

Despite the foolish hope I've clung to for so long, I know Scarlett is dead. If she were alive and part of some secular liberation movement, she would have come for me a long time ago. She wouldn't have left me for eight years in a situation she believed was dangerous, and she wouldn't have let me suffer through grieving her.

Yes, the Scarlett who was sent away to Greater Good to get off drugs was an angrier, scarier version of my sister than the one I'd known, but she still loved me.

So not Scarlett. Not Carrie. Which leaves…

"Dust," I whisper, letting my cell drop back onto the bed.

It's crazy, but it has to be him. After over a decade, he's back.

And he's a Hostile Force who wants to rip me away from my family and everything I've ever known,

BELLA JACOBS

precisely when I've been presented with an opportunity that could save my life.

Could give me a real life. Give me a future.

Or kill you, a soft voice in my head whispers.

Yes, or that…

The timing of the call and the letter is eerie. Could it be related to the procedure in some way? But if so, how did these mystery people find out I'm scheduled for treatment tomorrow? I didn't even know myself until thirty minutes ago, medical records are confidential, and I can't imagine that my parents would have mentioned it to anyone.

The thought gives me something to cling to, to investigate.

After hiding the note deep in my sock drawer—tucked into a pair of wool stockings I won't be wearing until next winter—I head back into the kitchen, arriving just as Mom is dumping pasta into a colander in the sink.

"Mom, you haven't mentioned tomorrow to anyone else, have you?" I ask, keeping my tone casual. "Like Aunt Sarah or Grammy P?"

Mom shakes her head as she sets the pot back on a cool burner and lifts the colander, giving it a shake, sending fresh steam swirling around her face, where her hair is already starting to curl into ringlets from the heat. "No, I didn't tell anyone. I thought that should be your choice, sweetheart. I'm not sure Grammy's up to dealing with this news, not with her own health so poor. But if you want to talk to her, we can. And we can absolutely get Aunt Sarah on the phone after dinner. It's

58

late, East Coast time, but she's a night owl and I know she'd love to hear from you."

I nod and say, "That sounds good," even though it doesn't.

I don't want to talk to Grammy or Aunt Sarah. I love them both, but the thought of having to put their minds at ease on something I'm still not 100 percent sure about myself doesn't sound like a great way to use up the last of my rapidly waning energy.

By the time we finish a quick dinner of pasta and fresh baby greens from the garden, I can barely keep my eyes open.

I need my meds, specifically the ones that keep my energy levels relatively consistent and allow me the luxury of having the strength to shower, brush my teeth, and read for an hour or so propped up in bed.

But when I grab my pillbox from the counter after dinner and tip the handful of red, white, blue, and yellow tablets into my palm, I don't pop them into my mouth and down them with the last of the water in my glass. Instead, I fake the tossing motion and pretend to swallow something more than water as I discreetly slip the pills into my jean pocket.

I don't know why I do it—I don't believe the author of that note knows what's best for me, and I haven't missed a dose of meds since I was a toddler.

It's like I'm possessed.

But not by demons or spirits, the way some of the movement's more orthodox elders might think. There's nothing supernatural in the prickling of my skin or the humming in my thoughts. It's plain old, garden-variety curiosity that has me hooked.

Safe and wise, or not, I want to know who sent that note. I want to look them in the eye and tell them that I'm fine and not even a little bit in need of saving.

And if it's Dust...

If it's Dust, I want to tell him that I've missed him and that he meant so much to me when we were children and that I'm glad he's alive, even if he has been enlisted into some crazy war. If I die tomorrow, I'll go out more peacefully after saying goodbye to one of the people who meant the most to me in my life.

And if it's someone else, then I'll deal with that when the time comes.

When the *sign* comes.

It could be any minute now...

After dinner, I assure Mom I'm okay with waiting to call Grammy and Aunt Sarah until we get back from the procedure, when I'll have good news to share with them. Mom, clearly approving of my positive thinking, sends me to bed with a kiss on the forehead and a promise to wake me early tomorrow so I'll have time to get ready, and I retreat to force myself through the usual bedtime ritual.

My parents don't think anything of me going to bed at eight. I rarely manage to stay conscious past nine or nine thirty. Exhaustion hits me hard after the sun goes down.

That's always the case, but tonight is far worse than usual. Without my drug cocktail to keep me semi-functional, my feet feel like leaden weights strapped to my legs. I shuffle into the bathroom—a zombie with sagging eyelids and limbs made of rubber. I flop through the washing of my face and the brushing of my teeth, knocking over my electric toothbrush, the hand towel holder, and my entire row of moisturizers before I'm finished.

In addition to nausea and a boatload of other fun side effects, my meds make my skin super dry, so thin and flaky I go through a small fortune in drugstore face cream each month. Tonight, however, I glop on more than I need and smear it in circles with clumsy fingers as I amble back to my room, not worried about wasting it.

I'm not worried about meeting my would-be savior in my pajamas with my hair up in a messy ponytail, either. I won't be going anywhere with him or her. The only place I'm going is to sleep—and soon.

Garble Voice better get moving with that "sign" if he wants me to be awake to see it.

"Vastly underestimated the power of exhaustion, he has," I grumble Yoda-style as I fumble the meds from my jean pocket before tossing my dirty clothes from today into the bin.

I'll wait fifteen more minutes, then I'm taking my pills, shutting my curtains, and crawling into bed. If Garble or his pet raccoon shows up in my backyard, they'll be as out of luck as the crack addict who tried to break into our house a few years ago. Our place may look quaint and cozy, but we've got one hell of a security system. Pops grew up in this neighborhood when it was truly the wrong side of the tracks and is a firm believer in being safe rather than sorry.

"Cops on 'im so fast his head will be swimming with the fishes." I'm with-it enough to realize that's not how that saying goes, but too floaty to figure out which part I've got wrong. My head is a helium balloon fighting to touch the ceiling, and my neck feels longer and thinner with every breath.

Fifteen minutes of continued vigilance might have been an overly ambitious goal.

Shuffling across the room, I open my sock drawer and grab my wool socks. Maybe rereading the note will help wake me up.

I worm my fingers into the tight curl of fabric, but no matter how deep I dig, there's nothing there but sock and more sock.

Have I accidentally grabbed the wrong pair?

With clumsy hands, I work my way through my entire sock drawer—even the summer stockings too thin to hide any secrets—without success. The note isn't hidden in my socks or anywhere in the drawer. The note is...gone.

Someone's been in my room.

Someone could *still* be in my room.

The thought is barely through my head when a hand covers my mouth, pulling me back against a wall of warm, unrelenting flesh.

CHAPTER 6

WREN

"**D**on't scream, and don't be afraid. It's me. I'm here to help." The deep voice rumbles softly into my ear, short-circuiting my shriek before it can emerge.

The voice is familiar.

So is the evergreen, sea spray, and campfire smell of this man.

"Kmmte?" I mumble into Kite's hand, sucking in a deep breath as he pulls his palm away. I turn to face him, the room spinning and blurring as I add in a slurred voice, "Wha' you doing here?"

Kite's three foreheads wrinkle and concern floods all seven or eight of his dark eyes. "We've got to get you out of here. You're going into detox crazy fast." He curses as he shakes his head, making his extra eyes kaleidoscope in and out in a way that makes my stomach uneasy. "They must have had you pumped full of enough drugs to take down an elephant."

BELLA JACOBS

I squint hard at his face, willing his features to hold still. "So you're the one? The one on the phone?"

The realization hurts, but my head is too cloudy to make sense of the misery flooding through me.

I'm having a hard enough time keeping my eyes open and my body upright. Even the shock of learning that I'm not alone in my bedroom isn't enough to banish the lethargy infecting me at a cellular level. No matter how much I want to give Kite a piece of my mind, pretty soon I'll be sacked out face first on my bed...

If I can make it across the room before I pass out.

"Easy, baby." He catches me as my knees buckle, swinging me up into his arms. "I've got you. It's okay. You're going to be safe soon, I promise."

I want to tell him not to call me baby—he's not my friend, he's a lying, crazy, undercover Hostile Force who took advantage of my trusting spirit and stupidly naïve heart—but the room is spinning faster now, and my lips refuse to obey orders. My throat is tight, and my stomach is pitching, and it's all I can do to roll my head onto Kite's chest as he swiftly crosses the room and shoves open the window.

The security system must be off.

It must have been off earlier, too, or it would have sounded when I opened the window the first time.

I curse myself for being so easily distracted by that note-delivering raccoon, as Kite sticks his head out into the near darkness and makes grunting sounds low in his throat. They're so soft I can't imagine anyone but me being able to hear them, but a moment later there's an

64

answering clicking sound from the garden. Someone's out there, his accomplice, and if I don't pull myself together soon, they're going to have me out this window and at their mercy.

"Help me," I whisper, swallowing hard as I will my clutching throat to relax. But when I try to call out to Mom and Pops, the only sound that emerges from my lips is a soft croak.

"Don't be afraid," Kite says again. "I promise I'll explain everything as soon as we're out of here, Bird Girl, but right now I need you to trust me."

Trust him? He's kidnapping me! He broke into my house, manipulated me into skipping the drugs that would have given me the strength to call for help, and now he's passing me through the window into the cool night air. I'm caught by another pair of arms—thinner than Kite's, but no less powerful—but I can't see the man's face. My head has fallen backward again, and this time I lack the strength to lift it.

The most I can do is blink faster to stay awake as the world bounces by upside down, the shadowy trees sprouting out of the sky as the ground bleeds from pale blue to cobalt stabbed through with the first bright white stars.

The moon is there, too, I realize as the stranger carrying me reaches the garden gate and quietly opens it, revealing more of the endless night spreading out around us, devouring all memories of the sun. The moon is the eye of a giant serpent hovering in the darkness, squinting down at my bared throat, debating whether or not to rip me open with its teeth.

And if it decides to strike, I won't be able to fight back. The serpent moon can do anything it wants with me, and so can Kite and his cohort. And even though a foolish part of me wants to believe that Kite is still my friend—or at least a well-meaning crazy kidnapper—I don't know this other man at all.

What if Kite leaves me alone with him?

Passed out and sick and completely unable to defend myself?

I've been sheltered from many of the ugliest realities of the world by my overprotective parents and the limitations of my illness, but I've worked with street kids long enough to know what happens to girls who are unlucky enough to find themselves vulnerable and unconscious around strange men.

Sometimes they wake up to find they've been raped.

Sometimes they don't wake up at all.

My pulse races faster, dumping adrenaline into my system. I use the burst of energy to thrash my arms and legs as hard as I can, which isn't all that hard, but thankfully the suddenness of the movement surprises Kidnapper Number Two.

He grunts—a high-pitched sound that's surprisingly breathy—and I roll from his arms into the grass.

Seconds later, I'm on my hands and knees, crawling back to the house, only to find my path blocked by an olive-skinned girl with dark, kohl-rimmed eyes and a shock of inch-long hair sticking up in spikes around her head.

Kite's accomplice is a *she*, not a he.

It's enough of a surprise to make me stop crawling

and stare up at her face, wondering why she looks so worried when *I'm* the one being kidnapped.

"I feel you, Mama," she says in a rich, husky voice that belongs on the radio advertising Kentucky bourbon. "I know this is scary, but there's seriously no time to explain shit, and you're safe with Kite. We go way back. I trust that boy with my life, and you can trust him with yours, but only if we get you out of here ASA-fucking-P."

She reaches for me, hooking her hands under my armpits as she stands, lifting me to my feet and pinning me to her side with a strength and ease that makes me suddenly, fiercely envious.

What would it be like to have a body that cooperates? A body that responds positively to proper diet and exercise? A body that can fight back and push through and experience the highs and lows of human existence in a way a sick kid benched at the side of the playing field never has?

If I make it to the procedure tomorrow, I might finally be able to find out. Which means I absolutely *cannot* let myself be taken. I have to get help, get Mom and Pops to call the police before it's too late.

"Mom, help!" I shout as I lunge out of Spiky Hair's arms, falling for a split second before she catches me around the waist with a grunt.

I claw at her fingers with my nails, making her curse, but she doesn't let me go. She simply flips me around like I'm a rag doll, shoves her shoulder into my stomach, and says, "Ain't got time for this, Mama. Sorry."

And then the world is upside down again, and I'm

bobbing along with my face in some strange woman's butt while my stomach churns and exhaustion seeps back into my limbs. I'm so pissed off I shout with every bit of strength left in me, "Help, I'm being kidnapped!"

A second later the front door swings open and light streams out onto the dark garden not three feet from my face. But before I can call out again, Spikey Hair breaks into a run. The sudden motion sends her shoulder jabbing even deeper into my gut, stealing my breath away, so I'm unable to answer when Pops calls out, "Who are you? Who's there? Get out of my yard before I call the police!"

Gasping for breath, I try to call out—to tell him it's me and I'm being taken and he absolutely should call the cops right freaking now—but Spikey picks that second to leap over the fence. My stomach flips in response, swooping into a sickening swan dive that ends in a crash landing as Spikey touches down on the other side and her bony shoulder slams into my solar plexus.

I clench my abdominal muscles against the invasion, avoiding losing my dinner by the barest of margins, and then immediately regret the choice to fight my gag reflex. I may not be able to kick ass, but I could have at least made a disgusting mess all over my kidnapper.

I'm coaxing my stomach back to the pitching place when tires squeal beside us and Spikey grinds to a stop. A second later, I'm upright again, staggering a step to the left before she grabs me by the shoulder and hip and tosses me bodily into the back of the car.

I land sprawled half on dank-smelling upholstery

and half on the floor, with one elbow wedged behind my back. By the time I pull myself together, Spikey is in the passenger's seat and Kite is swinging the car around in a swift circle.

I slide across the back, slamming into the door before Kite accelerates with another squeal of tires and gravity presses my shoulders into the seat.

"Took you long enough," Spikey mumbles, glancing over her shoulder. At first I think she's looking at me, but she's gazing over my head through the back window as if she expects something a heck of a lot scarier than Pops to be chasing after us.

"Sorry," Kite says. "I parked three streets over. I don't think they've got watchers on her, but you can't be too careful."

Spikey's gaze shifts to mine, and I narrow my eyes, glaring with as much fire as I can muster considering I'm on the verge of passing out again. Infuriatingly, she smiles at me and says, "You're cute when you're pissed."

"Shut...up," I rasp. Even the effort to speak those two words leaves me winded. Still, I force myself to keep going. "Take me back."

"We can't do that, Wren." Kite meets my eyes in the rearview mirror, dividing his attention between the road and me, captive in the back seat. "I know this seems crazy, but it's not. You were in danger there, more than you can imagine. And we're still not out of the woods. We won't be safe until we're out of the city. But as soon as we're safe and you're feeling up to it, Sierra and I will explain everything. Until then, I hope you can trust us." He holds my gaze a beat too long, making my stomach swoop as I wonder if we're on the verge of a traffic accident. "I swear on our friendship that I'm only doing what I have to do to keep you safe."

I want to tell Kite that friends don't kidnap friends, but my brain is melting, oozing, softening into a state where only minimal function is possible. I used up every bit of fight left in me during my last stand in my front yard, and I barely made enough of a commotion to get Pops to open the door.

How long until he realizes I'm gone and calls the police? Considering he thinks I've gone to bed for the night, it might not be until tomorrow morning, when he and Mom come to wake me for the journey to the clinic.

By that point, who knows where I'll be?

And even if he decides to go check on me now for some reason, there's still a good chance I won't be found.

Kite is making swift progress away from our cozy neighborhood, merging into the traffic streaming away from the city on the highway, the throng of commuters who stayed in the city for a late dinner, or to catch a band at one of the music venues, and are only now heading home.

Too late, I realize that I should have tried to jump out of the car sooner, and curse my sluggish brain. While Kite was going thirty or forty miles per hour, I probably would have survived the spill from the vehicle, but at seventy, a jump for freedom would be suicide.

Still, if my body would cooperate, I could scoot

closer to the door, get in position so I'd be ready the next time he slowed down.

But my body is done playing even remotely nice. The backs of my eyes are on fire with tiny pinpricks of agony, and my head feels like I'm trapped on a never-ending merry-go-round. Or like I'm swirling down the drain...

Swirling and swirling, picking up speed as gravity sucks me relentlessly downward, and then there is a squeeze as I pop through the drain and then—

Black.

CHAPTER 7

WREN

Consciousness attacks me like a prizefighter— swift and relentless, slamming me against the ropes.

Punch one— My eyes drag open to see large halogen lights zooming past overhead and hear Kite's engine groaning in protest as Sierra shouts, "Faster, man. We've got to get off the fucking freeway! We're sitting ducks out here!"

"I'm trying!" Kite jerks the car hard to the right and then the left, sending my pulsing, aching body sliding back and forth across the seat. "But the exits are all blocked. Find me an alternative route. If they get us on the bridge we're fucked."

Kite banks right again, skidding across at least three lanes of traffic. I slam into the door hard enough to send pain rocketing through my shoulder.

Should have put on your seat belt, genius.

The snide voice in my head is the last thing I hear before I snuff out again.

But consciousness isn't done with me yet.

Punch two— This time I wake to Sierra wailing into the phone, "You've got to get us out of here, motherfucker! I don't care who you have to put at risk. They're closing in fast from behind, and there are more of them waiting at the end of the bridge. I can fucking smell them, Ghost. Get us the fuck out of here!"

Kite shouts in an only slightly less hysterical voice, "I can get Wren to shore if we have to go into the water, but the current is too much for Sierra. You've got to get her out, man. Send air support. She's only ten pounds when—"

"Fuck!" Sierra cuts him off with a shout-sob as she tosses the cell into the cup holder between them. "He fucking hung up on me, that motherfucker. He's going to let us all fucking die out here."

"No one is going to die." Kite sits up straighter in the driver's seat, until his broad shoulders block what little I can see of the starry sky through the windshield.

Even in my spinning, melting, throbbing state I can feel the energy shift in the car as he takes control in that strong, seamless way of his. The way that once made me think he had a big future ahead of him, before I knew he was a kidnapper and a criminal.

"There's a maintenance shed a couple miles ahead," he continues in a no-nonsense voice. "Close to the middle of the bridge. We'll go over there, where we can be sure the water is deep enough, and double back toward Seattle. They won't be expecting us to swim back the way we came."

"Shit." Sierra's entire arm shakes as she braces a hand on the back of Kite's seat. "I was raised in the fucking hood, Kite. I can't swim. I mean, I can when I'm kin, but what if—"

"There's no time for what-ifs, mama." Kite puts a hand on the back of her neck, an affectionate touch that makes me wonder what these two are to each other. "You've got this, and I've got you. You shift on the way down and get out the window and onto whatever part of the car is still above water as soon as we land."

"As soon as we fucking *crash*," Sierra corrects, piercing the woozy fog around my brain that's been holding all of this at a distance.

She's right. We're going to crash. We're going to plummet off the edge of a bridge into the water, and who the hell knows if any of us will survive the impact with the river below, let alone whatever comes after.

I swallow hard and cut a glance to the door handle, knowing it's now or never, but my arm refuses to move. My fingers twitch uselessly at my sides, and I remain crumpled in my seat, as much a prisoner of my own body as the people who stole me away from my home, my family.

I'm sorry Mom and Pops, I think, hoping they can hear me, feel me somehow. *I'm sorry, and I love you, and I'm sorry. So sorry.*

"I'll shift as soon as I get Wren out of the car." Kite gives Sierra's neck a squeeze before returning his hand to the wheel. A moment later, freezing cold air blasts into the car as the windows all begin to slide open. "If you fall in, don't freak out," he adds in a louder voice, shouting to be heard over the rush of the breeze. "You'll only have to hold your own in the current for a minute or two and the Big Bad ferry will be open for service. Make sure Wren's buckled in. We're going in ten."

Sierra mutters something in a language I don't understand as she reaches over the seat, hesitating a beat as she sees my eyes staring up into hers. "Sorry, girl. I was hoping at least one of us wouldn't have to be awake for this." She lifts me upright and tugs the belt across my chest, clicking it into place. "Just hold onto your ass, okay? We're all going to be fine, and pretty soon you'll have your first Kin Born war story to share around the campfire."

She squeezes my knee and turns around before I can beg her to let me out.

I'm not at war with anyone. I'm a social worker, a book nerd, a goody-two-shoes who still lives with her parents even though she's twenty-four years old. Nothing in my life has set me on a trajectory to go out in a blaze of glory.

But sometimes life hijacks your free will and fate makes a mockery of all your carefully laid plans.

"And in seven, six, five," Kite says, his voice insanely calm considering how this countdown ends. "Four, three..."

A soft black mouth opens in the air in front of me, swallowing me whole before Kite can reach "one." This time, I go eagerly into oblivion, diving in head first, knowing whatever waits in the belly of this blackness is far better than what Kite has planned.

Punch three— I wake myself screaming, the sound howling from deep in my core before my eyes are even open.

I have a split second to acknowledge the sensation of falling, falling, the bottom dropping out of the world and chaos sucking my organs up through a straw, one by one, and then black.

Punch four— Cold. So cold. I'm soaking wet from the neck down, and I can't feel my fingers or my toes. Gasping in a deep breath, I tilt my head back, instinctively trying to keep my nose out of the water for as long as possible, and then there is a sharp jerk and pressure against my chest before my seatbelt falls away.

A moment later I'm pulled through the window, into the water, where the current tugs on my clothes like dozens of hungry toddlers demanding a snack, seeming innocent at first, but dangerous in numbers.

"Hold onto me, Bird Girl," Kite calls over the roar of the water streaming around the giant pillars of the bridge. "Hold on, baby, I've got you."

But he doesn't have me. He lets go, and I float away, sucked downstream so fast I'm half a dozen meters away from the sinking car by the time something large and hairy rises from the water beneath me.

My lips part on another scream, but instead I gasp and cough. Water I can't remember swallowing spills from between my lips while high above me—up where the bridge touches the sky—a wolf howls, baying at the moon, calling for my blood.

Somehow I know that's what the animal wants. I can feel its savage thirst, its rage, as powerfully as the terror thundering through my veins as whatever river monster has caught me carries me away.

This time I fight to stay awake, fearing I'll drown if I don't, but the darkness comes again because the darkness is an asshole who doesn't give a damn what I want.

Punch Five— The quiet wakes me this time.

Quiet like the quiet after a gunshot.

Dangerous quiet.

Deadly quiet.

Shh, don't make a sound, my inner voice whispers, and without a second thought, I obey, pinching my lips closed and holding my breath.

I want to be rescued; I don't want to be eaten alive.

Ripped apart. Torn to pieces and the bloodied trophies that were once my arms and legs thrust skyward in triumph by my enemies.

The creatures out there in the quiet dark haven't come to help me. They've come to *hunt* me. I can taste it in every sip of cool night air—metal, blood lust, hatred, and fear.

They're afraid of us, too.

Afraid of…*me*.

I can feel it as thick and real as the soggy fur beneath my cheek and the powerful arms holding me close to a warm, solid, not-at-all-human body.

My breath hitches, but I stay quiet, resisting the urge to pull away and see what the hell has me tucked against its chest. Whatever this massive creature is, it clearly doesn't mean me harm. It holds me firmly, but gently, its steady heartbeat sending waves of comforting energy pulsing across my skin.

But the things out there…

The monsters prowling through the night…

I squeeze my eyes closed, willing my pulse to go quiet, my breath to sip oh-so-softly in and out between my parted lips. If they find me, they will kill me, but not before torturing me a little first.

Or a lot…

Tucking my chin, I snuggle closer to the thick, damp fur. The creature—a bear, I think; there are no other furry animals this massive indigenous to the Pacific Northwest—covers my head with one paw. I can feel the slight pressure from its claws threading into my wet hair, but it doesn't frighten me.

The bear feels safe, almost familiar. And if it comes to a fight with the creatures hunting us, he will fight for me. I know it.

I know it the way I know that the sky is full of stars and the river is full of fish and the world is full of mysteries I've barely scratched the surface of before today. I've always known I was sheltered, but I'm beginning to think I've been kept even more ignorant than I ever imagined.

Hopefully, if I live through the night, I can start catching up on all the stuff I've missed.

Long minutes stretch into hours, and gradually the quiet is softened by cricket song. The frogs grow bold next, adding their percussive *croak* and *grog* to the mix, and then a night bird *coos* in the darkness, promising that everything is going to be all right.

I'm damp, exhausted, afraid, and far from home, but I'm alive and my head is no longer threatening to spin off my body. My stomach is still unsettled at best, my body aches in places I wasn't aware I had muscles, and my temples pulse and throb, but I'm in one piece and the worst of the danger has passed.

All around me, the night celebrates the return of the natural order, singing my protector and I off to sleep.

CHAPTER 8

WREN

This time, I'm not punched into unconsciousness.

This time, I'm lulled into rest, safe in the arms of the gentle animal that cradles me close. I sleep, and I dream for the first time in longer than I can remember. I dream of the fox in my sister's painting, and kind eyes, and a voice promising it's not too late, it's never too late, as long as there is hope.

Hope...

It's been the only thing that's kept me going for so long, the wind in the sails of my ship shot full of holes and held together with a string and prayer. I excel at hope. I've medaled in the Hope Olympics, taking gold though there was never any reason to believe I would survive to compete.

But when I wake up much later, just as dawn is smearing the sky above the evergreen trees grayish gold, I'm not sure what to hope for.

To escape my captors and get home to my parents?

To somehow make it to Dr. Highborn's clinic before my appointment is taken by someone else?

Or is there something else, something more?

I sit up, brushing damp leaves from my cheek and shivering in the early morning chill. God, my dreams were crazy last night—foxes and bears and monsters in the dark, hungry for my blood. All I needed was a lion and a tiger and I'd have had my own journey to Oz.

But now, I'm back on earth, my dream protector is gone, and I'm alone with nothing but the sound of the river rushing softly in the distance and the first bright chirps of morning birdsong to keep me company.

Drawing my now mostly dry pajama-pant-clad legs into my chest, I wrap my arms around my knees and wish I'd worn something warmer to bed. I have no idea how far downstream I was swept last night, but the absence of any rush or rumble noise of the city makes me think it was probably quite a ways.

It's going to be a long walk back to civilization, a walk I'm not sure I have the energy for.

"You have to at least try," I mumble, my voice rough from the adventures of the night before, "before someone tries to stop you."

I have no idea how I made it to shore or where Kite and Sierra are—I haven't seen them since we went off the bridge, and a terrified voice in my head whispers that they could be dead—but I don't have time to worry about that now. On the chance they are still alive, I need to be gone before they find me. Once I'm safe, I can call the police and tell them the entire story, ask them to send out a search party to look for two people who might have been swept farther downstream.

Yes, Kite and Sierra took me away from my family against my will, but I don't want either of them dead.

Especially Kite…

It's so hard to accept that I was wrong about him. A part of me is still certain that he's the good man I thought he was, a kind, strong, determined person who loves nature, his family, and his friends. I desperately want to believe that kiss we shared and the feeling of rightness when we touched was real, even if everything else Kite told me was a lie.

I hope he's alive. I do.

Even though I doubt I'll ever see him again.

I stand on shaky legs, bracing myself against a nearby tree as I take a few tentative steps away from the river, closer to the hill rising to my left. My socks don't offer much protection against the rocks and sticks on the forest floor, but it doesn't hurt that much. Pain is relative after the agony of last night. Bruised feet are child's play.

With one last glance at my surroundings, trying to memorize the slice of forest so I can describe it to the police—a circle of elms, a tangle of blackberry vines with tiny puckered white fruit concealing most of a fallen tree, and a boulder that resembles a giant's thumb poking up from the ground—I start up the hill.

I'm tired and weak, but I'm surprised to find the climb is easier than I expect it to be. My blood moves through my veins with an ease that's unfamiliar, and for the first time in months, I didn't wake up in the grips of gut-wrenching nausea. In fact, I'm actually...hungry.

Starving, in fact.

My belly mutters behind my ribs, a grumble of discontent that becomes a growl by the time I reach the first rise and a small clearing that offers a view of the city far away. Much farther than I thought. The Space Needle is barely the size of my pinkie finger from this distance, and Mount Rainier is a bump on the horizon.

"Shit," I curse, the sentiment echoed by another snarl from my stomach.

"Cussing so early in the morning? Didn't think you had it in you, Bird Girl." The voice comes from behind me, making me jump and yip softly in surprise.

I turn to see Kite cresting the hill, wearing nothing but some sort of leaf apron draped low on his hips and a tired smile. He holds out a hand, filled with a mound of tiny golden things that are roughly rice-shaped, though larger than any grains I've seen before. "I figured you would wake up hungry, so I went forest shopping. Your stomach was growling in your sleep."

"Wh-what's that?" I ask, instead of the hundred other questions running in circles around my brain.

"Why did you kidnap me and drive off a bridge" seems heavy for first thing in the morning. And then there's the fact that I can't seem to stop staring at his body, at his golden, nearly hairless skin that glows with health. And then there are the muscles... powerful muscles on his chest, and abdominal muscles more defined than I would have given him credit for seeing him in baggy sweatshirts and flannels, and equally powerful tree-trunk-sized-legs emerging from his leaf loincloth.

I have no idea what happened to his clothes, but he certainly looks good out of them. So good, I would probably be drooling if my mouth weren't so dry.

And if he weren't insane.

And dangerous.

And probably going to try to take me captive again as soon as we finish whatever he's dug up for breakfast.

"Termites." He pops one into his mouth, chewing with apparent satisfaction. "They're less likely to carry parasites than other edible insects around here. Until we find out how compromised your immune system is, I figure it's best to be careful."

"Um, yeah, thanks but no thanks," I say, taking a step back.

Kite arches a dark brow. "Why? Lots of cultures around the world eat insects. They're high in protein, low in fat, and better for your body than a greasy cow burger." He holds out his hand, his lips curving on one side as he adds, "And you're a bird girl, Bird Girl. Bugs should definitely be a part of your diet."

"I'm not eating termites," I insist, even as my stomach moans sadly, protesting the decision.

"Well, I could try to find some crickets, but we can't toast them, so you'd have to eat them raw. A fire is too risky. We gave the KB the slip last night, but once they realize they must have missed us somewhere along the river, they'll be back."

I cross my arms, fear sparking in my chest. "The KB... What is that?"

"The Kin Born. Their goons are the ones who ran us off the road last night. I'm not sure how they knew we were coming for you, since the Church of Humanity hates them as much as any other group of shifters, but having both bands of crazies on our ass is going to make things tricky. We'd better make tracks, which means you'd better eat."

"What?" I exhale sharply through my nose. "As far as I can recall, you ran yourself off the road and—"

"We can debate the finer points of our escape later, after we're safe. Now eat."

"Ugh," I mutter, my mouth watering despite the level of gross inherent in a pile of decapitated termites. "I can't believe I'm even considering it, but I'm so hungry."

Kite nods, his expression sobering. "Good. That means your systems are coming back online, kicking off the drugs. How are you feeling this morning? Any better?"

"Some," I admit cautiously, watching him through narrowed eyes as he moves closer, walking with a slow, easy gait, as if he isn't bothered in the slightest by the rough ground on his bare feet. "Where are your clothes?"

"They didn't survive the shift." He pauses a few feet away, as if he can sense exactly how close I'll allow him before I retreat. "They never do. Which means I've got spare clothes stashed all over the city. It's just a matter of getting to one of my lockers before someone sees me and starts asking me where I got my kick-ass leaf diaper and wanting to place an order with my designer."

I huff in surprise, and Kite smiles again—thin, but hopeful. "Not a laugh, but I'll take it."

"I'd rather you take me seriously and stop talking in riddles." I turn my head, studying him. "What is the shift? You said that last night, right before—"

"As soon as we're safe, I'll explain everything," he cuts in. "But first we need to move, and before we can move, we need to get something in your belly." He extends his insect offering again, his long arm bringing the mound of termites within easy reach. "Your body will be going through some serious shit for the next few days. You're going to need all the strength you can get."

"Serious shit, huh?" I echo as I shake my head. "Why do I feel like I'm never going to get any answers from you?"

"You will," he promises, his dark eyes boring into mine with an intensity that makes me dizzy all over again. "I swear on my mother's life, and you know how much I love that woman."

"I don't know anything about you, Kite." The backs of my eyes begin to sting. "How can I trust that anything you said was real? You've been lying to me from the moment we met. I have no idea who you really are. All I know is that you kidnapped me and put my life in danger and probably…" I choke on the words rising in my throat as I turn, scanning the forest around us. But aside from a squirrel racing up a nearby tree, the woods are still. "Where's Sierra?" I ask softly.

Kite's sighs sadly. "I don't know. The current was too fast. It took longer than I thought to get you out of the back seat. She was swept away before I could get to her."

"So it's my fault." I cover my mouth with my hand, fighting tears.

"Of course it's not your fault. Not even a little bit." He steps closer, warming me with his heat as the hand full of bugs drops to his side. I can feel how much he wants to wrap me up in his arms, and a part of me wants that, too—so freaking much—but I don't deserve comfort, and he can't be trusted.

"She's dead because you helped me first." I lift my chin, pinning him with a hard look. "You should have helped her. She's your friend."

"You're my friend, too," Kite says, pain tightening his features. "I care about you, Wren, every bit as much as I care about Sierra. But Sierra was a member of the resistance in peak physical condition who had agreed to risk her life for the cause, if necessary. You're a rescue who's had a steady dose of poison dumped into your body every day of your life. You needed my help more, so I went for you first, and I would do it again." He pauses, jaw clenching as he nods. "Sierra would have made the same call if she were big enough to carry you out of the river in her kin form. We both did what we had to do, and I for one believe she's still alive somewhere down stream. And maybe, if we stop talking and start walking, we'll find her." He lifts his hand, bringing the termite-rice-filled palm to hover beneath my nose. "But first you need to eat."

Lips pursed, I'm considering another flat refusal to eat insects or a demand to know what the hell he's talking about—I haven't been poisoned, and I didn't need to be rescued, and what the heck is a kin form—

but I can tell by the look in his eyes that he's done talking. He's entered stubborn mode, and I know from watching him with the kids at the shelter that there's no swaying him when he gets like this.

"Fine, I'll eat," I snap. "But when I'm done eating, you start talking. Last time I checked, you can walk and talk at the same time."

Kite's eyes narrow on mine. "All right. But only if you eat fast and keep up so I don't have to carry you. You're light, but I'll still be out of breath if I'm walking for two."

"Fine." I prop my hands on my hips.

"Fine, fine." He casts a pointed glance down at his hand.

Without breaking eye contact, I reach up, gather every single firm, bulgy little body in my fist, and slam them into my mouth. I chew slowly, thoroughly, refusing to let how creepy I find the feel of thorax bursting on my tongue show on my face. Kite watches me, respect blooming in his expression as I finish chewing and swallow the entire mess down without a flinch.

"How was that?" he asks, brows lifting.

"Crunchy," I offer in a monotone. "Gross. A little nutty. More acidic than expected, and at the earliest convenience I would like a drink of water."

Kite's lips curve. "There's a clear stream not far from here. I hit it this morning. Would have brought you some of that, too, but I didn't have anything suitable for carrying a drink back to my lady."

"I'm not your lady," I say, but when Kite leans close,

offering in a husky whisper—"Maybe not, but you're a badass. Even more than I thought. Can't wait to get to know who you're going to be now that you're out of your cage, Bird Girl."—I blush and forget how to form words.

By the time I whip up a comeback, he's already halfway across the clearing.

He pauses there, giving an impatient jerk of his head. "Come on, then, tough stuff. Gotta walk the walk if you want to talk the talk."

For a split second, I debate making a break in the other direction.

But even though I'm feeling better than I have most mornings in recent memory, I'm still weak, dehydrated, suffering from a chronic illness, and entirely outmatched when it comes to speed and strength. If I run, Kite will catch me without breaking a sweat, and then I might never have answers.

At least now, I have a bargain in place and reasonable certainty that Kite will hold up his end of the deal if I hold up mine.

Ignoring the discomfort in my feet as I scramble over the rough terrain in my soggy socks, I hurry after him, silently hoping I won't regret going deeper into the woods with this man.

CHAPTER 9

KITE

T*ake it slow, man. Take it slow and there's a chance you can get her back under lock and key before she decides to make a run for it.*

I cut a glance Wren's way as she pulls even with me on the deer trail winding through the woods, headed southwest. She's thin and frail and clearly still as weak as a newborn kitten, but that won't last long.

She's incredibly powerful, this girl.

So powerful it's a miracle that she's still alive.

The monsters who drug our kind into what they call "remission" have fine-tuned their medications over the years, but there still comes a point when they have to weigh risk vs. reward. The amount of meds it takes to suppress transformation in someone like Wren—a shifter from one of the most ancient bloodlines, dating all the way back to Mesopotamia and the cradle of civilization—often prove deadly. The line between "enough" and "too much" is razor thin, so sharp it leaves scars on those who do survive.

Even if Wren is as strong as she seems and is able to work through the mental and emotional anguish of learning everything she thought was true is a lie, she's going to bear the marks of these meds for the rest of her life. She might never be able to shift without pain, might never escape the chronic fatigue that plagues so many former captives, or she might lose her fucking mind.

A lot of us do.

Even those who have never swallowed a pill in our lives. Living a secret life on the fringes of society takes its toll on the spirit.

"I don't hear talking," she pants, her voice breathy, but stronger than it was even a half mile back.

"Just a second." I pretend to study the landscape ahead with a critical eye. "Just want to make sure we're not getting off course."

"One second, that's it," she says. She's bouncing back strong. The skin-to-skin contact between us last night definitely helped. It would have been more therapeutic for her if she'd been in her kin form, but until she's able to shift, fuzzy snuggles in her human skin will speed her healing.

And I will be happy to be the fuzzy in question.

I'm gone on this girl. Completely gone, crushing so hard that the fear in her eyes last night and the suspicion in them this morning are a knife stabbing into my chest.

She stops beside me with a frustrated huff and a stomp of her socked foot that is pretty adorable. *She's* adorable, in these baggy pink pajama pants and fuzzy gray long-sleeved tee, making me wish we were on an alternate timeline somewhere, snuggling in bed after an amazing night out catching some music, or wandering through a street market, or just cruising the beach collecting sea glass.

"That's it," she says, propping her hands low on her hips. "Answers, Kite. Now. Or I don't take another step and I don't trust you ever again."

Breath rasping in my throat, I turn to her, wishing we could put this off a little longer, but this girl is as stubborn as I am, and she's clearly reached her threshold for stalling tactics. "When I first started rescuing captives, I always rushed in too fast with too much information, and inevitably ended up scaring the shit out of the people I wanted to save." I rub a hand across my chest, not missing the way Wren's eyes flick down to my fingers and back up again, or the pink that stains her cheeks. At least she still thinks I'm pretty. That's something. If I can just convince her I'm not one of the bad guys, maybe she'll even let me kiss her again someday. "I'd end up with a hysterical kid in denial, weeping uncontrollably, begging me to let him stay in the shithole where I found him, or a pissed-off kid determined to maim me before I could get her out of danger. Either way, the end result was the same, so I eventually stopped trying to explain things beforehand."

"Kidnap first, explain later?" she asks, blue eyes icy.

"Something like that," I say gently, silently begging her to give me a break. "But I only want to help people like you, Bird Girl. It's my mission in life. My spirit work. It's something I do because I care. Especially about you."

"What do you mean, people like me?" she asks, ignoring my attempt to introduce emotions into the picture. "Sick people? Members of the movement? Which of those was my lucky lottery card?"

I bite my lip and shake my head, certain this conversation isn't going to end well. But we might as well get the worst out first, I guess. After that, there's nowhere to go but up. "Both. And you're not sick. They made you sick with all that shit they've been pumping into your body to keep you from figuring out who you really are. *What* you really are."

Wren rolls her eyes with a laugh. "I almost wish you were right. Seriously, I would love to be able to stop taking meds and magically be well, but that's not reality, Kite."

I shrug. "Listen, I get the denial—everyone I rescue goes through it to some degree—but sooner or later, you're going to be confronted with undeniable evidence that I'm telling the truth. And then you're going to have to deal with the fact that the people who adopted you aren't your family. Or your friends. They're crazy extremists who were willing to put your life on the line in order to make sure you never turned into something their messed-up religion doesn't approve of."

She shakes her head, her bottom lip jutting out as her expression hardens. "No. That's not true. You don't know anything about my family. Mom and Pops are nothing like that. They are the kindest, most generous—"

"They're monsters!" I say, frustration making my voice louder than I want it to be.

"No, they're not," she shouts. "They love me!"

"Fine. They may love you. Parents in India and East Africa who take their baby girls to have their genitals mutilated love those kids, too. That doesn't make what they do in the name of their religious beliefs any less barbaric."

Wren's lip curls. "You're crazy."

"I'm not," I say softly. "And that's what's really crazy. These people think we're marked by the beast, Wren. The devil. And the only way to save the earth from our 'wickedness' is to control those of us they can with drugs and slaughter the rest."

"Beast-marked?" she whispers, her face going even paler than usual. "But that's not part of the movement anymore, Kite. It never was, really. The elders purged that from the texts decades ago, along with the nonsense about ghosts and exorcisms and drowning vampires in holy water. That was insanity left over from the early days when the elders were old hippies who'd done too much LSD while watching cheesy horror movies. None of us actually believe beast-people or vampires are real anymore, and the sane members of the movement never did."

Now it's my turn to roll my eyes.

"We don't," she insists. "I'm mean, clearly you believe you're...special in some way, but I—"

"Ouch." I thump my fist gently against my chest, above my heart. "Special, huh? Is that your nice way of saying you think I should be locked in a padded room with no doorknobs?"

Wren clears her throat, suddenly very interested in a bit of mud caked on the back of her hand. "I didn't say that. I wouldn't presume to tell you where you belong, Kite, all I know is who *I* am. And I'm not a supernatural creature. I'm just an average girl with a Meltdown virus, like hundreds of others across the world."

"There's nothing average about you, Bird Girl," I say, my voice going husky. "You're one of the kindest, bravest, most good-hearted people I've ever met. There's nothing average about that. In the world we live in, that sort of kindness takes fucking guts."

She swallows and her forehead ripples. "Th-thank you. I..." She shakes her head, apparently thinking better of what she was going to say. "My parents, Hank and Abby, are the ones who taught me to be kind. And I've never heard them utter a single word about werewolves or ghosts or anything else. They're the least supernaturally or fictionally inclined people in the world. They don't even watch that kind of stuff on television. They're documentary and news-watching people, firmly grounded in reality and motivated by love and concern for me."

She stands up straighter, obviously buoyed by her own argument. "They would never hurt me, Kite. I can't even imagine it. They would die first. There is no doubt in my mind, and nothing you say is going to shake my faith in them. Hank and Abby are my parents, and we're a family, and they want me to get better more than anything else in the world. Truly, they're willing to do anything to make it happen."

"Even damn your soul to hell for all eternity?" I ask, though I know there's no way I'm getting through to her right now.

Shifting into bear form would certainly help with the whole "denial of the existence of shifters" thing, but I'd be wasting precious energy I need to get us both to safety, and her parents and the movement are too deep in her head for me to have any chance of deprogramming her this quickly.

It's going to take time, and time is one of the many things we don't have right now. The Kin Born soldiers who nearly killed us last night won't stop scouring the river and the forest until they find us, and we've already been vulnerable for too long.

"I believe you mean well, Kite, and that you *think* you're telling the truth, but I... I can't believe this. Not about my parents," Wren says, but there's hesitation that wasn't there before.

I should insist we take the rest of this convo on the road, but I'm too intrigued by the flicker of doubt in her pretty blue eyes to look away. "What about the rest of it?"

She meets my gaze, her throat working as she swallows. "There was something last night. Something I just remembered."

"Yeah?" I prompt after a moment. "What was that?"

She blinks faster. "I dreamt that I woke up and... There was someone, *something*, holding me and... It wasn't exactly…human." She glances up at me through her lashes.

I smile. "And how did it feel? This dream?"

"It felt…safe," she says, holding my gaze as electricity leaps between us, charging the early morning air. The attraction is still there. I can feel it prickling across my skin as her focus shifts from my eyes to my lips and back again.

I wonder if she's thinking about our kiss yesterday, and hope to all the gods she is, because I haven't been able to stop thinking about it.

I've never fallen for one of the people I've rescued before, but Wren is different, special. I've known for a while she and I might have a future together, but actually meeting her changed everything. From the moment our eyes met months ago, when she looked up at me from her desk where she was working on handwritten Valentine's Day cards for all one hundred and three kids under her care—each one personalized and overflowing with heart and humor—I was possessed by the urge not just to help her or save her, but to know her.

To get closer to her and see if she was as amazing as she seemed.

After four months, I know she's even better—kinder, funnier, stronger, fiercer and more passionate than anyone gives her credit for.

And sexy, too.

Like right now, the way she bites her lip as her eyes search mine…

It's enough to make me ache to hold her, to pull her close and crush my lips to hers and show her just what she does to me, all the incredible, overwhelming things she makes me feel. I haven't felt this kind of hope in so damned long, and it isn't just because Wren is the one who might finally put an end to all the terror and bloodshed plaguing our world. It's because she's a girl with the prettiest blue eyes and the sweetest heart, who tastes like moonlight and honeysuckle and who makes me long to be the one who gets to wake up to her kiss every morning.

"All I want to do is keep you safe," I finally say, neither confirming nor denying that I was the not-human someone in her "dream." There will be time for that later. For now, I just need her to know that, "As long as there's breath in my body, I'll do everything in my power to keep you out of harm's way, Wren. I'll give my life for yours if I have to."

She steps closer, her lips softly parting, and I realize she's going to kiss me, to push up on tiptoe and bring her lips to mine, and I experience a flash of anxiety that I'm going to embarrass myself. My leaf loincloth covers the subject now, but if Wren's kiss starts doing what it did to me yesterday, I'll soon be pitching a massive leaf tent. And when the leaf tent goes up, the berries are going to end up dangling in the breeze for all the world—and this girl I would really prefer not to be introduced to my balls this early in our relationship —to see.

I do not have attractive balls. Do any guys have attractive balls? Is Wren experienced enough to realize that my balls are merely equally ugly to all other balls and not uniquely hideous monstrosities that should never be allowed to dangle free in the forest or anywhere else?

I have no idea, but it's a risk I'm willing to take for another taste of her sweet mouth. I lean down, gently threading my fingers through her tangled hair, my pulse spiking as the heat of her body warms my lips, and the river and Wren scent of her fills my head.

My eyes are sliding closed, and I'm half a racing heartbeat away from claiming her mouth, when the sharp *whomp-whomp-whomp* of chopper blades thrums through the air, silencing the birds and sending any creature with sense diving for cover.

"Get down," I order urgently.

"What, I—"

"Down, now." I put an arm around Wren, dragging her to the ground with me as I back off the deer trail, tucking us both against the side of a tree, hoping the evergreen needles above will conceal our presence as the churning sound of the chopper blades grows closer.

Of course, if they have heat-seeking instruments in the copter, a lack of naked-eye visibility won't matter— our blood will give us away.

With a glance over my shoulder, I quickly estimate the time it will take me to carry Wren to the river versus the time it will take for the helicopter to reach our location. It's going to be tight—tight as hell—but I think I can make it.

I have to make it. I meant what I said to Wren. I'm going to keep her safe, and I'm willing to go to whatever lengths it takes.

A second later, I've got Wren in my arms, hauling ass

down the hill to the river bank while she clings to my shoulders and hisses, "What's happening, Kite? What's going on? Who's in the helicopter?"

"No time," I pant, staggering down the steep slope where grass and dirt becomes stony river bed. "No time. Just trust me. And I'm sorry."

"Sorry for what?"

"For this." I leap into the swiftly flowing water at the edge of the bank and charge through the current to where the riverbed is shadowed by tree limbs hanging low over the surface.

Wren sucks in a shocked breath as the frigid water soaks into her clothes, but when I lie down in the maybe two feet of river rushing over us, pinning her against me, she doesn't pull away. She presses closer, shivering silently as the helicopter roars overhead, pausing to hover over the place where we went into the river a few yards up the bank.

It makes me wonder if she can feel it—the danger. Empathy is my kin-born gift. I can feel what other people are feeling, even when they don't want me to. It's a gift that led to a lot of pain when I was younger, before I realized that feelings aren't always something we can control and a flash of loathing or contempt from someone I care about doesn't mean they don't still care about me. But these days it saves my life on an almost daily basis.

Like now...

I can feel the hate and fear roiling from whoever is in the chopper and know to stay the fuck down. I can feel how much they want to shoot to kill, to satisfy the blood lust that has their jaws locked tight and their fingers itchy on the trigger.

If Wren is what Ghost says she is, and I have no reason to doubt him, then she should be able to channel my gift, to absorb it through physical touch at first— mental touch once we've established a bond—and use it as her own. Moving slowly, carefully, I press my hand to the top of her chest beneath the water. Even with skin and bone between her heart and my palm, I can feel it thrashing behind her ribs.

She's terrified.

As she should be, but if she gets too worked up, she might trip the heat seeking equipment, even with the cold water streaming over us.

Bringing my lips to her ears, I say just loud enough to be heard over the storm of the chopper blades, "They aren't going to get us. Not today. We've still got too much left to do together. Try to relax if you can. The cooler we stay, the better."

After a beat, she nods, and some of the tension eases from her shoulders as her body melts against mine.

And even though the water is fucking freezing and I can barely feel my arms or legs, a crazy part of me celebrates the chance to be this close to her, to have her against my chest and her ass tucked to my hips and all the lovely length of her fitting into small-spoon position like we were made to fit together.

Maybe she's right. Maybe I am crazy, but as the helicopter finally swoops away, heading south following the curve of the river, I decide I don't give a shit. I stopped asking "why" a long time ago.

Most of the time, "why" doesn't matter. Things just are the way they are, and the sooner you start tackling how to deal with them, the better. Many a life has been lost to "why," to looking back and shifting puzzle pieces made of smoke and raging at people who are now ghosts.

I don't care about why, I only care that holding Wren feels like the rightest thing I've ever done, and I'm not going to stop fighting for her until she gives me a chance to show her how good we could be together.

How completely fucking perfect.

As if reading my mind—or my heart, I guess—Wren shifts in my arms, glancing over her shoulder into my eyes. "If you're thinking what I think you're thinking while we're submerged in forty-degree water and have just barely escaped being shot by bad guys, you really are out of your mind."

I laugh because sometime a man just has to cop to being a man, a less than logical creature ruled as much by what's between his legs as what's between his ears.

And then a miracle happens—Wren laughs, too, before coming to her feet in the water and announcing, "I want a hot coffee and a stack of pancakes as long as my arm. Then we can get back to our discussion. I haven't been this hungry in years, and I'm not going to be able to think straight until I eat something more than termites."

Grinning, I stand beside her. "I can make that happen."

"You can?" She arches a brow. "Because right now

neither of us is any state to cruise into the nearest diner."

I scoff as I offer my arm for her to hold onto for balance as we start toward shore. "Oh, I have my ways, Bird Girl. And a few tricks up my sleeve. You stick with me and I'll take care of your belly. We'll have you fattened up in no time."

She steps out of the river ahead of me, turning to cast a darker look my way. She doesn't say a word, but I can feel the silent battle waging inside her, the way she's suddenly torn between the lies of the past and the possibilities of the future. She's still not sold on me, on this great escape, and she might very well try to run if I give her the chance. But she doesn't hate me anymore, and that's a start.

"The journey of a thousand miles begins with one step," I whisper.

"Chinese philosophy so early in the morning?"

"Any time's a good time for Chinese philosophy." I squeeze her hand. "But that was also an offer of a piggy-back ride. I can get us where we're going faster if you'll let me carry you."

Wren hesitates, but after a moment she nods. "As long as you promise to put me down if you get tired."

"I don't get tired," I say with a wink. "But sure, in the unlikely event your scrawny scrap of a self starts feeling heavy, I'll put you down. Deal?"

Her lips twist. "Deal. For now."

And that's good enough.

For now.

CHAPTER 10

WREN

I'm probably losing my mind—or developing a swift and sudden case of Stockholm syndrome— but I can't worry about that right now. I can't seem to focus for too long on anything except how atrociously starved I am.

Starved to the core, to the bone, to the depths of my very being.

I thought I understood what it meant to be ravenous —childhood growth spurts and school days when lunch wasn't served until nearly one o'clock stand out in my memory as particularly belly-focused times—but I have never experienced anything like the hunger that catches fire inside me somewhere between the woods and Dupont, Washington. I only know that by the time we reach the U-Store at the edge of town, it feels like my stomach is about to inflict serious damage on the world at large.

"Are you going to be okay out here alone for a few

minutes?" Kite asks, squatting beside where I'm perched on a tree root in the woods a few yards from the storage facility's back fence.

I scrunch my nose and nod—just once.

"Are you sure?" Kite presses. "If you're scared, I can—"

"I'm not scared, I'm hangry," I snap. "I finally understand what hangry feels like, and it's not funny. Not even a little bit."

His lips twitch at the edges, but he seems to know better than to laugh at me. "Okay, then I'll hurry. Give me two minutes. Sit tight and try not to chew your arm off while I'm gone."

"I'll try," I respond in a sullen voice as he pats me on the back before loping away toward the fence and scaling it with the ease of one of those kids who uses the urban landscape as an obstacle course.

What is the name of that?

When they leap off of roofs and flip over stair railings?

I can't remember—my brain is a shriveled creature desperately in need of calories—and that makes me even angrier. I am full-on spitting mad at...nothing. No one. I'm enraged at the universe and fate and the layout of the greater Seattle-Tacoma metro area for being pock-marked by so many lakes and rivers that the sprawl has been contained to isolated pockets and Kite and I have not passed a single restaurant in our journey.

I'm not mad at Kite anymore. Not at all, which is *crazy*.

It doesn't matter that the helicopter gave me a case

of bad vibes unlike anything I can remember, or that I believe Kite's intentions are good. He still *kidnapped* me and took me away from my family and may have signed my death certificate.

I've missed the procedure for certain, now. Even if I manage to get home soon and put all this madness behind me, there's no guarantee I'll be able to score another appointment.

You might not need it. Can you remember the last time you felt this good? This awake and alive? And this is after you've missed two doses of your meds. You should be on the floor, too tired to lift your head up, but you're not.

I chew the edge of my thumb, not liking the suspicions these thoughts set to reeling through my head. There could still be another explanation. I could have been having a negative reaction to the meds my doctors didn't understand, or this could be the calm before the storm—my body surging back to life before it recovers sufficiently to return to attacking itself full time—but the constant snarling of my stomach is a nagging reminder that Kite might be telling the truth.

It's unfathomable, this idea that my parents might willingly poison me, but...

I shake my head. "No. They wouldn't. Never." My voice is thin and soft, barely audible over the distant rush of cars pulsing past on the highway miles away, but it does me good to hear it.

I saw the devastation on Mom and Pops's faces at the memorial service for Scarlett. They were shattered, every bit as broken by the loss of my sister as if she had been their biological daughter. They loved her, and they love me. They've gone into tens of thousands of dollars' worth of debt to treat my condition and put themselves through incalculable amounts of heartache.

My symptoms match the list for the Devour virus almost exactly. And I know better than to think that furry people are real.

So I had a crazy dream last night, so what? I was delirious and in the middle of withdrawal from my meds after being driven off a bridge and almost drowning in a freezing cold river. It was probably all a fever dream.

And my parents are no doubt worried sick about me, and not because they can't wait to get back to poisoning me. By now they will have realized I'm not in my bed, and that something terrible must have happened to me. They've probably already called the police and activated a movement positive-energy circle and are sitting by the phone, praying for me to reach out and let them know I'm okay.

There hasn't been any chance of getting to a phone until now—Kite has been watching me like a hawk, and we've been wandering around the middle of nowhere— but the storage facility might have a front office and someone on duty willing to let a girl in muddy sock feet use the phone.

I hesitate, guilt flashing through my chest as I contemplate breaking my promise to Kite to "sit tight" and how pissed he's going to be about me reaching out to the people he thinks are responsible for making me sick. But then I come to my senses and slip out from the tree line, scurrying around the closely shorn lawn that surrounds the rows of bright orange lockers toward the front of the complex.

Kite is a good guy, yes.

Kite is also someone I could see myself coming to care about—a lot—even if he is a radicalized kidnapping conspiracy theorist, but my parents are my *parents*.

Hank and Abby have been there for me almost every day of my life—good times and bad, happy and sad, miserable and silly and everything in between. My loyalty belongs to them, to the family we created together when they chose to rescue two hopeless kids and bring my sister and me into their home.

By the time I reach the entrance, I'm out of breath, but not nearly the way I would have been twenty-four hours earlier. My heart is beating faster, but I still have enough air left in my lungs to curse as I realize the front gate is controlled by remote and there isn't a sign of human life inside the rows and rows of identical orange boxes on the other side.

I'm about to give up and jog back to my hiding place, hoping I'll get there before Kite, when something catches my attention across the narrow county road running past the facility. It's a call box, one of those emergency phones that used to line highways before the proliferation of cell phones. My parents stopped to use one when our car broke down on the way to a camping trip when I was a little girl, after Pops realized he'd forgotten to charge his cell and Mom had left hers at home.

If I'm lucky, this one might still be functional.

Glancing both ways down the utterly isolated road, I

trot across the graying pavement and pry open the plastic box protecting the device inside. The puce-colored phone is coated with dirt, the cord connecting the receiver to the control box is cracked with age, and it looks like no one's serviced this sucker since long before I was born.

I expect to be disappointed, but when I lift the receiver, I hear a dial tone on the end of the line. It's distant and grainy, but there.

My heart leaps into my throat, frantically pulsing, as several soft clicking sounds are followed by ringing.

The phone is ringing! I'm about to make contact with the real world, to talk to someone who can help me get in touch with my parents and put this crazy night behind me.

"Nine-one-one, what's your emergency?" a faint voice asks, summoning a sob of relief from deep in my chest.

"I have to get in touch with my family. They're probably scared to death." Words spill out in a jumble as my brain tries to think clearly over the rush of excitement. "I was taken last night. From my house, I—"

"What's your name, ma'am?" the faint voice demands. "And are you in need of medical attention?"

"I don't think so," I say, my head still fuzzy from shock and hunger. "I think I'm okay, and my—"

Something blurs past my face and a second later an unfamiliar male hand snatches the phone from me and slams it back into the cradle, abruptly ending the call.

I reel around, stumbling backward. I'm about to fall into the weedy ditch at the side of the road when the man grips my elbow and draws me back onto solid ground. The second my feet are on the pavement, I wrench free and back away, watching the stranger warily.

He's only a couple inches taller than my five eight, with a slim but solid build, and slender fingers he threads together in front of his midsection. He's wearing expensive-looking gray suit pants that fit like they've been custom-made, a white button-up rolled at the sleeves to reveal surprisingly tan forearms for a guy who looks like he works with money, and a thin red tie that furthers the vintage vibe.

All things considered, he would be a fairly nonthreatening figure if he hadn't just put an end to my call for help with the whip-fast moves of a striking cobra.

And if he weren't so arresting to look at...

Broad shoulders, a shock of brown hair falling over a noble-looking forehead, and piercing gray eyes set in a face blessed with perfect masculine symmetry all contribute to the overall *Wow* effect. And then he opens his mouth and asks in an accent that's pure smooth and sexy Mark Darcy, "I'm sorry, but I couldn't allow you to complete that call."

"Who-who are you?" I take another step away, my admiration turning to trepidation as I wonder if this man is one of the people hunting us, one of the KB people Kite was talking about, one of those hate-filled things I could feel seething at us from the helicopter.

But he doesn't feel filled with hate, this random Brit seemingly spit out onto the pavement here in the middle of nowhere Washington. Presumably via a TARDIS?

No, he seems almost…familiar. Something about his eyes, his voice, and the particular sweep of his top lip, like the body of a priceless violin, all elegant curves.

"I'm a friend," he says, watching me with an intensity that's unnerving. "At least, I hope I can be again. We have a lot of lost time to make up for, you and I."

"Lost time," I echo, my chest filling with a strange swelling sensation as my body makes the connection seconds before my brain. But surely it can't be, this tall, powerful-looking man…

This clearly healthy person, who has probably never suffered through a sick day in his life…

There's no way this is… "Dust?"

A grin streaks across his face, revealing familiar, slightly crooked front teeth. "You remember."

"Of course I do. Oh my God, it's so good to see you, I can't believe you're here," I mutter, stepping toward him with my hands outstretched, only to check myself and back away again, snatching my hands to my chest. I'm instinctively drawn to Dust and dying to find out where he's been all these years, but even half starved and stupid with hunger, I know the odds that this meeting is a coincidence are slim to none.

Wasn't I just thinking of him yesterday, when I was trying to figure out who was responsible for that creepy phone call?

Forcing my arms to my sides, I ask, "Why did you do that?" I motion toward the call box. "I was trying to get help."

"I know." His smile fades. "But help's already here, and more is on the way. I trust Kite's done well by you." His gray eyes darken as he casts a glance over my shoulder. "Or as well as can be expected, considering he decided to drive you off a bridge less than half an hour after rescuing you from captivity."

"I did what I had to do, asshole." Kite's voice comes from behind me. I turn to see him hurrying across the road, now dressed in jeans and a simple white shirt that emphasizes the wedge shape of his torso, with a backpack slung over one shoulder. He stops behind me, putting a protective hand on my arm. "You okay, Bird Girl? Is Ghost creeping you out?"

This is Ghost? Dust is the person on the other end of the phone, the one Sierra was begging to send help? The one who hung up on her and left us all hanging?

I shrug Kite's hand off and step away from both of them. "No, I'm not okay. So you two know each other. You're friends?"

"Friends isn't the word I would use." Dust's voice is as crisp and politely cutting as it was every time he dressed down a bully on the playground when we were kids.

"Me either, Prince Charming." Kite smirks as he props his hands low on his hips, glancing my way as he jerks his chin toward Dust. "This one's royalty in our world; too good to get his hands dirty. Prefers to stay above it all, letting the rest of us risk our necks."

Dust sighs and rolls his eyes, seemingly bored. "That's such a preposterous misrepresentation of the truth, I'm not sure where to begin correcting you, Pooh-bie."

"Don't call me that," Kite growls.

"But sadly, we don't have time for a history lesson at the moment," Dust continues, adjusting the already impeccable fold of his right sleeve. "Kin Born forces were spotted less than ten miles from here, in the air and on the hunt."

"Yeah, we already ran into them," Kite says. "And gave them the slip. Last I saw the chopper was headed south, following the river."

"Helicopters are capable of reversing course," Dust says. "And so should we. The Church of Humanity activated reclamation protocols a little after nine p.m. last night. They've been looking for Wren for over twelve hours, and their resources are considerable. The sooner we get to the safe house and out of sight, the better."

Kite curses. "They called it in right after we took her? Sierra said she didn't think the old man got a good look at her. At least, not good enough to see that she had Wren slung over her shoulder."

"Apparently Sierra was wrong." Dust glances up at the sky, where storm clouds are beginning to gather, promising rain before afternoon. "Where *is* the trash panda? Celeste is worried."

"I...I don't know," Kite says, his chin dropping closer to his chest.

"You don't know?" Dust echoes, his voice cold.

"We lost her in the river. Wren was still out of it, withdrawing hard from the meds. I had to get her out of the car first, and by the time I did..."

"You shouldn't have gone into the river in the first place." Dust steps closer to Kite, his hands curling into fists as he moves. "Help was on the way. If you'd waited five damned minutes before you flew off the handle, we—"

"And how the hell was I supposed to know that?" Kite shouts. "You fucking hung up on us."

"I didn't hang up on you, the call was disconnected when—"

"Sure the hell sounded like it, and we were out of time, Mr. Perfect."

"Will you two, stop?" I say, raising my voice to be heard. "This isn't—"

"And we didn't have five minutes," Kite barrels on. "I had to make a call to try to save our skin, so I made it. And if you'll notice, Wren is here in one piece."

"And on the verge of alerting the authorities to our presence," Dust snaps. "If I hadn't stopped her, the movement would know exactly where she is right now."

"Seriously, stop it." I step between them, lifting my hands as if to hold them apart. "You're both—"

"And authorities are certainly on the way to this location right now," Dust cuts in, his manners not nearly as lovely as I remember. "So we should cut the shit and—"

"Hey, I'm talking, too!" I shout as Kite starts in with something about logistics. "Don't you know it's rude to talk over your kidnap victim? Especially when she's trying to tell you that she's not going anywhere with either of you until she gets some answers and is allowed to call her parents and tell them that she's not dead at the bottom of the river."

Dust gaze softens as it shifts my way. "I know how hard this is for you. Believe me, I do, but we can't allow you to stay here exposed. It isn't safe. Explanations will have to wait."

My lips part and I'm on the verge of using a few expletives to inform him how very tired I am of being told to wait for answers—he lost the right to be the leader of our merry band when he left town without saying a word and let me think he was dead for years—when a *whip-ping* sound whistles past my ear, so close it makes me flinch.

"What the…" I lift a hand to my ear, but before I can touch my fingers to the stinging place on the side of my head, the sharp *whip* comes again and again, three times in a row and a sensation like the worst bee sting in the world cuts into my chest, so close to my heart that for a moment I think I've been stabbed.

No, not stabbed…

Shot, I realize as Dust knocks me to the ground, rolling on top of me, while Kite pulls a gun from his backpack and takes aim at the field on the other side of the road. He fires again and again, not pausing a second, even when he's hit and red blooms across the virgin fabric of his white T-shirt.

Virgin, you're going to die a virgin, a voice in my head mumbles in a traumatized monotone as I watch Kite continue to fire and my chest fills with rocks—giant heavy rocks that weigh me down, cementing me to the warm pavement beneath my shoulders.

I try to pull in a breath, to call Kite's name, to tell whoever is out there firing on him to stop. But all I can manage is a wheezing gasp as Dust tucks his head close to mine, shielding me with his body.

I can't stand this—the senseless violence.

Our planet is already drowning in humanity's mistakes, the rising sea and resulting climate chaos putting all of us at greater risk of violent death and disease than our ancestors even just one generation ago would have believed possible. The only way we're going to survive as a species, as a planet, is to work together, to talk to each other, to empathize and share and remember the lessons we learned in kindergarten and forgot somewhere on the way to pretending to be grown-ups.

Seeing Kite shooting to kill—even knowing he's only shooting to protect the three of us—makes me physically ill. He is so gentle and good.

What kind of world do we live in where good people are forced to become monsters in order to survive?

But I want to survive, I realize.

Desperately. Frantically.

I don't want to die here in the road with so much left undone and unknown, with all the dreams I never let myself dream locked away inside me, and all my unanswered questions seething through my brain. There is so much left to discover, and for a moment it felt like I was on the verge of something new, something terrifying, but also thrilling and hopeful and freeing.

What would it be like to be free? To finally cast off

the shackles of this disease that's dragged me down and fenced me in every day of my life?

Dust has done it. Somehow.

In the shock of seeing him for the first time, I didn't connect the dots right away, but now, as he lifts me with seeming effortlessness, cradling me in his arms as he stands and runs across the road, through the grass, into the shelter of the trees, it's clear. The boy who was my partner in sick-kid crimes—whatever innocent infractions we could get away with, considering our finite energy reserves—is now a full-grown man.

A healthy man.

A man in command of himself and his surroundings, who doesn't hesitate to bark orders. "There's a car waiting for us at the edge of town. Run ahead to the corner of Pine and Fifth. Tell the driver to get the first aid kit out of the trunk and be ready to move."

"Is she okay?" Kite asks, his face bobbing above mine as he pulls even with Dust.

"No, she's been shot," Dust snaps. "And so have you. So move your ass, Kite. If we lose her, I'm holding you personally fucking responsible."

Kite's dark eyes flash with anger—then pain, guilt, shame, and so many other emotions he shouldn't be feeling. It isn't his fault that I was shot. It was the fault of the person who pulled the trigger.

I want to tell him that, but I'm beyond words.

Nearly beyond breath.

The rocks in my chest have multiplied and spread, rolling out to fill every inch of my body, dragging at my hips, my limbs, my head, my eyes—now far too heavy to remain open with boulders balanced on my lids, demanding I rest.

Demanding I go to a place deeper and darker than sleep.

Demanding I go...now.

CHAPTER 11

DUST

The ride to the safe house outside Port Townsend—careening up the highway and off onto side streets and then onto still smaller, even less trafficked country roads winding out into the middle of nowhere—as Wren bleeds on my lap is the longest in memory.

And I have a long memory.

A near perfect one, in fact.

I remember every second of my captivity, from the morning my new mother and father adopted me at the orphanage in Salisbury, to the illness that took hold soon after our move to the States, to every hard as hell day after as I struggled to finish the business of growing up while battling what I'd been told was a disease doing its best to devour me from the inside out.

There was only one bright spot—the girl with the big blue eyes and jet-black hair. The girl with the skin as

white as snow and lips as red as blood, just like
Snow White.

Until I met Wren, I'd assumed I was a Sleeping
Beauty kind of guy—all that long blond hair did something for me, even as a child—but Wren changed
all that.

I had never seen anyone that stunning in real life.
And it wasn't just her pretty face or her sweet smile or
the way she giggled like she was going to pass out when
I told one of the not-safe-for-grown-ups-to-overhear
stories she loved so much. It was all the things inside of
her—her hope and gentleness and her fierce loyalty to
those she claimed as her own.

For a time, I was part of Wren's tribe, one of her
people. I know she must have grieved when I left. It
must have torn her apart not to know where I was,
what I was doing, if I was okay or if I'd lost the battle
against the "virus" like so many of the kids we'd grown
up with in our school for the tragically ill.

If I could have reached out to her, I would have. But
it was too dangerous.

For both of us.

I'd hoped to explain myself now that we're adults, all
grown up and old enough to fight for our right to exist
together. But I might never get the chance.

"Can't you go any faster?" I growl to Creedence,
who's in the driver's seat, steering the car with a wrist
propped on top of the wheel.

"I'm going ten miles over, Captain," Creedence
drawls in response. "If I go any faster, we risk getting
pulled over, and I don't want to explain to small-town

cops why we've got two gunshot victims in this car. Do you?"

Curling my free hand—the one not cradling Wren's head—into a fist, I fight to keep a rein on my temper. "She needs medical attention. Now. It's worth the risk. Drive faster."

"No, she's going to be okay," Kite pipes up from beside me. "She's fighting back, digging deep. She's not going to be leaving us anytime soon."

I turn to see the bear shifter with his big hands wrapped tenderly around Wren's calves. He's pushed up her filthy pajama pants to achieve skin-to-skin contact, something that allows all shifters to bond more closely with each other—emotionally and supernaturally—but which is especially powerful for bear shifters. Empathy can become almost like telepathy if it's strong enough, and Kite is evidently the best of the best, the most devoted feeler his clan could offer. When we first met a few months ago, as we plotted our course and our rescue mission began to take shape, I actually liked the guy.

But that was before he went undercover to get closer to Wren.

Before he started flirting with her, teasing her, touching her way too often and hugging her goodbye in a way that made it clear he couldn't wait to get his paws all over her.

That was before the kiss yesterday, the one I was forced to watch from afar because it was my day to run security detail.

Now, I mostly want to rip his meaty hands off and

stuff them into his Wren-molesting mouth.

We all know what we're here for, and I'm as willing as the rest of them to share—assuming Wren decides there's a place in her heart for one or more of us and doesn't send off for another batch of mate candidates once she realizes how much is at stake—but Kite took unfair advantage of his early access to Wren. And I, for one, am pissed the fuck off about it.

Right, that's why you're pissed. Because he took off before the starting gun, not because deep down in your gut you will always think of her as yours. Your first best friend, your first crush, your Snow.

I lay my hand gently on her forehead, wishing I could feel what the bear can feel, that I could be as sure that she's going to make it to the safe house where we have supplies and medicine to help her heal.

But that's not where my power lies. So instead, I lift my free hand to the roof of the car and dig down into my core, summoning my own special skill.

"Drive faster," I calmly order as my marrow begins to hum and power sizzles up my arm, into my palm and out to hover in a bubble over the car. "I've got us covered."

"No, we can't risk it," Kite says. "What if there are other shifters around, Dust? Kin Born? They'll be able to feel you and—"

"That's a chance I'm willing to take. Drive faster!" I order.

"You're the boss." With an easy nod, Creedence mashes his foot down on the pedal and the car leaps forward. Soon we're speeding down the narrow country lane at nearly seventy miles per hour, but I'm not worried about losing control of the car. Creedence can be frustratingly laid-back and maddeningly shallow at times, but the man is one hell of a driver.

"It's not going to help Wren if we're all dead on the side of the road," Kite seethes through a clenched jaw.

"Relax, man," Creedence says. "I've got this. No one's getting hurt on my watch. I've been driving getaway cars since before you were out of diapers."

"Oh yeah, since you were seven?" Kite snaps back, clearly still irritated at being the youngest member of our crew. At least for now…

We're not sure who the wolves are sending. Wolves outnumber all other shifters three to one, but only very rarely bear the mate mark. Last I heard, the various pack leaders across the United States and Canada had been searching for a potential candidate for months without success and had decided to expand their search to wolves usually considered beyond the pale. Ideally, we'd prefer a marked wolf who isn't a criminal on the outs with his pack, but beggars can't be choosers.

"That's right." Creedence chuckles. "That's growing up with shit parents, Pooh Bear. As soon as you can see over the dashboard, you're ready to take over as designated driver while Ma and Pa get smashed."

"Don't call me that." Kite braces a hand on the roof with a wince as Creedence takes a hairpin turn fast enough to send all of us leaning hard to the left.

"It's Pooh-bie now," I offer, because fucking with Kite is preferable to watching Wren's lids flutter as she fights for her life. "I've shortened it for efficiency."

"Pooh-bie," Creedence echoes. "That does roll off the tongue, doesn't it?"

"You're a pair of assholes," Kite grumbles, but the irritation fades as he sits up straighter in his seat. "Is that the turn?"

"That's it." Creedence cuts hard to the left this time, sending us sliding back to the right. "Just a few minutes now, folks, and we'll be home sweet home."

"When we get there, take Wren up to her room," I tell Kite. "I'll get medicine, blood for a transfusion, and everything else we need from the basement and—"

"Nope, the basement is a no-go, Captain," Creedence cuts in. "Those items have been relocated to the pantry and the basement is off-limits for the time being."

My brows snap together. "And why's that? What happened in the basement?"

"*Who* happened in the basement," Creedence corrects. "While you two were out kidnapping damsels in distress and running from bad guys, we had a wolf special delivery. His name is Luke and he's been made as comfortable as possible until such time as we can figure out what to do with him."

"What to do with him?" Kite shakes his head. "What does that even mean? Doesn't he know why he's here?"

"Oh, he knows." Creedence nods. "But the man isn't too happy about it. He's what you might call...an unwilling volunteer."

I curse. "I was afraid of this. I told the pack leaders we needed cooperation, not a fucking captive of our own. We're in the business of liberating shifters, not locking them up. We'll have to let him go."

Creedence grunts. "Pardon my French, but the wolves do not give one sloppy shit about your orders, Captain. They do what they want, when they want. We're lucky they sent a candidate at all. If you cut this guy loose, we might not get another, and we have zero time to waste playing nice. Pooh-bie might be able to feel what this girl feels, but I can see what she'll be facing." He shakes his head, his tone uncharacteristically sober as he adds, "No toss of that coin looks particular rosy right now, but with the wolf, we have a chance. Not a great chance, but we might come out with at least some of our balls intact."

Silence falls as the small, unassuming ranch house tucked into a glen at the edge of the coastal rain forest comes into view.

Creedence comes from a long line of cat shifters with the ability to see different possible versions of the future. It's how his parents made a killing conning marks across three continents and twelve countries and how his sister knew to get out of the life before she lost the child she was carrying in a con gone wrong.

If he says we need the wolf, then we need the wolf.

"I'll figure out a way to get through to him," I say. "But Wren comes first."

"I'll make a meal and get her some clean clothes. Though I'm pretty sure everything I bought is going to be too big. You didn't tell me she was skin and bones," Creedence says, his initiative also surprising. He's been cooperative so far, but not nearly as enthusiastic about his role as a potential as the bear. Creedence gives off the strong impression that he's tolerating the new course his life has taken rather than embracing his destiny.

But maybe now that he's seen her, and seen what she's up against…

I want to ask what's coming next and how long we'll have to prepare for the battle we all know is coming, but there's no time. We're here, and Kite is already drawing Wren tenderly out of his side of the car.

I jump out, hurrying to open the front door for him, only to release an unearthly howling into the gray afternoon. "Shit," I mutter as Kite slides past me, heading for the stairs and the room I prepared for Wren.

"Yep, that's Luke. He's a real charmer so far." Creedence pauses beside me, leaning lazily against the doorframe before prowling inside with a grin. "Dogs, am I right? So fucking dramatic."

With a sharp sigh, I shut the door behind me, grateful we're miles from the nearest house and won't have to worry about the baying of our captive arousing suspicion. Mentally adding *Win over one pissed-off pup* to my to-do list, I head into the pantry to gather medical supplies.

Wren first. She's what matters most to our mission, and the one who's always mattered most to me.

Even if I didn't bear the mark, even if she were just another captive shifter in need of help, I would have fought for the chance to be here. She's that important to me, the light that kept me going through the darkest days of my life.

I just hope I get the chance to tell her that, and everything else that's in my heart.

CHAPTER 12
WREN

I wake up alone on a tiny island in the center of a vast blue ocean and sit up in the powdery white sand to look out at the waves. The water is cerulean, crystal clear, and glorious. The warm breeze carries the familiar salt of ocean air, but instead of the funky, murky notes of the sea breeze I've known all my life, the wind is perfumed with citrus and flowers.

Everything smells fresh and new, crisp with possibilities, and as I rise to my feet I'm filled with a joy so intense I'm not sure whether to laugh or cry as it rushes through me.

I lift my hands to the sun, fingers spread wide, feeling like every piece of creation is celebrating with me.

This is how it's supposed to be. This is how it was long ago, before we took too much too far too fast. This was how it was in the years when there was balance, before the disease took root and began to spread.

The disease…

But not the viruses released by the Meltdown.

This is something worse…

Someone worse…

The realization drifts through my head like poisoned smoke, carrying a whiff of sulfur and sweat, of things long left unwashed and important tasks neglected. As my thoughts darken, a cloud covers the sun, spreading out until it encompasses the entire sky, blocking out the light.

A storm is gathering, and at the center of the churning and frothing overhead is a face made of clouds, a man with a beard, mad eyes, and lips that spit rain as he promises, "You will fail, child. Challenge me and meet the same end as those who came before you."

The cloud face takes on sharper definition as the man opens his mouth, wider and grotesquely wider, a snake unhooking his jaw until I can see down the funnel cloud of his throat. And there, in his belly, dozens of people are writhing, screaming, suffering for all eternity as he digests them—still alive, always alive, yet always on the verge of death and in unimaginable pain.

I back away in horror, tripping in the sand and scuttling backward, but there are no trees on this island, nowhere to hide from the sky.

"Run, little one," the cloud man says. "Run and keep running and don't ever stop or I will catch you."

He spits more rain as he speaks, the hot drops stinging into my eyes. I reach up to wipe the wetness away and bring away red, sticky fingers.

Blood.

It's raining blood, the blood of all the innocent people this monster has devoured.

I hold my arms away from my body, trembling as streaks of red splash across my skin. I turn to run and the sky thunders with laughter—booming, exploding, splitting the world in two as the man in the clouds takes my measure and finds me lacking. Pitiful. Not even worth the trouble of plucking from the sand and popping into his endless mouth.

The shaking in the sky becomes an earthquake rocking the world beneath my feet and soon the island crashes in two, opening a chasm filled with fire in front of me, but I'm running too fast to stop. I dig my heels into the sand, fighting to reverse course, but I'm already stumbling, tumbling, hurtling into the void, burning so hot my skin begins to melt from my bones.

I'm so hot, miserably hot...

And thirsty, so thirsty...

"There you go, Slim, open up those pretty eyes," an unfamiliar voice murmurs close to my ear. "I've got something to wet your whistle."

My eyes creak open to see an angel by my bedside—a rumpled angel in a wrinkled T-shirt and battered blue jeans, with sandy-blond hair, golden whiskers on his chin, and a wicked smile on his impossibly handsome face. His eyes are gold with a brown patina on top and absolutely the most mesmerizing thing I've ever seen.

I blame the eyes for the fact that I don't notice the straw wresting lightly on my bottom lip until Golden Boy reaches out, adjusting it as he insists, "Here you go.

Big drink, Slim, or the captain is going to hook you up to an IV again and that's no fun."

I pucker around the straw, sucking gently, drawing something sweet and tangy—lemonade—into my mouth. The citrus hits my taste buds, clean and refreshing, reminding me of the dream.

The first part. Before the monster in the sky.

I release the straw and swallow with a shudder.

"Bad dreams?" Golden Boy asks.

I nod, wincing as the movement causes an ache to spread through my chest and memories to come rushing back. The kidnapping, Kite, the sudden appearance of Dust, getting shot down in the middle of the road—images flash across my mental screen, but none of them are as scary as the Devouring God.

"Well, you're safe now," Golden says, his handsome face breaking into a smile so charming my lips curve instinctively in response. "Well, as safe as you're ever going to be. Must suck being the chosen one, huh?"

My forehead furrows, but before I can discover if my pain will allow me to speak, a voice comes from the doorway, "She doesn't know what you're talking about, Creedence. Shut your trap and let her rest," Kite says, meeting my gaze as my attention shifts his way. His lips curve in a tentative smile. "Hey, there. You're looking a lot better than you did yesterday."

"Don't...want rest," I force out, finding my voice does indeed work, though sucking in the air needed to speak isn't exactly pleasant. "Want...answers."

"You heard that, Pooh-bie," Golden Boy—Creedence —says with a wink. "Slim wants answers, and I think we ought to give 'em to her. I'm Creedence." He holds out a hand, waiting patiently as I shakily maneuver my palm into his and then giving my fingers a careful squeeze. "I'm low in the pecking order around here, but I'm on your side." He lifts a shoulder in a loose shrug, but the look in his extraordinary eyes isn't the least bit easy-going as he adds in a voice for my ears only, "Don't take any more shit from these clowns until they put their cards on the table, okay? You deserve at least that much."

"What was that?" Kite strides across the room, his head cocked at a suspicious angle.

"I said we should all play cards." Creedence stretches lazily, once again the laid-back Golden Boy. "I've been bored out of my skull sitting here waiting for Slim to wake up and wolf boy to stop screaming. Someone really should have considered cable. I mean, can't we save the world and binge watch all six seasons of *Buffy the Vampire Slayer* at the same time?"

"Seven," I correct in a slightly stronger croak.

Creedence sucks in a breath through his teeth. "Oh, no, Slim. I meant six. Season six is an abomination, and I prefer to pretend it never existed."

I narrow my eyes into slits. "No. Musical episode. Brilliant."

"What are you're talking about?" Kite asks, clearly bewildered. "Is this a television show?"

I blink up at Kite, horrified, as Creedence gasps in disbelief.

"Only the best television show ever, hippy boy," Creedence says, rising from his chair and punching Kite lightly on his arm. "I'm telling you, you missed out on some incredible storytelling out there in the pristine wilderness drawing in the dirt with sticks or whatever it is you bears do for fun."

"And yet somehow, I've survived," Kite says dryly, slugging Creedence back, making the other man dance to the side with a good-natured laugh.

Creedence is slimmer than Kite, but just as tall, and moves with a grace that makes me wonder if he's a dancer or an athlete—someone who makes a living with his body. From what I remember, they definitely seem to get along better than Kite and Dust, though that encounter became very fraught, very fast.

"How long have I been out?" I gently push up into a seated position, testing the limits of my post-gunshot-wound body. Thankfully, aside from a flash of pain as my pectoral muscles engage, I'm not feeling nearly as bad as I would have expected.

"Two days." Kite reaches out to help as I toss the covers from my legs, revealing my new duds—a loose-fitting pair of dark jeans and a baggy T-shirt with a bunny wearing a pink bow on the front that would be more at home on an eight-year-old.

I frown down at the clothes, but Creedence answers my question before I can say a word—"Sorry about those. I didn't have much time at the Goodwill and I wasn't sure what size you were. I can grab you something better next time I'm in town."

"No, it's fine," I say. "It's nice to have something clean to wear." Brushing my hair over my shoulder, I realize that it's clean, too, and that my skin feels fresh beneath my new clothes.

Someone must have bathed me, I realize, but I'm too shy to ask who did the honors. I'm alive and seem to be healing well, and I decide to be grateful for that and conserve my energy for more important questions.

"It's time to tell me what's going on, Kite," I say, pinning him with a firm gaze. "Everything. Now."

He nods. "I'll go get Dust."

"No, I'll go to him." I swing my legs over the edge of the bed. "I need to get some fresh air." I also need to get away from that dream, to feel the sun on my face and remember that nightmare monsters, no matter how terrifying, can't hurt me.

"I'll grab the shoes I bought you," Creedence says, shaking his head as he glances down at my sock-clad feet. "Those are going to be too big, too."

"I don't care," I say. "Shoes of any kind are appreciated."

Creedence grunts. "Low maintenance is a good thing, but don't be a doormat, kid."

"I won't." I hold his gaze and then Kite's, hoping they can see how deeply I mean business. "Just choosing my battles. And I'm not a kid."

Kite nods. "No you're not. I'll go tell Dust we're meeting out on the deck."

CHAPTER 13

WREN

Outside, we settle into chairs around a wrought iron table on a deck overlooking a field filled with purple spring flowers and a forest beyond so bright green it looks like it's been freshly painted.

It's beautiful, this place. A lovely retreat from reality.

Looking out across the rolling pastoral splendor, the insanity of the past two days seems like a bad dream.

But bad dreams don't leave you with a bullet wound in your chest and so many unanswered questions your head feels like it's been infested by a swarm of killer bees. I'm overflowing with curiosity, but I'm also sore from my trip down the stairs, so I keep things brief, "Tell me everything. I'll hold up hand if I need you to stop and clarify." I sit tall in my chair, not wanting to show weakness or give Dust any reason to insist I should return to bed and save this discussion for a later date.

He studies me for a long beat, as if debating doing just that, but before he can speak, Creedence cuts in, "Just tell her, Captain. She's got a right to know, and spreading it out isn't going to make it easier. Shit or get off the pot already."

I lift my eyebrows and blink, indicating my whole-hearted agreement with his statement. Creedence is still a stranger, but so far, I like him.

A lot. His no-bullshit attitude is refreshing.

"I'll start," Kite offers, leaning forward to brace his arms on the table, framing the gently-sweating beer bottle between them. "The people who ran us off the road and the piece of shit who shot you are part of the Kin Born alliance. They're born shifters and they think that's the only kind that should exist." He holds up a large hand, ticking off one finger for each of the items on his list as he continues, "So other kinds—shifters made by mate-bite, shifters who become kin after being exposed to shifter blood, and the handful who are created in labs by doctors—the Kin Born want those people to die and us to die for standing up for them. I have a reputation for helping what they call 'artificials' escape. One of the Kin Born must have followed me the other night, assumed you were an artificial shifter, and decided to take us all out." His chin drops to his chest with a sigh. "I'm sorry. I tried to be so careful, but obviously things didn't end well. You were shot, Sierra is still missing…"

"That's not your fault." I want to reassure him that I don't blame him for my injury, but I'm not sure what to make of half of what he just said. It sounds like something from a twisted fairy tale.

"It is, though. At least partly," Kite says. "I was sent in undercover, posing as a shelter worker, so I could determine the easiest way to get you out. I should have come up with something safe and seamless faster. I was told I had until August to finalize the details and get the moving pieces in place, but then Dust found out your parents had gotten you an appointment with Dr. Death, and we had no choice but to move fast."

I frown, and Dust jumps in to offer, "Dr. Highborn's procedure, the one you were scheduled for... It doesn't cure any virus; it permanently alters a shifter's DNA, making it impossible for them to take their kin form. It also ends in death for about seventy percent of his patients, though he doesn't own up to that when sharing his statistics." Dust's jaw clenches. "A lot of his victims are shifter street kids his people lure in with promises of free food and board in exchange for participating in a drug trial. They're never processed into the clinic through official channels, so we can only estimate how many are lost on the operating table. But from our research and tracking the kids who have gone missing in the past few years, we're guessing it's close to a ninety percent fatality rate."

My eyes fly wide.

"Highborn tests his procedures on the homeless kids," Kite says softly. "He uses them to find out what's safest for his Church of Humanity patients and then only the movement deaths are recorded."

"And only patients referred through a Church of

Humanity physician are serviced at the clinic," Dust says, crossing his arms over his chest. "Every other patient with Devour virus who applies for treatment is turned down. We hacked into their database and verified it for ourselves. Dr. Highborn isn't a member of the movement—he actually has a history of clashing with C of H charities in the past—so why make his 'cure' available only to their members?"

"Ooh, ooh, I know this one." Creedence bounces lightly in his chair as he lifts his arm in the air like an overeager student. "It's because he's full of shit and also a human supremacist motherfucker."

Dust inclines his head and offers a dry, "Tell him what he's won, Johnny."

I shake my head gently, brows pinching tight.

"I know it's difficult to hear," Dust says. "I've been in your shoes. When I found out my adopted parents had been making me sick..." His gaze shifts over my shoulder, a shadow falling behind his eyes, as if for a moment he's back in his little boy's body, helpless and sick and praying for a reason to believe that someday he would get well. "Belinda and George weren't nearly as good to me as Hank and Abby were to you and your sister, but I still didn't want to believe it. They were my parents. They took care of me, said they loved me..."

Dust's lips curve in a bitter smile. "But that's part of what makes this so insidious, Wren. Love and the willingness to brutally torture another living being because he or she isn't something you think God approves of— both can exist in the same person. Most of the time these people feel they have no choice. The more a

Church of Humanity parent loves the child they're trying to save from the beast mark, the more passionately they'll set about poisoning them."

"They literally think the devil made us and sent us to earth to serve him." Kite glares at his beer as he spins the bottle on the tabletop. "And that every time we shift we're sucked further under Satan's control until we become pure darkness, pure evil."

"Which is offensive." Creedence winks as he takes a pull on his IPA. "I like to take full responsibility for my bad behavior."

All of the men have beers, but I didn't ask to join them. I've never tried alcohol—my meds had enough unpredictable side effects without adding that into the mix—and I figure two days into recovering from a gunshot wound isn't the time to start experimenting with new things.

Though, considering all I've been through, I actually don't feel *that* bad. In fact, I would swear I feel stronger now than I did thirty minutes ago when I woke up.

"I'm feeling better." I motion in the general direction of my chest, not sure what to say in response to everything they've just told me. "You did a good job patching me up."

Dust's expression brightens. "Good. I guided the bullet out, and we got several bags of fluid into you the first six hours after. But if you were human you'd still be down for the count."

"We heal faster than regular folk," Creedence offers.

"And if you could shift, you would heal even faster." Kite smiles. "But don't worry about that now. It can take a month or more to get the drugs out of your system enough to make a shift possible. When the time is right and you're ready, it'll come naturally."

With a soft huff, I lift a hand.

"Or it won't," Creedence says with a contrary grin. "Some people never come all the way back from the meds. Sometimes the poison just got in too deep."

I lift both hands now, fingers spread wide in the universal sign for "slow the heck down."

"Not for Wren." Kite frowns at the other man. "She's going to be fine. She's got a kin form moving inside her. I can feel it."

I wave my hands in the air, but Creedence is already saying, "Yeah, well I have a few feelings of my own, Pooh-bie, and I think it might not be as simple as all that."

"Stop!" I smack my hands onto the table hard enough to make Kite jump and Creedence shift back in his chair, studying me out of the corners of his golden eyes. "I don't believe in this. At least, not most of it."

"In what? That your parents were drugging you?" Dust cocks his head inquisitively. "Then how do you explain the rapid improvement in your health? Stopping the meds alleviated your symptoms. That's just cause and effect, Wren. No faith or suspension of disbelief required."

"No, I mean shifters," I say, though I'm not sure about the other stuff, either, at least not that my parents knew the drugs were responsible for my sickness and not the other way around. Hank and Abby are trusting people, hardworking, but uneducated, and they've never been far outside the Seattle city limits. Someone else—the elders or some crazy person like this doctor who treats humans like lab rats—could have tricked them into hurting me.

But the shifter thing...

Seriously, how gullible do they think I am? And what are they hoping to accomplish by convincing me they're supernatural creatures? I mean, from what I've seen of Creedence so far, he seems like the type who might go along with a gag for fun, but Kite is a serious person and Dust seems to have gotten downright stuffy by the ripe old age of twenty-six.

"Well, that's easy enough to sort out." Creedence tips his beer back, draining the last of the golden liquid before plunking it down on the table on its side. "Ready for a game of spin the bottle, gentlemen? I spin, winner gets a shift and a kiss?"

Creedence glances my way, arching a suggestive brow. "Assuming that's acceptable to the lady? I assure you I excel at all boudoir activities, the captain's a stuffy Brit, but he keeps his mouth clean, and Pooh-bie here is a sweet kid. You could do worse."

Kite's scowl is the most menacing expression I've ever seen on his face. "Call me Pooh-bie one more fucking time, and I will end you, cat."

"Pooh-bie?" I blush as Kite looks my way. I guess he hasn't told anyone about our kiss, which makes me strangely happy. I like that it's still between us, our secret. It makes me think it might have meant as much to Kite as it did to me.

"Short for Pooh Bear." Kite runs a hand over the top of his silky hair as he rolls his eyes. "Because my kin form is a bear. Aren't they creative?"

I smile, but it fades quickly.

A bear…

Like the bear in my dream, the one who held me close and made me feel so safe, even when surrounded by evil things slinking through the darkness.

Kite's eyes light up, almost as if he's read my mind. "No need to spin the bottle. I'll do it."

"You'll do no such thing," Dust says, his voice cool and brisk, "You've been injured, and you've already shifted too often in the past few days. You need to rest and conserve your energy in case we need it for something more pressing than a parlor trick."

"You're just saying that because you want the kiss, Captain," Creedence teases, guiding the bottle back and forth, like the arm of a metronome. "But you underestimate how good I am at getting a bottle to stop where I want it to. I've had more than my share of experience with this game." Creedence's mischievous gaze cuts my way. "Completely unsupervised childhood. Got into all sorts of trouble. Upside, I'm really good at trouble."

I bite my lip, fighting a smile, not wanting to encourage him or this strange rivalry he seems to be trying to stir up. But the man has an infectious grin and an air about him that makes even his more outrageous comments seem harmless. I have a feeling he could say just about anything and get away with it, as long he flashed that "I-can't-help-being-bad-baby smile" after.

"I'm sure you have incredible bottle-twirling skill." Dust's lids slide to half mast. "But I prefer to use logic, not games of chance, to make decisions. I can't risk shifting out in the open—my kin form is large enough to show up on radar if our enemies are watching—and the farmhouse interior isn't of sufficient size to accommodate me. With Kite needing to continue to heal, it makes the most sense for you to shift, Creedence."

"Sweet. I could use a run, anyway. Been cooped up too long." He stands, gripping the bottom of his light-brown tee and tugging it up and over his head, revealing the most incredible body I've ever seen. Golden skin covers lean, powerful muscles and abs an underwear model would kill for, with crisp, curly golden hair that dusts his chest, making it clear Creedence is a *man*, not a boy. The sight of him—so powerful and sensual and clearly completely at ease in his body—makes me blush even before he reaches for the top button on his jeans and pops it open.

I jerk my head to the left, averting my gaze so fast it sends a flash of pain through my chest.

Creedence chuckles, and Dust snaps, "You could have undressed inside."

"I'm just trying to keep everything above board and out in the open," Creedence says, amusement thick in his voice. Clearly, he's finding this all a lot more entertaining than the rest of us. "Transparency, Captain. That's the key to building trust."

"Interesting advice from a con man," Kite says. "Wouldn't think you would know much about trust."

"Con men know more about trust than anyone. Before you break it, you have to make it." Creedence pauses, and I hear more rustling, making my face flame hotter as I realize there is likely a completely nude man standing a few feet behind me. "You want to turn around, Slim?" he asks. "See the entire show from start to finish?"

"Um, I..." I swallow, wondering if it's possible to burst a blood vessel from embarrassment. "I—"

"Cover up, Creedence," Dust says, clearly sensing my distress. "She's never been out of the human world. She's not used to strangers stripping down to the altogether five minutes after she's met them."

"We've known each other nearly an hour now," Creedence says, mock hurt in his tone. "I thought we were ready to take the next step."

"Sorry, I'm old fashioned," I say, fighting to pull myself together. "I need at least two hours to acclimate to full nudity."

Creedence laughs, and even Dust's scowl backs away from his face. He glances my way, his lips curving in silent approval. But he always did appreciate spunk, and I can't keep blushing and averting my eyes forever.

I asked for this. I should at least be woman enough to give Creedence my full attention as he does...whatever he's planning to do.

Fifty percent of me is still sure this is some kind of prank or maybe a case of group psychosis, in which all three of these men have convinced themselves that they possess the power to transform into animals.

But the other half...

Memories of that dream bear and waking up to find Kite wearing a leaf apron because his clothes "didn't survive the shift" keep squirming through my head. Why would he engage in such elaborate mind games while we were in mortal danger? And if that bear was real, then shifters are the only explanation. An actual purely-animal bear would have zero interest in snuggling a half-drowned woman he'd pulled from the river.

All right then, time to woman up and face this head on. Rolling my shoulders back, I turn back to Creedence, who has mercifully grabbed his T-shirt from the ground and is holding it in front of his hips, shielding the part of a man I've never seen in real life before.

Yes, I did my share of sneaking peeks at kinky websites in college, back when I was supposed to be using my internet waiver to study and nothing more. And yes, I've seen naked statues of men, but statues and the internet are nothing like a flesh and blood man standing in front of you. And call me old-fashioned for real, but I would like for the first man I see naked to be someone I care about.

Though, if I were simply looking for man candy, Creedence would certainly fit the bill. From his sandy head to his tanned toes, he is incredible to behold, and he knows it.

He smirks as he shifts his weight from one foot to the other, studying me from behind the shaggy hair that's fallen into his face. "You ready, Slim? Seen enough to be positive I don't have any tricks up my sleeve? Or do you want to see the view from the back?"

I give a small shake of my head.

"Are you sure?" He cocks one hip to the side as if preparing to turn around. "The view from the back is nice. Or so the ladies tell me."

"Just get on with it, asshole," Kite grumbles at the same moment Dust sighs, "Give me a fucking break."

Creedence's grin widens, and I can't help but laugh. The man is pure mischief. It makes the crazy half of me wonder what sort of animal he'll turn into—a ferret, maybe, or a crow, though it's hard to imagine this golden creature growing midnight feathers.

"Then without further bullshitting." Creedence gives a slight bow, his chin dropping to his chest, concealing his face as the rest of his skin begins to ripple like the surface of a lake after a handful of stones hits the surface.

My jaw drops, but the rest happens so fast that by the time a soft cry of surprise makes its way from my parted lips, a miniature-pony-sized cat is standing beside me on the deck, its large paws soft and fluffy-looking against the weathered wood. I gape at the creature, unable to remember what this particular cat is called, the one with golden fur painted with wisps of dark brown, a jaunty white beard beneath its powerful jaws, and tufts of feather-like fur sticking up from the tops of its ears.

"Lynx," I finally sputter, huffing in surprise as the cat rises onto its hind legs, bringing his paws to rest on the arms of my chair and his head even with mine. I gaze into eyes the same golden as Creedence's, but with pupils shaped liked tiny seeds instead of the circles of his human form.

But it is unmistakably Creedence. Even his grin is the same—smug, but charming and roguishly full of himself.

"Well, then," I finally say. "That settles that, I guess. Thank you, Creedence."

He cocks his head, and a soft rumble, like a distant motorcycle engine trying to turn over, fills the air. It takes me a moment to realize he's purring—it's a deeper, more gravelly sound than a house cat—but when I do, I grin. "You're a charmer in all your forms, aren't you?" I reach out, scratching the soft fur around his neck, smile widening as his rumbling grows louder.

"Shameless," Kite says. "Completely shameless. Just remember he hasn't been declawed, Bird Girl. Keep your guard up with him when he's human. Don't let the fluffy purring kitty crap fool you."

Creedence glances Kite's way, slitting his golden eyes as his lips peel away from his teeth in a soft hiss.

Kite laughs. "I like you better in your kin form, Tigger. Harder to run your mouth this way."

Creedence pushes off from my chair and prowls slowly around the table, his short tail whipping ominously from side to side.

"What, you don't like being called Tigger, wittle kitty?" Kite asks in an over-the-top baby voice. "Since you like calling me Pooh Bear so much, I thought it would tickle your whiskers."

This time the rumble emerging from Creedence's throat is clearly a growl, not a purr, but Kite doesn't seem worried about what the claws hiding in the other man's fluffy paws might do to him.

Still, I would rather they hold off on any further teasing or scratching until I've fully wrapped my head around all this.

"Shifters are real." I test the words, finding they're easier to digest than I expect. "And I am one..."

Dust nods, relief clear in his expression. "You are."

"What am I? Is there any way to know?"

Dust casts a glance Kite's way. Kite purses his lips, silently communicating something I can't get a read on. Whatever it is, it makes Dust turn back to me and say, "Not yet. It's too soon."

I frown. He's bad liar—and I'm about to tell him so—when an unearthly howl fills the air, making me flinch and cringe lower in my seat. It's a horrible sound, simultaneously threatening and pitiful, the cry of a wounded animal caught in a trap. It is protest, prayer for mercy, and promise to seek vengeance all in one, and I instantly know it doesn't belong to a normal wolf.

I can also tell it isn't coming from the hills outside.

It's coming from much closer, from…inside the house.

"Another shifter?" I scan the faces surrounding the table, but none of them look surprised. Uncomfortable, but not surprised. "Who is it? Why aren't they out here with us?"

"Luke is…complicated," Dust offers.

"Definitely not all we'd hoped he would be," Kite agrees. "But he's coming around."

Creedence simply rolls his cat's eyes before dropping onto the deck and stretching out in the sun, apparently deciding a nap is in order before that run he wanted to take. No answers coming from that corner—at least, not for now—which leaves me to squeeze the truth out of the other two.

"Explain," I demand. "And then take me to him."

Kite visibly balks. "You don't want to do that, Wren.

He's definitely not up for making new friends right now."

"And why's that? Is he hurt?" I ask. "He sounds hurt."

"Not hurt," Dust hedges. "He's a bit...uncomfortable, due to factors beyond our control at the moment. That's why he's currently in containment in the basement."

"Containment in the basement?" I blink fast. "You mean you've got him locked up down there? You've got a man locked in the basement?"

Kite lifts his hands off the table, bringing his palms to his chest and slowly lowering them to his midsection, one of the tai chi moves I know he uses to soothe himself and others, but I'm not in the mood to be soothed.

"Talk, Kite."

"Relax," he says in his Zen-master voice. "He's okay. He's being fed and taken care of. We're not monsters. We just can't have him running off just yet."

Dust stands with a sigh. "Give it up, man. One whiff of injustice and she's like a dog with a bone."

"Yeah, well, Luke is like a wolf with rabies," Kite counters as he comes to his feet. "We just got her believing that we exist and we're here to help her. Are you sure you want to undo all that by making introductions to Mr. Tall, Mean, and Scary?"

"*She* can decide for herself." I stand, proud of how steady my legs remain—even when another unearthly howl shatters the silence, lifting the hairs at the back of my neck. "And I want to know what the hell is going on. All of it—including why there's a man... A wolf..." I wave a hand through the air. "A shifter person locked in the basement. Let's go. Now."

"There's more you need to know first." Dust crosses to stand beside me, making me marvel all over again that the frail boy I used to know is now a man I have to tilt my head back to look up at. "Luke is important. We need him. Until you understand why and how he fits in to the big picture, there's no chance you'll find the current situation tolerable."

"That's stuffy Brit for you're going to lose your shit," Kite mumbles.

I prop my hands on my hips, finding this situation less tolerable with every passing second. "Then tell me, but I'm warning you right now, it's going to have to be a pretty compelling story for me to even *consider* that locking a man up against his will is necessary for whatever you three have planned."

"It's not just us. It's so much bigger than that," Dust says. "But the best way to tell you is to show you." He lifts a hand, his fingers spreading wide as the lines on his palm begin to glow a bright, piercing white. "May I touch you, Wren?"

The way he says "touch" makes it clear he doesn't mean it in any sense of the word I've ever known. He means something bigger, deeper, more intimate than simply skin on skin.

For a moment, I hesitate—I would have trusted the Dust I used to know with my life, but this man isn't the boy who told me stories in his tree fort while our parents had dinner inside. This man is for, all intents and purposes, a stranger, and one who seems comfort-

able with a lot of things—kidnapping, for example—
that aren't on my approved behaviors list.

"I promise it won't hurt," he whispers, his gray eyes
cloudy with what looks like regret. "I would never, and
will never hurt you, Wren. I swear it on my life. My
touch can conceal things, but it can also reveal them, if
you're open to receiving what I have to give."

I hold his gaze, looking deeper, deeper until I see
him again, my friend, the silly yet solemn, curious but
wounded child who once knew all my secrets.

He's still there. And though I have no idea what he
might do to the man locked in the basement or anyone
else who threatens the success of this mission he's on,
he won't hurt me. Instinctively, I know I can trust him
to keep me safe or die trying.

So I nod, shoulders relaxing away from my ears as
Dust says, "Thank you," and reaches out, wrapping his
glowing hand gently around the back of my neck.

For a moment, there is only the warmth of his skin
and a slight tickling sensation, like a faint current of
electricity buzzing between us. And then the world goes
white, vanishing in a flash as bright as the flare from an
atomic bomb.

CHAPTER 15
WREN

My lips part on a scream, but the sound is lost in the wind howling in my ears. It stings my face and tears at my clothes, tugging me back in time, in space, through a thick gray fog to the place where this story begins as Dust's voice rumbles softly through the air.

"Atlas was born just after the Peloponnesian War, the son of a Spartan merchant and a woman who had fought on the front lines for the fate of the city state. They called her Wolf Mother, but very few knew how apt the title was."

The fog clears, and I see the shadow of a woman in a short tunic holding a sword, who transforms into a wolf as she leaps at her enemy's throat.

"Her husband was human, but she prayed for her children to inherit her shifter blood and grow to be great warriors. Her wish was granted on her youngest son's third birthday, but his kin form proved unlike anything she'd encountered before."

The violence playing out of the battlefield gives way to a more domestic scene, drawing me into the cozy main room of an ancient home. A toddler plays with his carved horses in front of the hearth. As he stares into the flames, he suddenly transforms into a ball of fire with a delighted laugh.

"He was a Fata Morgana, a rare shifter who can take the form of multiple animals and elements and who requires intense training to grow successfully into his or her power. Knowing she would never be able to keep her son's exotic abilities concealed in their village, his mother took Atlas to a temple in the mountains to be raised by the oracle. The prophet there was a lioness shifter who had dedicated her life to the service of the gods. She graciously offered to take the babe under her wing and to educate him until such time as he gained control over his powers. And for a time, all was well."

The toddler's mother hands him into the arms of a woman swathed in a long white robe. The child hugs her tightly around the neck before squirming free, leaping to the ground where he transforms from a dog to a mouse to a dragon rearing onto its hind legs and finally into a sure-footed goat that dashes up the rocky cliff toward a marble temple.

As he runs, time speeds faster.

"But as he grew in age, Atlas also grew in lust for power. It soon became a sickness that consumed his soul, a hunger he would go to any lengths to feed."

I watch the boy grow ten years in the blink of an eye,

and then he's back in the robed oracle's arms again. But this time, instead of embracing the woman who raised him, his fingers close around her throat and squeeze—tighter, tighter, until her knees buckle and her bulging eyes roll shut.

I suck in a horrified breath and the scene vanishes, the shadows of both murderer and victim dissolving into ash as the wind stings my face once more and the fog rolls back in.

"The oracle was his first victim, and his first human mask," Dust's disembodied voice intones. "He stitched her skin into a suit he wore as he made his way down the mountain, and practiced living inside her form until he could take on the oracle's appearance at will."

Gorge rises in my throat, but I press a fist to my mouth and force it down. I can't be sick. I need to focus, to absorb every detail of this story. I don't know why, but I almost feel as if I know this man, this monster who strides into Sparta wearing the face of his adopted mother and sets a terrible series of events into motion.

"Disguised as the prophet, Atlas summoned the Spartan army into the service of the gods, insisting it was the holy mission of their people to rid the world of demons masquerading in human form. With the army's help, he rounded up shifters from across the Greek city-states and into Persia, imprisoning them until he found what he was searching for."

I watch as weeping women are herded into pens not fit for animals, some of them clinging to children until the soldiers rip them out of their arms, some of them not much more than children themselves.

"The oracle had told Atlas that there would be shifter women who bore the mark of a potential Fata Morgana mate, and that forming bonds with these women would make him even more powerful than he was already. And so he set about choosing four brides, one from each of the kin groups—canine, feline, forest kin, and the beasts of antiquity. He took them from their families and gave them the choice—bond with him or die."

Atlas strides into the pens, selecting his prey, chaining them around the neck before dragging them back to his quarters where the scene thankfully fades to black before I'm forced to watch any more.

"As the oracle foretold, he did grow in power. He began to be able to sense the whereabouts of others like him, those rare shifters with the capacity to express the entire spectrum of creation, and to hate that there was anything living that might someday challenge his supremacy. So he began to hunt."

The taller, broader, even more powerful Atlas creeps into a man's home and kills him in his sleep, slits a woman's throat while she's bathing in the river, and rips a babe apart with his bare hands only seconds after the child has emerged from its mother's womb.

This time I can't control my visceral response to the carnage. I groan as if I've been punched in the gut and clutch at my stomach, but thankfully the scene is already fading and the wind picking up again.

"Soon there were none left to challenge him, but Atlas's thirst for power was unquenchable. He began to seek out oracles and prophets, craving mystical secrets that would make him even stronger still. And finally, one day, he found someone willing to tell him what the others had not."

A man with his feet thrust into a fire screams something in a language I can't understand, and Atlas turns toward his wives with a terrible smile. The next tableau to emerge from the fog is so horrific I can only watch for a moment before I have to squeeze my eyes shut with a whimper.

But I know I'll never forget the images burned into my brain—the sight of Atlas sitting at a giant table feasting on the roasted bodies of the women he'd forced to marry him.

"Atlas claimed more mates and the cycle continued, until he was as mighty as a god. Until his magic and influence became so strong it began to shape the course of history."

Images flash faster now. I watch as the darkness and drudgery of the Middle Ages gives way to the modern horrors of the twentieth century—scenes of progress turned to poison as greed leads to putting profit before the health of the planet and the things living upon it. I see species die out and rainforests disappear and eventually the superstorms rise and the Meltdown flood the coastlines of the world.

"But all power comes at a price and Atlas paid for his with his sanity. With each spouse he consumes, he loses more of his own humanity. And as he declines, the health of our world declines with him."

The wind grows warmer, and I feel it pulling me forward, back toward my own space and time. When the fog clears now I see a burly man with a thick gray and black beard seated on a throne, his bloodshot eyes burning with a mad intelligence and his fingers gnarled into claws that clutch the gilded arms of his seat. His face makes me shiver in terror and recognition, and again I'm filled with the sense that I know him—or that I *will* know him.

That we're connected in some way...

"If he isn't stopped, there won't be a planet left worth saving. A new Fata Morgana must rise. And fight. And win, no matter what the cost."

The skin on the back of my neck lifts and I turn to see the silhouette of a woman striding through the mist. Slowly, one by one, the shadowy forms of four men come to stand beside her, each one lending her strength and his own special gifts until she's glowing with potential energy, a bright golden light poised to take back the dark throne behind me.

And then she steps out of the shadows and my heart stops.

It's me. My face, my slim shoulders bearing the weight of the world, my hands balling into fists at my sides as I face down a being of ancient and utter evil with nothing but good intentions and a seventh-grade self-defense class under my belt.

I'm once again on the verge of being sick when suddenly the world goes bright white, and I open my eyes to find myself back in the present, but with my reality permanently altered.

I've just finished shifting back into my human form and tugged my clothes into place when Slim comes back from her vision quest. She looks even more worn and fragile than she did before, her face pale even in the warm sunset light.

It makes me want to box the Brit's ears and slug Pooh Bear in the stomach for good measure.

Not many things make me violent anymore—I've made peace with the shit in my past, and these days I prefer to make love not war—but the way these two are treating the girl chaps my ass.

But there's not a damned thing I can do about any of it. I'm as much a pawn as Wren is, one of many moving pieces in a game played by people who have far more money and power and influence than either one of us can even dream about.

Though, she could, conceivably, be the most powerful being in the world one day, this tiny thing with her big blue eyes, knobby elbows, and soft-spoken gentleness. Even her smart-ass comments come out so sweet, you just want to ruffle her hair and lay a kiss on her pink cheek.

She's so innocent, so terrifyingly new and unspoiled. I want to believe she's got what it takes to succeed where so many have failed, to live when so many have died, but it doesn't look good for sweet Slim.

Even if she weren't about as threatening as a baby deer wearing angel wings, recent history proves her chances aren't great. Every Fata Morgana born in the past fifty years has been killed in the cradle, assassinated while they were still kids, or slaughtered on the road to Atlas's stronghold before they reached the field of battle.

Atlas does not play fair.

Atlas does not have a single moral qualm about killing unarmed women and children.

And Atlas grows stronger with every mate he marries and devours, meaning each child born to challenge him has a smaller and smaller chance of taking that crazy motherfucker down.

But if things keep going the way they've been going —floods and famines, war and terror, plagues and cancers and new diseases being born every day—there won't be a world to fight for much longer. Atlas and his shitty reign of unchecked evil will send this entire planet straight to hell, and every man, woman, child, shifter, animal, fruit, veggie, and spore will be destroyed in the flames.

Except maybe the spores...

Spores are some hardy motherfuckers.

In my next life, I'm coming back as a spore, I decide as Slim's gaze moves from Dust to Kite to me and then back down the row, apparently seeing us with fresh eyes now that she knows what we're really here for.

"I'm in charge of saving the world." The fear in her tone makes it clear Dust's psychic story time filled the gaps in her education. "Are you sure? There isn't someone else? Another Fata Morgana out there somewhere?"

Dust shakes his head. "You're the only one who's lived this long, and you might be our last chance to fight back before it's too late."

"And you're positive I am what you think I am?" she asks, desperation warring with resignation in her eyes. "I've never shifted into anything before, let alone lots of different things."

"Without a shadow of a doubt," Kite says. "I sent a strand of your hair into the resistance leaders to be sure. The DNA sequence is a match to every Fata Morgana on record."

Her shoulders slump in defeat as she lifts her gaze to the darkening sky. "Well...I guess Fate could have picked someone worse." She pokes out her bottom lip, rocking her head side to side. "Maybe. If she tried really hard."

"I disagree," Dust says softly, for once seeming to understand that people need time to adjust before he pushes on to the next item on his agenda. "You're stronger than you know, and you're going to get stronger every day. And we're all here to help you. We'll train, prepare, make sure you're in top physical, mental, and shifter condition before we get anywhere near Atlas."

"So you all have that mark?" she asks, blinking fast as she pulls her gaze from the nearly full moon rising overhead.

Dust draws up his sleeve, showing the star-shaped birthmark on his inner arm. Kite lifts his shirt and turns, baring an identical mark at the small of his back.

When Wren's attention shifts my way I bite my thumb and bat my eyes, hoping to make her laugh as I say, "I don't think you're ready to see my mark, Slim. On account of you not being a butt girl and all."

Her lips swoop up on the sides for half a heartbeat before going flat again, but even that is enough to make it worth playing the fool. I'm basically a prisoner here— or would be if I had been stupid enough to put up a fight like the wolf. My future, my life, my destiny no longer belong to me.

Nothing belongs to me, but when I can make people laugh, bring them out of the dark and into the light for even a second, I don't feel like a piece of shit. I feel powerful, useful, like I have worth beyond serving as cannon fodder for a doomed cause.

It's very likely we're all going to die with her, or get picked off—one by one—along the way. Especially if we can't win over the wolf.

I know that. The moment I was recruited as one of the Fata's potential mates, I signed on the dotted line, swearing to give my life for her if necessary. I am replaceable; she's not. I get it. It's not personal, that's just fucking logic.

But it still pissed me off.

Up until the moment Dust and Kite carried that bleeding girl into my car, I wasn't happy about my role as an expendable bodyguard to some Chosen One chick I'd never met.

Then I laid eyes on her for the first time—this poor kid already poisoned, weak, and shot full of holes because fate decided she was born to die—and the chip on my shoulder fell clean off. And then she woke up in her sick bed and smiled at me, and something even crazier happened in my chest. If I didn't know better, I would think it was my heart melting every time she looks at me with her old-new eyes, but I don't have that kind of heart.

I'm not built for any of that sappy shit. Growing up, I learned the hard way that love never lasts and romantic love is the biggest con of all.

But I am built to be loyal to those who prove they deserve my loyalty. Somehow, within those first few seconds of eye contact, with those first few words, this girl earned mine, so when she says, "I guess we'll all have to get to know each other better, huh?" and blushes pink for the fifth time this afternoon, I do my best to make things easy on her.

"But you set the pace, Slim," I say, all joking aside. "You decide when you're ready and what you're ready for, and you don't do anything because you feel obligated to do it. You do it because it feels right. Understood?"

"The bonds will strengthen you, no matter what you feel or don't feel for any of us," Dust says. "But bonds chosen out of affection and desire, maybe even love, those will give you the kind of power you'll need to have a chance in this fight."

"More importantly, it's what we all want," Kite pipes up, increasing my respect for our youngest boy scout. "I don't want you to feel pressured into being with me, Wren. I want you to choose me because you want to choose me, the way I want to choose you."

Wren and Kite lock eyes and some secret something passes between them that gives me no choice but to give them shit, "Okay, Romeo and Juliet, save it for when you're alone. I'm too old to watch youngsters making puppy dog eyes at each other without getting sick to my stomach."

Wren's eyes cut my way. "Exactly how old are you, grandpa? You don't look like you're at death's door."

"Twenty-eight," I say, nodding with mock seriousness. "So basically the only adult around this daycare center."

Dust snorts and Wren's mouth wrinkles as she clearly fights a smile. "So two years older than Dust, four years older than me, six years older than Kite..." She nods as if accepting the years separating us as vast and unbridgeable. "You're practically a geriatric. Maybe we should check you into an assisted living center on the way to fight this crazy guy who eats his wives. Wouldn't want you to break a hip on the battlefield."

I grin. "I like you more with every passing minute,

Slim. I appreciate this smart-ass side of yours. Helps balance out all that sweetness and light."

Her smile fades as she turns back to Dust. "Speaking of sweetness and light, I don't want to be the only one free to make choices that feel right around here. If the man in the basement doesn't want to be here, it's our obligation to let him go."

"You'll need a marked member from one of the canine clans to reach your full power," Dust says, clearly underestimating Wren's bleeding heart. I've only known the girl a little over an hour, and I can tell already that "the ends justify the means" defense isn't going to fly with Slim.

As expected she shrugs. "Then we'll have to find to find someone else, someone who's willing to be part of this."

Dust shakes his head. "You don't understand. The mark is very rare in wolf shifters and their kin cousins. If we lose Luke, we might not be able to find another marked wolf in time. It could take years, and we don't have that. We have months, if we're lucky and manage to avoid the Kin Born and keep you off Atlas's radar. Right now, he has no idea you exist. Being medicated suppressed your powers and his ability to track you, but when he finds out you're a Fata Morgana—"

"Then we'll move forward with four of us instead of five." Wren slices a hand through the air when Dust starts to speak again. "This isn't up for debate. If I become like Atlas, forcing people to serve me against their will, then I'll be no better than this monster we're trying to get rid of."

"Not eating people would still be better," I offer. I absolutely admire her for standing up for what she believes in, but we'll all be safer if we're five instead of four. "So you could just promise not to eat Luke—or any of us, really. If that's something you're comfortable promising this early in the courtship."

Wren rolls her eyes, but I can tell she's charmed, at least a little. "Of course I won't…" She shudders, her lashes fluttering. "I can't even say the words, but yes. I intend to respect every one of you. From the start of this until the end and whatever lies between." She pulls in a breath as she scans the three of us. "And I expect the same from you. So when I draw a hard moral line because I cannot, in good conscience, do what you're asking me to do, I need you to respect that."

Dust's lips part but, after a moment he sighs, his shoulders drooping as the fight goes out of him. "All right. Then let's go see Luke. But I recommend we explain what you've decided first, and free him after. Less chance of having our throats ripped out that way."

Kite grunts as he ambles around the table. "I could take that guy. He's even shorter than you, Dust."

"He's also a felon who just got paroled after serving seven years for a gang-related murder," I remind Kite, in case the kid gets any dumb ideas about fighting Luke on his way out. "He's lean, but he's hard and fast, and he will absolutely fuck you up. Stay back and let the big kids handle this one, buddy. In fact, maybe you should head upstairs and have a nap, instead."

Kite glowers at me but doesn't respond.

"Nap time can be fun, Pooh-bie," I wheedle.

Kite moves to take a swipe at me, but Wren steps between us at the last moment and Kite jerks his hand back so fast he nearly slaps himself in the face. "Don't let him get a rise out of you. The more you respond, the more he's going to mess with you. You know how to deal with guys like him. I saw you do it every day at the shelter."

"I know." Kite bites his lip as he shakes his head. "Sorry. He just gets under my skin for some reason."

I get under his skin because he's falling for this girl and he doesn't want to share her. That's as clear to me as the big bad moon rising in the sky and the anxiety creasing Wren's pretty face as we turn to follow Dust inside.

But some things even *I* won't say aloud.

I won't shame this kid for falling in love, I won't rub his nose in the fact that—unless she shuns me outright —I'm going to end up taking the girl he loves to bed. I'll push the limits for a laugh, but I don't believe in adding to the cruelty in the world.

There's already plenty of that going around.

So I just clap Kite on the back in silent apology and follow the rest of them inside, wishing I'd stayed in my cat form. I haven't learned many lessons that have stuck in my life, but "more human, more problems" is absolutely one of them.

CHAPTER 17

WREN

I follow Dust down the stairs into the semi-darkness of the basement with Kite and Creedence not far behind. Slowly, my eyes adjust to the gloom, and by the time I step off the final stair and onto the concrete floor, I can see well enough to pick my way through the stacks of boxes.

"We've got enough food, medical supplies, and training equipment to get us through two months without having to leave to restock," Dust says, glancing over his shoulder as he circles around the staircase toward the darker portion of the basement. "Once you're fully healed, we won't have to worry about anything but training."

"Or *you* won't," Creedence pipes up. "Dust has already assigned me laundry duty, and Kite's in charge of meal prep and—"

He's cut off by another howl of pain and outrage that makes me flinch, but Creedence simply smiles and adds, "And Luke's in charge of screaming. So far, he's kicking ass in his field."

Dust stops in front of me, and I move to stand beside him, forcing myself to come fully into the small circle of light surrounding the man chained to the heavy chair in front of me, instead of peeking at him from behind Dust's shoulder. I have nothing to be ashamed of here, but I can't help but feel guilty. The olive-skinned man in front of me with the buzz cut and stubble thick on his face is clearly in pain. I knew that from the moment I heard him cry out, but instead of rushing to help him I took a break to hear a story about the end of the world.

But I can fix that right now.

I start toward the bound man, but Dust stops me, gripping my upper arm tight as Luke lets out a bone-chilling growl from low in his throat.

"That's right, stay back," he says, the words rough and raw. "Because if you get close enough, I'm going to rip your throat out first and ask questions never."

"I was going to take off your chains," I say, hating the way my voice trembles. "I'm not going to hurt you, I just—"

Luke's bark of laughter is so caustic I can feel it stinging my skin. "That's right, you're *not* going to hurt me. You have no power here, princess. I know what you want, and you're not going to get it from me. I'm nobody's pawn, and I wouldn't fuck you if you were the last woman of the face of the earth."

I blink faster, but stand up straight as I say, "Last I checked I hadn't made any offers. And for what it's worth I had no idea what was going on around here until a few minutes ago. I had no idea what I was, who I was, or how any of you were involved. But if I had known, I would have made certain that no one was brought here against his will. That's not who I am. So assuming you can refrain from ripping my throat out for a few minutes, I'm prepared to let you go."

His dark eyes narrow, glittering with suspicion. "That's it? You're just going to let me go?"

I nod. "Yes."

"You realize I'm one of the only wolf shifters with this stupid mark, right?" he asks. "It's rare. So rare the pack from L.A. had exactly zero issues with throwing me into a van and dragging me here in chains, even though I've never shown those fucks anything but loyalty."

"I'm sorry," I say, meaning it. "Being betrayed by people you think you can trust is awful. And I was kidnapped, too, so I can empathize."

Luke's lip curls in a sneer. "You don't look like a captive to me, sweetheart. You look like you're the queen bee walking around free as you please."

I sigh as I roll my shoulders, shocked by how much better my chest feels. "I'm not a queen and none of us is really free, not if the story Dust told me is true. And I'm inclined to believe it is. In my experience, people lie about a lot of things, but the fate of the world resting on the five of us joining forces to take down a cannibalistic monster would be a first."

"The stranger the tale, the more likely it is to be true," Creedence says, earning another growl from Luke, to which he responds, "Yeah, yeah, we get that you're pissed, bucko. What you fail to realize is that this sucks for everyone, but you're the only one pitching a big whiny diaper baby fit about it. Wren took the news like three times the man you are."

"That's not helpful, Creedence," I cut in before Luke can say whatever is about to burst from his curled lips. "And I didn't take the news like a man. I took it like a woman. Growing up female, you get used to dealing with unexpectedly crappy news. Like when I was twelve and my mother explained I'd be getting my period every month for the rest of my life." Dust arches his brows in surprise and Creedence looks amused, but I press on. "Seriously. I mean, maybe that was *slightly* less of a bummer than finding out I'm the chosen one, but it still sucked. Periods are the worst."

"My sister gets wicked cramps," Creedence says with a nod. "They lay her up for days sometimes."

"My ex-girlfriend, too," Luke adds in an unexpectedly calm voice.

I glance his way to see his shoulders finally relaxed away from his ears and a thoughtful expression on his sculpted face. He's a handsome man when he's not snarling and spitting—even with the inch-long scar marring one cheek and the scary wolf tattoo curling around his neck.

"So, yeah," I say, breath rushing out. "It was kind of like that. I'm taking the news in stride and trying to make the best of it, but I understand why you want out. If I weren't the only Fata Morgana alive, I would want out, too. But as of now, I don't see that I really have a choice, so—"

"Of course you have a choice." Luke's brow furrows in what looks like genuine confusion. "You tell these assholes to fuck themselves and get out of here. Run, hide, enjoy what's left of your life. Let the world save itself."

"The world isn't going to save itself," Dust says softly.

"Then let it burn." Luke shrugs before nodding my way. "She didn't start any of this. It's not her responsibility to fix it. And it isn't mine, either. I already spent seven year behind bars. I'm not going to spend the rest of my life fighting and dying for a lost cause."

"Then you can go. Just promise not to hurt us on your way out." I start forward, holding a hand out to Dust when he tries to stop me again. "No, this is my choice. I know what's at risk, and I want to let him go. I would rather be weaker than steal strength from someone who's not willing to give it. I need the key for the lock." I wait, hand outstretched, until Dust finally digs into the front pocket of his black suit pants and places the key in my palm with a sigh.

Luke cocks his head as I approach, watching me with guarded eyes when I crouch down beside him and work open the padlock holding his chains in place. "You're a decent person, princess."

"Thank you," I say, trying not to be distracted by the intensity of his personal energy. He has the aura of an explosive that might detonate at any moment, and I don't want to be caught in the blast.

"You're also going to die," he says flatly. "Decent

people don't last long on the streets or the battlefield. You better toughen up and toughen up quick."

I loosen his chains and step back as he shrugs them off. "I'll take that under advisement."

I feel the men tense behind me, ready to jump in if Luke tries to hurt me, but he simply stands, holding my gaze in the murky light as he says, "You need someone to teach you how to not die."

"That would probably be helpful."

Luke scrubs a hand across his jaw, his whiskers making a shushing sound that's strangely pleasant. "And I need a new life somewhere they won't send me back to prison for violating my parole." He glances over my shoulder at Dust. "Maybe we can find a way to work together. At least for a little while. I train your princess the way you wanted. In exchange, you get me across the border with new I.D., new papers, everything I need for a fresh start."

Dust grunts. "And why would I do that? If you aren't willing to commit to keeping her alive long term? Anyone can teach her how to fight."

"Not the way I can," Luke says simply. The lack of arrogance in his tone makes me believe him, though I can't imagine myself becoming much of a fighter, no matter who's in charge of my training.

"What we need is a canine shifter with the mark willing to go all in," Dust insists. "Without that, our chances of living through this go down by twenty-five percent."

"Not my problem," Luke says callously. "And that's my final offer. Take it or leave it." His eyes lift to the ceiling. "But I would suggest you make a decision quickly, friend, before someone else makes it for you."

"What does—"

Creedence cuts Dust off with a hand in the air and a shushing sound. His brow furrows as he cocks his head. "Sirens. Maybe three miles out, but closing in fast."

Dust spins back to Luke to growl, "What have you done?"

"Nothing I had any control over. No one asked if I was tagged before they threw me in the back of their van or locked me up in their basement." He lifts the leg of his jeans, revealing an ankle bracelet ringed by flashing red lights. "You're lucky my parole officer is a junkie who forgets what day it is half the time or this would have been over a lot sooner."

Creedence curses while Kite backs across the room, saying, "I'll grab the emergency bags. Creedence get the car to the rendezvous spot. We'll meet you there."

"No, let me do it." Dust claps Creedence on the back. "You and Wren head for the woods. We'll meet you on the other side."

"What about him?" Creedence jabs a thumb toward Luke.

"He's coming with me." Dust turns to Luke, his eyes narrowing as he nods curtly. "I accept your terms, but no papers until you hold up your end of the bargain."

"I keep my word," Luke says, jaw clenched tight. "I'll train her like no shifter's been trained before. Assuming I don't end up leaving here in cuffs."

Dust's lips tilt up on one side. "I'm good at hiding

things that don't want to be found. But we need to get out of here. Now."

Luke hesitates a second, but apparently decides he's out of options—he either takes a chance on us or stays put and gets taken into police custody—and hurries after Dust as the other man starts for the stairs.

Creedence arches a brow as he closes the distance between us. "Well, this is it, Slim. Are you staying the course or making a run for the nearest cop car?"

I blink, surprised that the thought hadn't crossed my mind until this instant.

"I wouldn't blame you," Creedence says, lowering his voice as he adds, "And I'll let you go if that's what you want. Like you, I think people ought to choose their own quests. Especially when the chances of dying on said quest are unusually high."

I hesitate, searching his golden eyes. "And if I walk away..."

"Things have a way of working out or...*not* working out." He rolls a nonchalant shoulder as he studies the chains strewn across the floor. "Personally, I would like to leave my nieces and nephews a world better than this one, but despite all the shit I've seen in my life, I tend to think there's something more. Something after this life for those who've lived right." He turns back to me, holding my gaze. "And those kids are already living right. They'll be okay, even if we don't save the world."

His words break my heart and make my decision for me. "I'm not ready to give up on this planet. Or the people I love finding happiness while they're still on it."

Creedence smiles. "Then we should get going.

Judging by the sirens, our police friends aren't obeying posted speed limits. They're going to be here soon."

I'm about to ask how long we have when I hear the sirens keening through the air, not nearly distant enough for comfort. Without another word, I bolt for the stairs, moving fast for a girl with a gunshot wound. Still, by the time Creedence and I reach the back deck, where dusk is giving way to night, I hear wheels churning in the gravel of the front drive.

"Jump, I'll catch you." Creedence leaps easily over the deck railing to land softly in the grass on the other side. I swing one leg over the wooden rail, hesitating a split second before forcing myself to make the five-foot leap to the ground.

As promised, Creedence catches me, swinging me in a circle before setting me down on the grass and taking my hand. And then we run, sprinting for the tree line behind the property as a voice on a bullhorn shouts for us to stop and put our hands up.

But we don't. We cling tight to each other's fingers as we disappear into the shadows of the forest.

CHAPTER 18

WREN

Creedence and I emerge from the woods onto a gravel road fifteen minutes later and tumble into the softly idling car crouched in the near darkness with the lights off.

We did it! We made it out without anyone getting hurt, shot, or arrested!

But inside, the car it isn't as crowded as I expect it to be.

Buckling up, I scan the cab—Dust is driving and Kite is in the passenger's seat, leaving the back for Creedence and me. "Where's Luke?"

Kite jabs a thumb over his shoulder. "Trunk. Figured better safe than sorry in case we get pulled over."

"I'm cloaking the signal on the tracking device, so we should be fine," Dust says, shifting the car into drive. "Of course, if he'd been checked before he was chained I would have known it was there earlier, all of this could have been avoided, and we'd still have a safe house."

"I apologize." A hard smile curves Creedence's lips, his teeth bright in the shadows as Dust picks up speed and moonlight flashes into the car through the trees. "I'm sorry, friends, for forgetting to check to see if the wolf a bunch of other wolves delivered to our hideout in chains was wearing an ankle bracelet. Though, in my defense, one would think the pack would have taken care of that themselves if they were truly interested in helping our cause and not intending to royally fuck up our world-saving plans. They had to have known he was on parole."

Kite grunts. "You think it was deliberate."

"I try not to think," Creedence says. "Thinking causes wrinkles, but I'm sure Dust can figure out if we're being deliberately fucked up the ass. Since he's the brains of the operation and all."

"Cut the shit, Creedence," Dust mutters.

"I'm serious. No shit, Sherlock. You're the fearless leader. I just work here." Creedence stretches his arms out across the back of the seat, tapping me lightly on the shoulder as he adds in a softer voice, "How you holding up, Slim?"

"Good." I give my ribs an experimental wiggle. "My chest was aching a bit while we were running, but I think I'm almost back to normal. Better than normal. Is that possible? So quickly?"

"Not for me," Creedence says with a wink. "But I'm not the chosen one. Who knows what you'll be able to do once we get you patched up and shifting and hurling thunderbolts or whatever your thing is."

Before I can ask what kind of powers a Fata

Morgana might have aside from being able to shift into multiple forms, Dust clears his throat pointedly from the front seat.

"She's never going to figure out what her 'thing' is if we're detained by the police or hunted down by Kin Born forces before Wren has time to heal and train. That safe house was supposed to be our home base for the next three months."

"We can find another one," Kite says. "There are lots of vacation rentals up here."

"That's going to require I.D., a bank account, and a paper trail," Creedence says. "All things we either don't have or can't afford to share."

"And money is tight until my next meeting with our handler, which isn't for three more weeks," Dust says. "I have an emergency number, but that's only for use in an actual emergency, not because one of us was too stupid to make sure we stayed off human law enforcement's radar."

"You are such a passive-aggressive shit," Creedence says pleasantly. "Where I come from, you're lucky to get one 'I'm sorry.' Keep pushing and I'll take my apology and go home."

"Speaking of home," Kite says, a hopeful note threading into his voice. "We're not far from my tribe's land, and normal cops don't have jurisdiction there. Our tribal police force calls the shots and one of my sisters is the captain. She'll make sure we're safe if anyone comes looking."

"What about your family?" Creedence asks. "The human authorities aren't the only threat, or even the worst one. If the Kin Born track you down while you're shacking up with the other pooh bears, they won't spare the innocent. They'll kill every man, woman, and child to send a message to anyone else who thinks peace, love, and acceptance are good ideas. They aren't fucking around, and you know it."

Kite turns, his eyes shadowed in the dark as he says, "My people know what I'm signed up for, and they're on board for whatever comes next."

Creedence makes a doubtful sound low in his throat.

"We're coastal people," Kite continues. "Half the land we were originally deeded is underwater, and the U.S. government isn't in any rush to approve our petition for an expansion inland. If environmental damage continues and the sea levels keep rising, in a hundred years there won't be any reservation left. My people's way of life, traditions dating back thousands of years, and the safety our tribal lands have provided to our community will be lost. Our success is my tribe's only chance of survival, and they're willing to take risks to win back the future."

I reach out, giving Kite's shoulder a gentle squeeze. "That's very brave of them. Of you. But let's keep brainstorming. Surely we can find somewhere to lay low that won't put anyone else at risk."

But by the time we reach the outskirts of Conway—a one-horse town with a faded main street about two blocks long—an hour later, no one has come up with a better idea and a visit to Kite's neck of the woods is looking like our only option.

Dust pulls into the parking lot of what was once

Paco's Mexican Grill and around to the back of the clearly abandoned restaurant. The roof of the building sags ominously in the middle, weeds sprout from the cracks in the sidewalk near the entrance, and as we emerge into the cool night air, the scent of mothballs and rotting wood wheezes from the building like a sad perfume.

"I'll get Luke out and take him for a walk," Dust says, circling around to the back of the car. "Let him get some air and stretch his legs while I keep the cloaking active on the device. It looks like there's a hardware store at the end of the street, but it won't open until morning. Creedence, you come with me to do recon. Kite, you're in charge of keeping an eye on Wren."

"Afraid to be alone with the ex-con, huh?" Creedence asks as he joins Dust beside the trunk. "Need me to hold your hand?"

"If we run into trouble, I won't be able to fight and keep him cloaked at the same time," Dust says tiredly, clearly in no mood for teasing.

"Want to take a walk?" Kite asks me, nodding toward the rear of the parking lot and the open field behind it. "If you're feeling up to it?"

"Sure. A walk sounds good."

"Check in every thirty minutes," Dust says. "You have your cell with the cloaking device, correct? Please tell me we didn't leave that at the house along with all the food and medical supplies."

Kite pulls his phone from his front pocket. "I've got it. I'll give my family a call while we're out, too, let them know we're on our way."

Dust nods as he pops the trunk. "At least for now it seems like our best option." He reaches down, helping Luke out of the trunk. The slightly shorter man emerges with a graceful roll, landing on his feet and immediately turning to scan his surroundings, his hands lifting and curling lightly into fists. But he seems more relaxed than he did before, making me think his vigilance is more habit than inspired by anything that's happened in the past hour.

He even thanks Dust for the hand up before stretching his neck sharply to one side, sending an audible crack through the quiet darkness.

Creedence winces and lifts a hand our way. "Later, Romeo and Juliet. Don't do anything I wouldn't do."

"I have a feeling he'd do just about anything," I say to Kite. "So that gives us plenty of options."

"Sassy wench," Creedence says, making me laugh as we go our separate ways.

CHAPTER 19

WREN

"Well, at least one of us is back on your good side," Kite says as we amble off the cracked and crumbling pavement into the short grass at the edge of the field. "Creedence is one of those people, though. You can't stay mad at him. Even when he deserves it."

I smile. "Seems that way. I obviously haven't known him long, but he's funny. And kinder than he would like people to believe, I think."

"Agreed," Kite says. "He'll tease you until you're ready to rip his hair out, but he's not a bad guy. And at least he's here of his own free will."

"Luke is now, too." I amend with a sigh, "For now."

"What about you?' Kite studies my face as we start across the sea of hay, all silver in the moonlight. "Still planning to ditch us all at the earliest opportunity?"

I shake my head. "No. Dust's vision-sharing was pretty convincing."

"He could have been making it up," Kite says, playing devil's advocate.

"He could have," I agree. "But I knew Dust pretty well back in the day. He had his faults, but he was never a liar. He was actually a good friend to me when were kids."

"Hard to imagine him as a kid. Was he stuffy even back then?"

I smile. "No, he wasn't. He was kind of a rascal. Funny, too."

Kite pulls a face. "Nah. I'm not buying that, Bird Girl. That man's about as funny as a sack of smashed crackers."

I laugh. "Nothing sadder than a bag of smashed crackers. But I swear, it's true." I cross my arms over my waist, sobering as I add, "The vision felt true, too. It almost felt like I'd seen that monster, Atlas, before." I pause, brow furrowing as pieces of my dream come back to me. "Right before I woke up at the farmhouse, I dreamt about a face in the sky. A man's face, and when he opened his mouth, there were people writhing inside of him."

Kite makes an unhappy noise low in his throat. "You should tell Dust about that. He's supposed to communicate any sign that your powers are coming online to the higher ups. You should tell my mom about it, too, once we get to my family's place. She has prophecy dreams. She might be able to help you sort out what your dream meant, see if there's anything there that might help us get ready to face Atlas."

I blink, the strangeness of my new life hitting me all

over again. "My first instinct is still to say there's no way I could be prophesizing the future in my dreams, but...maybe I am." I look up at the moon, so big and nearly full in the sky. "I mean, from what I've gathered, there are shifters with supernatural powers spread out all over the world, fighting their own battles and dreaming their own dreams, and up until a few hours ago I would have sworn all of that was fiction. Horror movie stuff."

Kite steps closer, his arm brushing my shoulder. "So you think we're scary?"

Tilting my head back, I search his face, but his eyes are cast in shadow. "No, I don't think you're scary. I'm sorry, that came out wrong. I think this situation is scary—terrifying, really—but not you." I pause, unable to resist adding, "especially not you."

He turns to me, his hand coming to cup my cheek. "So you think you can forgive me someday?"

"Yes," I whisper. "Though, I am confused. I keep wondering what was a lie and what was the truth, you know?"

"This is the truth," he says, leaning down to press his lips to mine.

Instantly, sparks ignite behind my closed eyes and awareness ripples across my skin. My breath comes faster, and my arms go around his neck, and I barely notice the twinge in my chest as he hugs me close, lifting me off my feet, bringing me up to his level. He parts my lips with his tongue as I thread my fingers into his soft hair and hold on tight as our kiss goes from zero to sixty in seconds flat.

I don't know if it's the fact that we've survived so much together in the past few days, the improvement in my health since the last time his lips met mine, or just the magic of the moonlight and the star-filled sky, but our second kiss is so much more intense than our first.

Hotter, deeper, and urgent in a way I've never experienced before.

This is *passion*, this hunger that claws away inside me, demanding to be satisfied, demanding I wrap my legs around Kite's hips and squeeze. So I do, gasping into his mouth as I feel him, hard behind the fly of his jeans.

"I want you so much." He squeezes my hips, building the sweet ache spreading through my core. "From the moment I met you. It's not about the mark or the mission for me. It's all you, Bird Girl. You're incredible." His breath rushes out as I dig my nails into his neck. "And so damned sexy. I like you off your meds."

"Me, too," I murmur against his lips. "I almost don't know what to do with all this extra energy."

"I have a few ideas," Kite says, one hand skimming up to cup my breast through my T-shirt, stoking the fire building inside of me as I kiss him again, long and deep, taking the lead for the first time in my life.

I've only kissed five guys—most of them while I was in remission in college—and none of them ever made me feel anything like this, like the fierce thrill that rips through me from head to toe as Kite lays me down in the sweet-smelling hay, bracing his arms on either side of my head.

"Can I kiss you?" His voice is soft and husky, warm and shiver inducing at the same time.

"I think it's a little late to ask that question," I tease.

"I don't mean on your lips. Can I kiss you other places, beautiful Wren?"

I swallow, pulse fluttering in my throat. "Places like where?"

"Like here," he says, his fingers skimming lightly over my nipple, making me suck in a sharp breath as electricity surges between my legs. "And here." Now his hand slides between my thighs, gliding over places no one has ever touched but me, not even through my jeans the way he is now. It is...incredible. Terrifying. Magnificently overwhelming.

I exhale, shivering harder.

"Cold?" he asks.

I shake my head, holding his gaze in the moonlight, hoping he can see how much I want him to kiss me in those places, to strip me bare and show me how a woman my age is supposed to feel with a man.

But I'm still too shy to say the words aloud, a part of me trapped in the version of myself that always had to be so careful, so reserved, who was always so fearful of not having enough energy to handle love or relationships or much of anything else.

Kite's thumb drags across my bottom lip, making my blood burn even hotter. "It's okay to say no. I don't want to push you. I'll wait as long as you want to wait."

"I don't want to wait," I whisper. "I just... I don't know what to do. Everything is so new. The things I'm feeling, the fact that I have enough energy to feel them in the first place. But, I want you, too. So much."

"Then let me take the lead," he says, giving my hip a gentle squeeze. "I'll make you feel good, and that's where it ends tonight. No pressure, no stress, just relax and let me take care of you."

"Sounds selfish," I say, but I can't stop the soft moan of pleasure that escapes my lips as his hand skims beneath my shirt and his fingers brush over my tightly puckered nipple, making disco lights spin behind my eyes.

"Not selfish. I get off on giving," Kite says, guiding my T-shirt up and over my head, baring my breasts to the moonlight. He looks down, an almost pained expression flashing across his face as he says, "God, you're beautiful. So perfect..."

He runs his fingers up my breastbone to hover over the slightly puckered flesh above my left breast that is all that remains of the gunshot wound. "It doesn't hurt at all?" he asks, wonder in his voice.

"Not much, no," I whisper. "But it's starting to hurt in other places. To ache..."

His lips curve as his focus shifts back to my face. "Let me see if I can help you out with that, baby."

And then he dips his head, his hair tumbling around us to slide, dark and silky, against my pale ribs as he presses a kiss to the underside of my breast and then another and another, building the tension swirling inside me until he finally gives me what I didn't realize I was craving. His mouth closes around my nipple, and he sucks me into his mouth, making the stars spin and the ache between my legs become a sharp, sweet tug.

He continues to kiss and lick, to suck and then to bite—oh God, he bites me, and I would never have imagined I would want someone to bite me there, where I'm so sensitive, but it feels so incredibly good. So sexy, so hot that by the time he reaches for the button on my borrowed jeans, my shyness has vanished.

I'm not anxious about a man seeing that part of me for the first time, I'm too desperate for him to touch me, stroke me, do something to take the edge off this hunger that feels like it will devour me whole if I don't find something else to feed it.

He slips his hand down the front of my panties, his fingers curling until he finds where I'm wet. We groan together as he glides a single finger inside me, but even that slight penetration is enough to drive me wild.

"Yes," I gasp into his mouth as he kisses me again. "I want that so much. I want you so much."

"You drive me crazy, beautiful," he murmurs. "I'm dying to taste you. Can I taste you, Wren?"

"Yes." I nod even though I'm not exactly sure what he means. But everything Kite has done to me so far— every kiss, every caress—has been so perfect, I'm sure whatever he wants to do next will be perfect, too.

I shiver, biting my lip as he strips my jeans and panties swiftly down my legs and tosses them aside. I experience a fleeting moment of shyness as he parts my thighs and settles his broad shoulders between them, but before I can worry too much he leans in, pressing a kiss to the place where I ache, and a rush of pleasure banishes my anxiety. I suck in a shocked breath as his tongue circles the top of my sex, building the pressure dragging at my core until I'm lifting shamelessly into his mouth, desperate for that release I've only ever found by my own hand.

But I can already tell this is going to be a hundred times more intense than any self-delivered orgasm. And that's before his palms glide up my ribs to find my breasts, cupping and squeezing, teasing my nipples as his tongue continues to work its dark magic between my legs.

Soon I'm bucking into Kite's tongue, panting and writhing beneath his hands, his mouth, as he takes me to a place I've never been before. And finally, when I'm certain I can't bear another moment of anticipation, I tumble over. I swoop and soar, crying out in bliss as my body locks down around Kite's hand. He glides two fingers inside me, driving them slowly in and out as I come, drawing out my pleasure until I'm trembling on the grass beneath him.

"Oh God," I whisper, too shattered to think of anything more eloquent to say. "Oh my God."

He lifts himself onto his forearms, grinning at me from between my legs. "Good?"

"Mind-blowing," I say, my next words tumbling from my lips before I realize what I intend to say. "I want to do that to you. I want you in my mouth."

Kite's breath rushes out as his eyes darken. "No, Wren. Like I said, tonight is about you. Your pleasure."

"It will give me pleasure to know what you taste like, too," I say, knowing I'm winning this fight when Kite's jaw clenches and a soft groan escapes from low in his throat. "But you'll have to show me what to do. I've never done that before."

I'm reaching for him, determined to give him the same magical release he just gave me or die trying when a musical flute noise fills the air, coming from the general direction of...Kite's butt.

"Sorry. I have to take it." He curses as he sits back on his heels in the grass, breath still coming faster as he tugs his phone out of his pocket. "It's home. Probably Mom responding to the text I sent about letting us hide out there for a while."

He stands, pacing a few steps away as he begins conversing in a language I don't understand. It's beautiful, lilting and soft around the edges, with a few random guttural inflections here and there that Kite makes sound incredibly sexy. So sexy it's hard to resist the urge to slip up behind him and kiss his neck while he talks.

Surely, I can't be this desperate for more after he's already given me the kind of mind-bending, soul-transporting release I thought was just the fictional fodder of sexy books and racy movies?

But as I stand, pulling on my clothes with trembling hands, every second that I have to wait to touch him again feels like an eternity. I find myself clenching my jaw as I exercise my willpower in a way I've never had to before. I mean, I crave sweets as much as the next sugar addict, but what Kite does to me makes walking by Gypsy Donuts without popping in for a red velvet special seem like child's play.

I must be getting greedy in my old age, drunk on my newfound health and all the previously unimagined possibilities unfurling in front of me, a road as filled with excitement and adventure as danger and uncertainty.

You're also becoming a heartless asshole. There's a phone right there, Wren. You've got to call Mom and Pops and let them know that you're not dead. No matter what anyone else thinks, no matter how confusing all of this is, you know they love you and must be desperately worried.

The inner voice is right. So when Kite hangs up, instead of rushing back into his arms and picking up where we left off, I thread my fingers together and ask softly, "I know this is probably off-limits, but I was wondering if I could call my parents? Just to let them know I'm okay."

Kite shakes his head, but I hurry on, not ready to give up yet. If any of these men are going to help me break this rule, it's Kite. Family is as important to him as it is to me. So is kindness, and it isn't kind to let the people who love me most worry when I could put their minds at ease. "There's a cloaking device on the phone, right?" I press. "So if the police are with them, they won't be able to track the call."

Kite nods, but he's still clearly not a fan of this idea.

"I won't tell them where we are or what's happening or anything else," I promise. "I'll just tell them that I'm alive and fine and that they shouldn't worry. Would that be okay?"

"I know you love them, Wren." Kite brushes a stray hair from my face, holding it there as a breeze rushes across the field, doing its best to undo his work. "But your parents are in deep with some incredibly dangerous people. Even if they are simply ignorant or misguided, the people who arranged for them to adopt you aren't. They knew exactly what they were doing when they tracked you down and took you away from your parents. They are highly organized, driven, and fueled by a kind of hate we can't even understand. There is no doubt in my mind they've got people on your parents, tailing them everywhere they go on the chance that you make contact." He shakes his head as his hand drops from my face. "I'm sorry, but I can't risk it."

"Then what about Carrie Ann?" I ask, inspiration striking. "What if I called her and gave her a message for my parents?"

He exhales through his teeth, casting a glance over his shoulder.

"We don't have to tell the others," I whisper. "I'll call really fast, and then we can delete it from the call history."

"Dust will have my ass if he finds out," Kite mutters, but he finally holds the phone out my way. "Text her, don't call. You're less likely to say things you shouldn't if you have to type them out first."

"Thank you so much, Kite." I press up on tiptoe to kiss his cheek as I take the phone. "I promise I won't tell her anything I shouldn't."

"Just be quick, Bird Girl." He kisses my forehead before stepping back and pointing a finger at my chest. "And as soon as you're done, we block her number so she can't call or text back later when we're surrounded by people who will have my ass for breaking protocol."

I nod quickly. "I promise."

"Call me if you need me," he says, walking toward the tree line at the opposite end of the field, giving me privacy. I glance up at the limbs rocking gently above him in the breeze, a flash in the shadows beneath the canopy making me hesitate.

I catch what looks like a pair of eyes, glinting in the darkness, but they vanish so quickly I'm not sure I saw them at all. I hesitate, wondering if I should call out to Kite to warn him we might be being watched—knowing our enemies could come for us in animal form has brought an entire new dimension into this flight—but then I remember the way Kite always seemed to know when danger was coming. If there was something malevolent watching us from the woods, he would sense it. And he certainly doesn't look worried.

I watch him go, his stride light and easy despite his large size, and things low in my body start humming all over again.

All I want to do is hide away in a cave with my sweet, sexy bear for a week or two—until we've discovered all the ways we can give each other pleasure, all the ways our bodies fit together—but for now I settle on admiring his broad shoulders and the moonlight reflecting off his dark hair before I tap Carrie's number into the phone and cast a line back into my old life.

The one that already seems so very far away...

CHAPTER 20

Text log: Wren Frame and Carrie Ann Cutler

Wren: Carrie Ann, it's me. Wren. I'm on a borrowed phone and I'm okay.
I'm safe for now, and I'm going to call you and my parents as soon as I can.

Carrie Ann: Oh my God! Wren! I've been so worried. We're all freaking out! We thought you were dead. It's been so insanely scary around here. There have been cops all over the shelter, looking for clues and bagging up everything in your office. What happened, babe? They said you were kidnapped!

Wren: I was, but it's okay. They're actually good people. Just misguided in their methods.

Carrie Ann: You've lost me, honey. Are they with you

right now? Are they making you say this shit? Because taking a chronically ill person away from her family and her friends and her meds isn't fucking okay.

How are you feeling by the way?

Are you holding up all right?

I've been lying awake every night imaging the worst, so scared that you were out there dying, and plotting how I was going to kill these monsters who took you away from us. Just tell me where you are, babe, and I will be there with all the fucking cops in a heartbeat.

Wren: I can't tell you that, and please don't tell the police about this or try to have this number traced. There's a cloaking system on the phone, and I'm going to have to block you in a few minutes, anyway. But I promise that I'm in my right mind and no one is making me say or do anything.

And I'm actually feeling so good.

Better than I have in my entire life.

Carrie Ann: Wow. Seriously? How is that even possible? Your mom said all of your meds were still there at the house.

Wren: Turns out I don't need those meds.

I'm not sick, Carrie, and I probably never have been.

Carrie Ann: Holy. Shit.

What does that mean, Wren?

How could the doctors have had it so wrong all this time?

God, your parents are going to be so happy! And so relieved.

Wren: I think so, too. I'd love for you to tell them that for me—that I'm feeling good and getting better every day, and as soon as it's safe to make a call, I'll be contacting them. And tell them I love them and I believe in them and that they will always be a part of my heart, okay?

Carrie Ann: I will tell them exactly that, honey, but can you tell ME what the actual hell is happening? Reading between the lines here, my mind starts going to some pretty dark places.
Like…Munchausen by Proxy places.
You know those people who poison their own children to get attention when the kids get sick? You honestly don't think your parents…

Wren: I don't know, Carrie. I hope not, I hope for that with everything in me, but there are so many crazy things happening right now that I'm not sure what to think anymore. All I know for sure is that I believe they love me and I don't want them to be scared.

Carrie Ann: Got it.
Dude…this is so messed up.
Are you sure you can't tell me where you are, babe?
I promise not to tell the cops if you don't want me to, but I would feel so much better knowing where you are on this big blue planet I can't imagine continuing to

spin without you. You know you're like the sister I never had, right? That I love you like family? Better than family, since mine was utter shit?

Wren: I love you like family, too, sweets. And I promise I'll tell you more as soon as I can. But right now I have to go.

Carrie Ann: Okay, but you have to tell me one thing first! Kite isn't involved in this, is he? He didn't show up for work this morning, and his roommates said they haven't seen him since Thursday afternoon. The police thought he might be the one who took you, but I told them that was crazy. He's not that kind of guy.

Wren: No, he isn't. And no, he didn't take me.
Got to go. Take care of the kids for me. Tell them I'm sorry I let them down.

Carrie Ann: No, I won't tell them that. Because you didn't let them down—you were taken from your home against your will—and you're going to be back here changing lives before you know it. You're going to get out of whatever crazy mess you're in, and now that you're well enough to move out of the family home-stead, we can get our own place together. It's going to be epic!
You and me, single ladies taking Seattle.
Just wait and see.
And don't lose hope on me.

You know that's the one thing a girl can't ever afford to lose.

Wren: I know. Love you.
Take care of yourself, okay?

Carrie Ann: I will. And I'll take care of you, too, any time you need me. Reach out as soon as you can, babe, and I'll be there.

CHAPTER 21

WREN

Smearing tears from my cheeks, I delete the text record and block Carrie's phone number. By the time I'm finished, Kite is by my side. He takes the cell and then my hand, lifting it to his lips to press a kiss to my knuckles in silent apology.

I force a smile and fall into step beside him as we walk hand in hand back to the car. My life is crazy right now, but it isn't Kite's fault.

Or my fault. Or the fault of anyone I know, really, not even my parents.

If I hadn't been hidden in a human family, Atlas would have tracked me down when I was a baby and killed me the way he did all the Fata Morgana children before me. I would never have had the chance to grow up, let alone get a degree, do good work, make dear friends, or find out what it feels to fall for an incredible man.

I pause at the edge of the parking lot, tugging lightly

on Kite's arm. He turns back to me, curiosity and affection mixing in his expression, making me feel as cozy as a cup of hot tea on a winter morning.

"Can we keep everything that happened out there just between us?" I whisper. "I mean, I'm sure secrets are going to be hard to keep as we move forward, but…"

He squeezes my hand. "I would never tell anyone about anything that happens while we're together like that," he says with a quiet intensity. "It's too precious to me. Too private."

I bite my lip, blinking fast against a sudden wave of emotion as I lean into his side, wrapping my arms around him as I say, "Me, too."

I want to tell him that it was my first time doing most of what we did together and how much it means to me that he is so gentle and patient and generous with me, but Creedence is slinking across the pavement and is probably already within ear shot. So I settle for a quick squeeze, which Kite returns before stepping away.

"Hello, young people," Creedence says, playing up the old man act again. "How was your walk?"

"Good," Kite says. "Where are Dust and Luke?"

Creedence's brows lift as he jabs a thumb over his shoulder. "They decided to head into town and hit the hardware store early."

"But I thought it wasn't open?" I ask, confused.

"Oh, it's not," Creedence says, pleasantly. "But Luke is apparently very handy with a lock pick, and Dust is apparently not a fan of listening to other people having fun while he's left out in the cold, so…"

My cheeks go from cool to burning hot in two seconds flat.

"Yeah, we could hear." Creedence shrugs. "We're shifters, Slim, we've got excellent hearing. But it's not a big deal, nothing to be embarrassed about. Wouldn't have mentioned it, in fact, except I thought you would want to know. Just so you could be a little quieter next time if you're hoping to keep your private life private."

I nod, wishing I weren't so horrifically inexperienced. I can't imagine ever being as laid-back about sex as Creedence apparently is. But I appreciate him not making this any more uncomfortable than it has to be.

And how quickly he changes the subject.

"So, I think we should hop in the car and be ready to roll when those two get back." He reaches for the driver's side door. "Even if we don't know where we're headed, it's not smart to stick around a small town for too long. These people will definitely remember a pretty girl and four strange dudes hanging around Main Street if they're questioned by the police."

"We're clear to head up Fidalgo Island way. I heard from my mom," Kite says, opening the back door for me. "The tribe is going to put us up in the cabins we used to rent out to tourists back in the day. The state made us close them down when high tide got within twenty feet of the campground, but we'll be safe as long as there isn't a bad storm or a tidal wave."

"That's comforting," Creedence says as we all pile into the car. "Not a fan of the water, myself."

"Because you're a cat?" I tease.

"Because my old man taught my sister and I how to

swim by throwing us in the deep end of a swimming pool in Vegas." Creedence slips the key into the ignition and the engine purrs quietly to life. "Needless to say, that didn't go so well, and he and his buddies were so drunk it took them a few tries to fish us both out again. To this day Fiona won't even take a bath."

He says it all in his usual, laid-back way, but I can tell this is a painful story. There's something in his shoulders as he pulls around to the front of the restaurant, a stiffness that usually isn't there.

"I'm sorry," I say. "That sounds traumatizing."

Creedence casts a quick grin over his shoulder as he pulls to a stop under a tree at the edge of the lot, just barely in view of the rest of Main Street. "It was. Will you hold my hand if I get scared near the water?"

"I will," I promise seriously, though I know he's trying to deflect attention with a joke. "Be happy to, in fact."

I don't remember anything about my childhood before going to live with Hank and Abby in a warm and loving home, but I know those wounds can haunt a person long after they've grown up and left the abuse behind. Half of the scars on the kids I work with are on the inside, damage to their souls and psyches from abuse that took place when they were too little to know how to process the terrible things that were happening to them.

So often, they blame themselves for the trauma, either because their abuser made them believe it was their fault or because their child's mind embraced the logic of "if something bad happened to me, that means I must be bad. I must have done something to deserve it."

It's actually more empowering to think that way.

To think that there is a logical cause and effect at work, and that one's future behavior can be modified in order to keep those bad things from happening again. The truth—that evil is loose in the world and that it preys on the weak at random and at will, and often there's nothing that can be done to stop it—is so much more traumatizing.

Or at least I used to believe there was nothing that could be done...

Now I have a sliver of hope that things can change, that the runaway train barreling toward the certain painful annihilation of humanity can be stopped.

I just wish Fate had picked a tougher customer to lead the charge.

Yes, I'm getting stronger every day, but I'm still just one scrawny, sheltered girl who's never had to fight a day in her life. At least, not with my fists. I fought to survive, to keep going while the virus inherited from my addict mother...

My brain stutters and my thoughts screech to stop.

"My mother wasn't a drug addict, was she?" I blurt into the silence, breath rushing out as I shake my head. "I don't know why I didn't think of that before. How dumb am I?"

"Give yourself a break," Kite says, laying a hand on my knee. "Your entire world has been turned upside down and dumped out on the floor. It's going to take some time to pick it all up and make sense of the pieces."

"Who was she?" I ask, still feeling foolish. I'm a counselor; I should be quicker than the average person to realize I'm clinging to outdated stories. "And my father? Does anyone know?"

Kite shakes his head. "I don't know. We're all told as little as possible, to make it easier in case we're captured and interrogated. The less we know, the less we can be forced to reveal to the enemy."

"Dust knows more than most of us," Creedence offers. "You could try asking him. Assuming he's in a better mood when he gets back than when he left."

"And my sister." I nibble on my thumb as new pathways appear in my mind, narrow roads that could lead to a completely revised version of my personal history. "She wasn't sick, either."

Kite shakes his head and gives my knee another squeeze.

But his touch isn't comforting this time, and the realization breaks my heart. Not only did Scarlett have to fight the same pointless, agonizing war I've battled my entire life, but she died before she could be rescued, before she knew what it feels like to be well and free.

It's so sad.

It's also...enraging.

For the first time since the truth started bursting through the strained seams of my life, the rage crouched deep inside of me turns its red eyes Hank and Abby's way. Maybe they *were* simply ignorant or doing what they were told. Maybe they were poisoning us out of love.

But it doesn't matter if they killed her with love or with hate—my sister is still dead.

My sister is dead, and I will never know who she could have been if she hadn't been tortured and then sent away when she turned to street drugs to escape the suffering.

It makes me burn with anger, a hot fire that roars to life inside me, spreading through my veins and *whooshing* into my chest like the flames leaping into a forge as a blacksmith pumps his bellows.

"Whoa." Kite pulls his hand away from my leg as if I've burned him, and Creedence curses as he jumps out of the car. I have split second to realize that something's seriously wrong before the seat beneath me bursts into flames.

CHAPTER 22

DUST

I pride myself on excellence in all things.

If I don't excel at something initially, I keep at it until I achieve mastery, or I abandon the pastime, leaving it for those with more natural ability.

Life is too short to settle for mediocrity.

So I do not play tennis. I do not write code. I do not touch paints, colored pencils, or pens because I have the artistic aptitude of a monkey wearing a blindfold and no wish to torture the eyeballs of my friends or family, let alone the public at large.

But I am a skilled marksman—months of drills with Celeste and the other resistance leaders ensured that I rarely miss my target—and I can take just about any machine apart and rebuild it from the lug nuts up.

But I can't rebuild a vehicle that's a smoldering hunk of metal, and I'm beginning to think my skills as mission leader are as deeply fucked as our getaway car.

Abandoning the roaring inferno that's bound to

attract the wrong kind of attention, we toss Luke's recently removed ankle bracelet into the flames and flee north on foot, moving fast enough that we're miles outside of town by the time the sirens begin to wail behind us.

Still, it was another close fucking call. Too close.

Nothing is going as planned, and spending an entire day hiking definitely wasn't on the agenda. It's soon late afternoon, but we keep moving deeper into the woods —hoping to avoid detection by the human authorities until we can reach a town where we can hop a bus or a taxi bound for Fidalgo Island—and I'm wondering how long I can keep my four cold, hungry, and, in Kite's case, slightly singed, compatriots motivated to move forward.

Kite knows what's at stake in a visceral way—we've both lost people we love in the fight against the Kin Born, including Sierra, Celeste's lover, just a few days past—but Luke is an apathetic participant at best. And though he's doing what he's told and appearing to toe the party line, Creedence gives off the distinct impression that, all in all, he would rather be getting declawed without anesthesia.

And Wren...

I glance her way, at her bare legs sticking out of Luke's massive jean jacket and the dejected droop to her head as she sloughs through the leaves in the too-big sneakers that thankfully survived the fire that burned away the rest of her clothes, and my chest aches. I knew extracting her from the cult wouldn't be easy, but I'd hoped for a smoother transition than this. So far she's been shot, chased off a bridge, dragged naked from a burning car, and forced to flee the authorities twice in less than a few hours.

It's time to raise the damned bar.

I don't want to simply keep her alive; I want her to feel liberated, empowered, maybe even excited about the future. Yes, it's going to be a dangerous and challenging fight, but we have the chance to change the world, to give the next generation of both shifters and human beings a better place to live and love and grow old without fear that there won't be a world left for their grandchildren. I want Wren to feel the intoxicating promise of the future we can create together. I want her strong and hopeful and delighted by the powers that are coming online for her faster than even the most optimistic projections.

Instead, she looks about five seconds from sitting down in the dirt, dropping her face into her hands, and crying her eyes out. She's miserable and ashamed, and I can't seem to think of anything to say to make this better.

At least not anything I feel comfortable saying in front of the other men.

If only I could have a moment alone with her, just a few minutes to connect the way we used to. I know we're older now, different people in so many ways, but deep down I'm still that boy who would do anything for his best friend.

For his Snow, his Wren.

But she's not mine anymore, and she might never be. She could very well decide to choose Kite as the only man for her and give the rest of us our walking papers.

Embracing the possibility of taking multiple mates is a lot to ask of a woman who was raised to believe she would be married *one* time to *one* man and anything else would be a violation of the promises she'd made to the movement. It's part of the pledge the Church of Humanity made us say every morning before class —*Lord keep me strong and pure of heart, body, and mind, so I may better serve you, humanity, my one true husband or wife, and myself.*

I got out of the movement over a decade before she did, and it still took time for me to adjust to the shifter community. The freedom, the lack of shame, the focus on the gifts and consequences of the present rather than the imaginary treasures or punishments waiting in the future—it was all a lot to get my head around at thirteen.

Maybe that's all she needs, too—time.

If we can just get to the bear kin lands where we'll hopefully find that time without anyone else getting shot or catching fire...

At least things can't get worse.

No sooner has the thought drifted through my mind than thunder rumbles in the distance—a long, low, sky belly-growl that doesn't bode well. Kite pauses, turning to meet my gaze over the heads of the other three.

"Is it coming this way?" I ask, silently praying for a break in our shitty luck.

Kite's mouth tightens as he cocks his head, listening as the thunder comes again. After a moment, he nods.

"It is. We've got ten minutes. Maybe fifteen if we're lucky."

Balls, I silently curse even as I calmly point Creedence's way. "Creedence, you and Luke head up to the ridge and see if you can find anything that might serve as shelter. We'll keep going straight and meet up with you in no more than eight minutes. That should give us time to find cover before the storm hits."

"Should we split up?" Kite asks, casting a suspicious look Luke's way. "Isn't it more important that we stay together?"

"It's more important that we aren't killed by falling tree limbs or a flash flood," I say, circling my arm, signaling for Creedence and Luke to get moving. "Let's go. If we're separated, we meet up in Anacortes by the marina tomorrow." I meet Wren's gaze for a quick beat. "You okay to run?"

Wren nods. "Lead the way, I'll follow."

I motion to Kite. "Call out if you see anything. A hollow tree or even something with a big enough root system to offer shelter if the runoff starts rolling down fast from uphill."

"Got it." Kite pauses to usher Wren gently in front of him—as attentive as he's been since the moment I pulled her from the car, making it clear he isn't holding a grudge for his burned hand, presently bandaged in a strip of Creedence's T-shirt.

I should be pleased that she's bonding with one of her potential suitors and that he's clearly so smitten with her—the sooner she forms mate bonds, the sooner she'll be strong, centered, and prepared for battle—but I can't help the bitter taste that rises in my throat every time he touches her.

Logically, I knew from the moment I took this mission that, if everything went as planned, I would eventually be sharing Wren. But I secretly assumed I would be the first to form a connection. I know Wren, I've cared about her since we were kids, and I've watched over her for years, using the charmed coin I gave her to make sure she was still alive and fighting back against the poison.

And the coin worked every time.

Every. Single. Time.

Assuring me Wren had never forgotten about me. If she had, the charm would have lost its power, and our connection would have faded away.

Some magic stands alone, but it takes two to hold onto a love spell.

That's what the charm is really about. On the surface it's a tracking spell, designed to help me home in on Wren's location when we're far apart. But at its core it's a gift from a little boy who loved a little girl and wanted to make sure she would always be safe.

Or as safe as he could make her...

As the wind whips faster, tossing the tops of the trees back and forth like slam dancers at a punk club, and dark clouds sweep in from the west, carrying the fierce rattle-drum of thunder closer to our part of the woods, I have to fight the insane urge to stop, pull Wren into my arms, and tell her I'm sorry for all the ways I've let her down. To tell her that I care, that I still want to be someone she can trust and confide in, and that I will do whatever it takes to earn the right to be her friend again.

But there isn't even a second to waste, let alone the time it would take for that conversation. Storms aren't what they used to be back in the days before the Meltdown. As the ice caps disappeared and the climate shifted in response, storms grew teeth and claws. They became predators who prey on the weak and unprepared.

Flooding caused by super storms is now responsible for as many deaths per year as heart disease, and I would personally rather face down an armed member of the Kin Born army than weather a monster storm in unknown territory with no shelter.

"There!" Kite shouts to be heard over the rush of the tossing leaves, and jabs a finger at a large, hollowed-out log not far off the trail. It's on a slight rise, lifted above the rest of the forest floor by the rock formation it tumbled down onto long ago. It should give us the protection from runoff we need. "You and Wren take cover," Kite continues, holding his hair away from his face as he turns his back to the wind that's whipping faster with every passing minute. "I'll get the others and guide them back."

I nod and reach for Wren's hand, knowing Kite has a better chance of finding his way back than I do. I was trained in tracking, but that was in the domesticated woods of Southern England, where the forest has been beaten into submission by thousands of years of humanity stubbornly imposing its will on nature on an island with limited land mass.

Here, the forests are still wild and new, untamed and determined to stay that way. These woods fight back, a fact I'm reminded of when Wren trips on something lurking unseen beneath the leaves and falls to the ground, Luke's coat riding up to expose the bare back of her thighs and the curve of her bottom.

I avert my eyes as I reach down to help her up, able to read the mortification on her pinched face. I keep my arm around her waist as we close the distance to the fallen tree, wishing there was something I could do to make at least this one thing better.

But maybe there is...

We climb into the hole on the side of the tree and crawl deeper in, over to the higher elevation on the right. It's a large space, with room enough for both Wren and I to sit comfortably without hitting our heads, and it's been dead long enough that rot has given way to a smooth, hard petrification. It will do for all five of us, though I would like to get one piece of business done before the others arrive.

As the first hard drops of rain begin splattering down outside our shelter, I reach for the close of my pants.

Wren glances over, her brows lifting sharply.

"I'm going to give you my boxers," I explain. "So you'll have something to wear on bottom as well."

She nods, her face creasing with a mixture of embarrassment and gratitude. "Thank you. That's very sweet."

"It would have been sweet if I'd thought of it before." I strip off my khakis, pausing for a moment to glance Wren's way.

She averts her gaze with a soft laugh. "Sorry. I was distracted."

"By my manly thighs?" I tease as I quickly guide my boxers off and my pants back on, not liking being exposed from the waist down any more than she must have for the past day. Empathy—I need to get fucking better at it if I'm going to mean something to her again.

"No, distracted by the flamingos," she says, a smile in her voice. "I didn't take you for a secret flamingos under your pants kind of guy."

"I'm full of surprises." I pass the boxers over and take my turn averting my gaze as she tugs them on. "I'm also sorry," I add softly. "I'm sorry I haven't made this easier on you and that I couldn't get you out sooner. And that I haven't made time to tell you how happy I am to see you again. You were never far from my thoughts."

She stills, the rustling sounds fading away now that she's dressed. I could turn back to her now, but I continue to study the swirls in the stony wood, wishing it were that easy to read the story of a human life. If I could just roll up my sleeve and show Wren the rings, the slim, sickly years of sickness followed by years that were hard in a different way. Hard because I was weighed down by a destiny that was so much bigger than anything I had ever imagined—griffins are princes in our world, Kite wasn't kidding, and a shifter royal court is as fraught as any other—all while a weak part of me wished I was back in Seattle.

Back with Wren, where I was sick, but at least I was just a kid expected to do kid things, like playing and pretending with my best friend.

"Do you remember the story you used to tell about the man trapped in the tree?" Wren asks, raising her voice to be heard over another crash of thunder. "The one where he had to be cut down, losing both of his legs, before he could remember who he was and go find the wizard who had stolen his family away?"

"I do." I turn, studying her face in the rapidly fading light. The storm is almost here, and the world is nearly night black. If the others don't get here soon, they're going to be stuck in the downpour.

"I think this is kind of like that," she says. "No matter how hard anyone tries to make it easy for me, there's still going to be pain and bleeding. There's no way to get from who I was to who I need to be without it. Birth is a beautiful thing, but it's also…violent." Her forehead wrinkles as she adds in a softer voice, "And dangerous. But that's not your fault."

I reach out, covering her hand with mine, amazed by her all over again. "You always were smarter than I was."

Her lips curve. "Not true. I seem to remember my math homework being more of a joint effort than my parents would have preferred."

"I'm good with numbers. You're smart in the ways that count." I pull in a breath, holding it for a beat as I debate the wisdom of further confessions, but in the end, I can't help myself. "I've missed you, Snow. More than I can say."

Wren shifts her hand, turning it over until her palm presses against mine, and our fingers have space to twine together. "I've missed you, too. Thank you for the flamingos."

"You can have my flamingos any time," I say, loving the way she smiles in response. She's so beautiful, so brave, and I want to kiss her so much it takes my breath away.

I'm debating the wisdom of asking if I can kiss her, of leaning in and seeing how we might fit together as more than friends, when bright-white light pulses through the air. It's a strobe effect so intense it leaves a shadowy imprint of Wren's profile on the backs of my eyes as the world goes dark once more.

A beat later, thunder cracks open the sky, the boom fierce enough to make the wood beneath us tremble and Wren clutch my hand. A moment later the skies open and the clouds unleash their full fury, pummeling the wood over our heads, making conversation impossible.

I'm about to stick my head out into the rain to see if I can spy the others when the tree trembles again, this time from the force of the impact as first Creedence, then Luke, then Kite land on the damp wood at the entrance and quickly crawl up to dry ground.

Wren releases my hand as she scoots closer, making more room for the others, sending a flash of irritation through my chest. But it isn't as strong as the jealousy that squirmed through me when the sounds of Wren enjoying Kite's intimate company threatened to make me physically ill.

Now, I have the memory of her hand in mine and her smile and a flash of connection that gives me hope that someday I may have a chance to show her how I feel about her.

And blow Kite's performance out of the water while I'm at it.

Pleasuring a woman is definitely one of the pastimes at which I excel, and I can't wait to put my skill to use making Wren come apart beneath my hands, my lips, my tongue...

Creedence interrupts my less than pure thoughts—holding up a hand with three fingers raised and shouting something I can't hear over another explosion of thunder. I shake my head, but he's already repeating himself. "Three shifters to the north, following the road. No way to know if they're Kin Born from a distance, but Kite was getting a bad vibe."

Kite nods, his face suddenly paling as another pulse of lightning illuminates our hiding place.

We weather the next quake of thunder in silence, the five of us in closer quarters than we've shared thus far, making me keenly aware of our differences. There's the evergreen and earth smell of bear, the muskier aroma of wolf, the salty-sweet scent of cat, and beneath it the new smoke and cedar scent of Wren.

Up until a little over an hour ago, I'd had no clue that she might start developing powers so quickly, and I have no idea how to help her control them. My handlers only gave me enough information to complete the first stage of this mission, assuring me guidance would be provided for Wren when the time was right.

I don't know what's normal for a Fata Morgana or extraordinary or somewhere in the middle, but I can't help but find Wren's fiery display impressive and her smell comforting. Sure, she's capable of torching our shelter, burning it to the ground in moments with all of us in it, but her scent ties us together, uniting the separate notes into a perfume that smells safe and...cozy.

We aren't safe, of course, but sitting here surrounded by people who are the best bet for a future for the planet, I can't help but feel hopeful.

"Then when the storm stops we'll stay away from the roads," I say when it's finally quiet enough for conversation. "And veer west to look for a town with a bus station."

There are nods all around, and then, one by one, eyes grow heavy and fall closed. It isn't long before the rest of them are asleep, Luke and Creedence with their feet propped up the opposite side of the log, Kite passed out while still sitting cross-legged with his head tipped back against the wood, and Wren with her cheek on my shoulder.

I'm tired, too, but I fight to stay awake a little longer, stealing a moment of peace in the relative safety of this warm, dry place, with Wren finally close and safe, the way I've been dreaming of for so long.

CHAPTER 23
WREN

The bus we jumped on at a hamlet so small I'm not even sure it had a name dumps us out in Anacortes, Washington several hours later, right on the coast of beautiful Fidalgo Island. It's a perfect early summer day with clear blue skies washed cleaned by yesterday's storm, wispy white clouds, and all the sunshine a beach lover could ask for. Along the rocky shoreline, white daisies sprout from between the stones, seeming to promise that life will find a way to be beautiful no matter how hard things get.

But my hope is faltering fast.

Every time I see Kite's bandaged palm and the exhaustion clear on the other men's faces from being forced to spend the night in a log before trekking eight more miles on foot to the bus station, guilt rises inside me so fast it feels like I'm choking on it. I'm an accident waiting to happen, and I have no idea how to control myself or the dangerous potential lurking in my body.

I didn't mean to catch fire, but I did.

Who knows what I might do next time?

Shoot lasers out of my eyes? Spit poison?

And what if something like that had happened while Kite and I were in a more intimate situation than with his hand on my knee? The thought of what I could have done to him is horrifying. Stomach turning. I haven't eaten in over twenty-four hours, but when Luke plunks a muffin onto the picnic table in front of me, I don't hurry to unwrap it.

I just sit, staring at the blueberries smeared against the plastic wrap, feeling a strange sense of empathy with the squashed fruit.

"You should eat," Luke says, taking a massive bite of what looks like a ham sandwich. "It's another ten miles to the reservation and Kite said we'll be walking. Better to sneak in the back way in case the Kin Born have spies watching the entrance at the road. They know he's worked for the resistance in the past, and threatened to attack his family if he tries to come home so…"

I know he's right, but the most I can bring myself to do is scratch at the top of the wrapper, peeling a corner free from the rest, before dropping my hands back into my lap with a sigh.

Luke doesn't say a word, but that isn't unusual. Since his first "I'm not a fan of you assholes" sentiments down in the basement, he's been pretty tight lipped. He's either the strong, silent type by nature, or he's plotting to kill us all in our sleep.

I peek up at him through my lashes, hoping he'll look less intimidating in the cheery sunshine, but no dice. With the snarling wolf tattoo on his neck—the fangs partly visible before the design disappears beneath the collar of his tight black tee—his eyes so dark brown they're almost black, and the inch-long scar on his right cheek, he looks like a man who could kill you with his bare hands without breaking a sweat and then go right back to eating his sandwich.

"Yeah, I'm scary. But I can't catch fire and walk away without a mark on me," he says, making me blink faster. "So you're still holding the trump card."

"I'm sorry," I say, ducking my head. "I can't believe I said that out loud. I must be losing it."

"You didn't. I've seen that look in enough eyes to know what you were thinking." He takes another bite of his sandwich, chewing and swallowing before he adds, "But you don't have to be scared of me. I'm not going to hurt you. Like I said back at the house—as long as Dust gives me what I want, I'm on your side. Growing up the way I did, you learn the importance of loyalty pretty fucking quick. Besides, I don't hurt women," he adds, swiping a crumb from the corner of his lips. "Especially women who can burn my skin off."

"I don't know how I did it. It was an accident."

He grunts. "Too bad, I picked up some marshmallows at the shop just now. Was hoping we could make s'mores later." His tone is so flat and emotionless it takes me a moment to realize he's joking.

I exhale through my nose as my lips twitch at the edges.

"Eat." He reaches across the table, finishing the job of unwrapping my breakfast. Or brunch, I guess, since it's nearly eleven in the morning. "Take this and put it in your face. You're too skinny. You're never going to survive the workouts I've got planned for you unless you get some meat on your bones. As soon as we get to our new digs, we're going to up your protein intake. I want you loading at every meal."

My eyebrows lift as I reach for the muffin, breaking it in half. "What kind of workouts? You do realize I have exactly zero experience in a gym."

"That's all right," he says. "I can get anyone in fighting shape. We'll get you running, punching, kicking boxing, add in some dirty street moves. The people we're up against use weapons, but in the shifter world it comes down to hand-to-hand combat more often than you would think. You need to be able to kill a man with nothing but your body if you have to."

I balk, blinking faster. "Oh, well... I guess learning to defend myself is important, but I can't... I can't even imagine."

He studies me, brow lifted. "You can't imagine offing someone?"

I shake my head. "No, I...I can't. I couldn't. I take spiders outside to set them free. Life is important to me."

I pop a bite between my lips and force myself to chew, even though my mouth suddenly feels desert-wasteland dry. Luke was in prison, for murder, they said. I haven't had time to wonder who he killed and why before, but now...

"The Kin Born killed my little brother," Luke says, making me wonder if he's secretly a mind reader. "I killed all six of the men who jumped him while he was at the movies with his girlfriend—who they killed, too, even though she was just a sweet kid from West Covina who did nails for a living. And I don't regret it. I would do it all again in a heartbeat."

"I'm sorry." I feel like I say that a lot lately, even more than I did when counseling troubled kids.

Sadly, it doesn't seem like any of these men have travelled an easy road.

But that's probably why it's so easy to start caring about them. I've never been able to identify with people whose personal history is all sweetness and light and well-lit paths through fields full of flowers. The damaged souls who've fought their way out of the woods to emerge barely breathing at the fringes of society are the ones that speak to me, the ones whose hearts vibrate at the same frequency as mine.

It's a sad vibration sometimes, but it has a depth and beauty those well-lit people lack.

"I can absolutely understand the impulse to get revenge," I say, not wanting him to think I'm judging him. "I just don't think that I, personally, am capable of doing something like that. No matter how much I might want to."

He shoos a fly away from my muffin with a tight flick of his wrist. "You'd be surprised what you're capable of when properly motivated."

I make a noncommittal sound as I press crumbs into the tip of my finger. "So is that why you went to prison? The police found out you'd killed those men?"

"They could only pin one of the deaths on me, and

BELLA JACOBS

that was the one with witnesses willing to testify that he'd jumped me first." He shrugs. "I did seven years inside, and I'll be going back if the cops catch up with us. I was only out on parole for a few weeks before the L.A. pack motherfuckers jumped me on my way to work and threw me in a van. They shot me up with something, and I woke up chained in your basement."

"Not *my* basement," I clarify. "Before I came down the stairs to meet you, that basement and I were total strangers."

"You're funny," he says, his eyes as flat as his voice.

I bite the inside of my lip as I tear off another piece of muffin top. "You're hard to read."

"Something you learn in prison. Never let 'em see you sweat or smile or anything else. Best way to stay out of the fucking drama." Luke wads his sandwich wrapper into a ball and tosses it at the trash can six feet away at the next picnic table over. It lands perfectly inside, disturbing the swarming flies, sending them buzzing in dizzy circles before they resettle on what looks like the remains of a rotisserie chicken.

He shifts his attention back to me, "So let's get real with each other before the rest of them get out here, all right?"

I nod, anxiety prickling across my skin as I hurry to finish chewing the bite of muffin already in my mouth. "What's on your mind?"

"From what I've heard so far, it sounds like the only way to complete your mission is to kill this Atlas guy, is that right?"

I pull in a deep breath and exhale. "Yes, but I'm hoping we can find another way."

"Like what? Supernatural bad guy jail? Because I'm pretty sure that doesn't exist. At least, not a jail prepared to hold a guy who can shapeshift into over a thousand different forms and counting."

I shake my head. "I don't know. Everything is so new to me right now. I'm going to need time and more information to have any real idea of what is possible and what isn't." Sitting up straighter, I add, "But I'm determined to proceed with as much compassion and empathy as possible. Violence isn't the antidote to violence. If we have to fight to survive, we will, but as soon as the fight is over, we're going to show our enemies mercy. That's what separates the good guys from the bad guys."

Luke's eyes glitter. "That's what separates the living from the dead, chica. You leave enemies like that alive, and they'll come back to stab you in your sleep. With an enemy like that, you take him out. Then you take out anyone who ever swore loyalty to the bastard. Then, if you're really serious about shutting that shit down, you take his kids away and send them somewhere else to grow up, some-where far away where they will never learn the story of what happened to their dear old dad and decide fucking up the people who killed him sounds like a good idea."

Jaw clenched, I shrug. "None of that is on my agenda."

"It should be."

"I guess we'll have to agree to disagree."

"And I guess you're deciding to lay down and die before you even get started." He stands, untangling himself from the bench with languid movements at odds with his harsh words. "And in that case, I'm not interested in signing up for long-term service. I'll train you and help you and your boys get across the border. Then I'm out."

I frown as I nod. "All right. That's your choice."

He turns his head, studying me from the corners of his eyes. "But you'll make sure Harry Potter keeps his promise? That I get a Canadian passport and everything else I'll need to start over as someone new north of the border?"

"Harry Potter, huh?" I shift my gaze as Dust, Kite, and Creedence amble of the market's front porch and start across the lawn toward us. "No glasses, but I can see a resemblance. Did you like the movies?"

"The books were better," Luke says.

I glance back at him, brows lifting. "You read them all?"

"Twice. I had a lot of time to kill the past few years." His dark eyes narrow. "You didn't answer my question."

"Yes, I'll do everything I can to make sure Dust keeps his promise. But you have to remember that I'm not the one in charge here, Luke."

He smiles for the first time in memory, a wide grin that transforms his face into something almost boyishly handsome. "Oh, yes you are, chica," he says, with a soft laugh. "You are absolutely in charge. And the sooner you realize it, the better. For everyone involved."

Before I can argue with him—or ask him to explain

himself—the others arrive, and Dust asks, "Everything all right out here?"

"Everything's fine," I say, watching Luke's expression darken once more. I make a mental note to ask Dust the next time we're alone to stop treating Luke like a second-class citizen and stand, wadding what's left of my muffin in my fist. "But I'm ready to get going, how about you?"

"No sense wasting daylight," Kite agrees. "The sooner we get moving, the sooner we'll be somewhere safe where we can get showers and a real meal."

"Sounds wonderful." I draw my arm back, tossing my trash at the same bin Luke scored on a few minutes ago. But I don't expect to get anywhere close. I've never played sports and I can freely admit that I "throw like a girl," though Carrie Ann, a star softball pitcher, would have a fit if she heard me say that.

But to my surprise, the muffin ball finds its target, sending the increasingly large swarm of flies frothing into the air with irritation as it lands in the can.

"I made it!" I thrust my arms into the air, a grin breaking out across my face as I turn back to my companions. "I never make the basket. Never, not once in my entire life."

"Your life is changing fast, Slim," Creedence says, a smile on his face. "Best open up your mind and get used to all kinds of exciting new developments."

He's right. I do need to open my mind. But as we head down to the marina to hook up with a trail leading farther up the coast, I vow to keep some parts of my self on lockdown.

I don't care what Luke or anyone else says—I refuse to violate the beliefs that are most sacred to me.

Hank always said that "if you stand for nothing, you'll fall for anything."

In this new world, with so much coming at me every minute, standing for what I believe in may be the only thing I can count on to keep my head above water.

CHAPTER 24

THE SWARM

We rise from the trash bin, lifting higher in the air to watch the girl and her four marked men cross the lawn toward the path. Seeing her now, it's impossible to fathom how we didn't sense her sooner. How we were ever fooled by the pretender we've been hunting unsuccessfully for so long.

She glows with power.

Burns with it.

Rays of energy stream out from beneath her skin to pierce the continuum, making her shine like a star.

We could see her from the highest mountain.

From the moon.

But soon, she will take mates whose auras will cloud hers, smearing it thin, making it harder to track, to find and pluck her out before she metastasizes. Soon she will have other powers, other forms that will make it impossible to pinpoint her kin shape in the sea of shifters over-populating this corner of the world.

The raccoon is right.

Best to give her to the doctor now.

It means we forfeit the power to be gained by consuming that bright, blazing light, but better…

What is the phrase? The one the little beast used?

Better to be safe than to be sorry. Yes, that's it.

We buzz approvingly as the cowering young one crawls on her belly from beneath the bin, trembling and wringing her small black paws as she gazes up at us with bright marble eyes. Her kin form is pleasing, but her human form leaves much to be desired.

She prefers women, she talks too loudly, and she turned on her comrades only a few days into her torture, just forty-eight hours after being pulled, half-drowned, from the river.

The fact that she bears the mark of a possible mate wasn't enough to tempt us into keeping her alive. But she has proven useful these past few days.

She had the connections that allowed us to learn of the planned attack. She had the knowledge that led to the swift assassination of those providing the girl and her men with financial and tactical assistance.

And she will contact the doctor and give him our blessing to proceed.

By this time tomorrow, the baby Fata Morgana's light will be snuffed out, and we will be peerless once more.

Unrivaled. Matchless. Unequaled…as it should be.

We are pleased.

We communicate this to the fawning creature below us, slipping the thought easily into her malleable mind as we rise higher—higher and higher until we reach the air above the clouds and allow the breeze to carry us north, back to our stronghold where the rest of us waits on the throne, ready to return to business as usual.

CHAPTER 25
WREN

We cut away from the coast and into a cool redwood forest, stopping only once to drink from a crystal-clear stream before pushing on toward our destination. It seems we're all feeling the powerful draw of safety, showers, and a meal that doesn't come from a supermarket shelf.

Even with my shorter, considerably less in-shape legs slowing us down, we make excellent time, cresting the final hill at the edge of the Samish reservation by midafternoon and making our way down to the collection of longhouses and larger, communal buildings in a glow of welcoming light. Instantly, I feel at home here where the cliffs and the forest meet the sea. There is no seawall here, in this place where nature has been allowed to run its course.

Kite explains how the village reorganized farther inland a few decades ago, once it became clear that the rising ocean levels were only going to get worse. He points out islands that were once part of the mainland and details how the tribe's oyster farming practices changed in response to the new normal.

"The saddest part about it is how much harder it is to see the orcas," he says, pointing out toward the waves sparkling gold in the afternoon light. "My grandmother said they used to jump so close to land that you could see every detail of their markings. She used to name them, keep track of who the matriarch was and how many babies were born into the pod."

"Orcas do it right, man." Creedence's hand comes to shield his eyes as he squints toward the horizon. "If women were in charge, shit would suck so much less."

"Or just suck in a different way," Luke pipes up. He's been chattier since our talk, offering a total of five or six sentences in the past two and half hours.

"I'm on team suck less," Kite says, leading the way down the path onto the main dirt road running through this part of the reservation. "I think women understand how vulnerable we all are in a visceral way most men don't."

"Because they're the weaker sex?" Dust asks, clearly not on board with that assumption.

Kite shakes his head. "No, because they bring life into the world. A woman is vulnerable when she's pregnant, unable to protect herself the way she could before, and then she gives birth to this tiny life completely dependent on the adults around it to keep it alive…" He shrugs. "I think that makes most women see how precious and fragile life is. Makes them more compassionate, less prone to violence without thinking through the consequences."

I meet Luke's gaze behind Kite's back, arching a pointed brow. For the second time today, his lips curve, communicating a wry "point taken" that I appreciate.

Maybe he isn't a lost cause, after all, this man who was raised in a world so much more savage than my own. Maybe he just needs a chance to learn that there are other ways of solving conflict than the slash and burn method he's known until now.

Though, I can't really blame him for killing the men who killed his brother. My flame attack yesterday proved how much rage I'm capable of when it comes to the people who matter most.

I'm going to have to keep a close eye on myself and make sure to use my new powers with the same compassion I valued when I was one of the most vulnerable among us. Mercy when you're desperately in need of it yourself is easier, I would think, than mercy when you're an apex predator, capable of destroying anyone who stands in your way.

Though the thought of me, scrawny Wren Frame, as a predator is still laughable.

"You ready?" Kite turns to me with an expectant look that makes me think I might have missed part of what he said.

I shake my head with a smile. "Ready for what?"

He nods to the road in front of us. "That's my mom. Don't be scared. She's harmless, I promise."

I turn, eyes flying wide as a laugh bursts from my lips. In front of us, standing on her hind legs next to a brightly painted totem pole featuring animals native to the Samish lands, is a grizzly bear nearly as tall as the masterpiece beside her. From her clawed toes to the tip of her black nose, she's at least ten feet, and the roar that rumbles from her throat as Kite jogs toward her is loud enough to make the ground tremble.

"Wow," I murmur as Kite hurls himself into her outstretched arms. She wraps him up tight, giving me a new appreciation for the term "bear hug," even as a whisper of unease tickles the back of my brain.

"First time meeting the boyfriend's mama is always fun, right?" Creedence murmurs softly, his winning grin in place as he lifts a hand to the men and women stepping down from shaded porches and hurrying up the beach to greet us.

"He's not my boyfriend," I whisper back. "Not officially."

Creedence makes a dismissive sound. "Oh, stop. You're friends, you like making out with him, and your fates are entwined by destiny and an epic quest and shit. He's your boyfriend. Own it." He nudges me in the ribs with his elbow. "And own that monster-in-law of yours. Think you can win her over?"

I swallow. "I hope so. Kite's always talked about how nice she is."

"Nice to her baby boy, I'm sure. We'll see how much she likes the girl taking him away from his tribe and putting him in mortal danger." Creedence lays a gentle hand on my shoulder that does little to offer comfort before he steps away, moving to greet a man with silver-streaked black hair even longer than Kite's with an outstretched hand.

Swallowing the ball of anxiety forming in my throat, I force a smile as I wade into the crush of bodies, accepting hugs and greetings from more tall, beautiful people, several of whom announce they are Kite's sisters or cousins, all of them with a welcoming smile on their faces.

But when I reach Kite and his mother—who has dropped onto all fours now, making her slightly less intimidating, but only slightly—I'm not sure what to expect.

"Wren, this is Mina, my sweet little mama." Kite motions to me. "Mama, this is Wren, the girl I was telling you about."

"Thank you so much for taking us in," I say, meeting the bear's intelligent brown eyes. "And thank you for raising such a wonderful person. Kite's one of the kindest people I've ever met."

Kite looks embarrassed, but his mother smiles, baring her teeth in a way that's a little scary until she lets out a soft rumble and leans in to nuzzle my stomach with her nose. Smiling I lay a gentle hand on her head in appreciation, able to feel the warmth and affection in the connection the same way I can feel tenderness flowing from Kite every time we touch.

After a moment, she pulls away, turning to grunt rapidly to Kite in a bear language he clearly understands.

"Mom says we should all be ashamed of ourselves for making you hike all over creation in a pair of old boxer shorts and oversize shoes," he says, extending a hand my way. "She insists I take you to her place and get you some decent clothes from my sister Selkie's closet. You're about the same size." He glances over my head as our fingers twine together. "The rest of you can head into the main lodge. My cousins will get you set up with clothes and show you to your cabins."

"You'll be all right, Wren?" Dust asks, his gaze meeting mine.

"I'll be fine." I glance around, warmth filling my chest as I'm suddenly able to feel the love flowing in from every beating heart in this tribe. Touching Kite has something to do with it, I know, but now that I've felt this love, this truth, I know I'll never doubt that I'm welcome here again. "Better than fine," I add with a smile. "Feels like home already."

Kite grins a proud, pleased grin that fills me with a badly needed shot of hope. We aren't as alone as I thought. And maybe we never really are, even the most lost souls among us.

CHAPTER 26
WREN

After a hot and heavenly shower—I will never take the glory of clean hair and dirt-free nails for granted again—I change into a long red cotton skirt and a soft clingy white tee Kite borrowed from his littlest sister and slip on a pair of sinfully comfortable black sandals that soothe every sore spot on my feet.

Beneath the piles of clothes and shoes, I discover a pair of earrings carved from dark gray granite and lift them to the light.

"Bears," I whisper with a smile as I slip them into my ears and turn to the mirror.

What I see there shocks me.

My jaw drops and the lips of the girl in the reflection part, too. But this girl isn't the pale, dark-circled, sickly person I remember seeing the last time I took a hard look at my reflection. This girl's skin is clear and bright, and her blue eyes shine with a sharp curiosity. Her cheeks are flushed, and her lips are raspberry red, and the thick hair drying around her shoulders gleams with health.

I pull in a deep breath and roll my shoulders back, standing up straight. I even look taller than I was a week ago.

Is that possible? To hit a growth spurt after your twenty-fourth birthday?

A soft knock on the door interrupts my self-inspection. "Wren? It's Kite. I brought some other stuff you might want—deodorant, lotion, some sort of oil…shaping, smoothing stuff my sister told me would be good for your hair. They're all pretty horrified that I sent you in there with nothing but shampoo and soap."

I crack open the door with a smile, my grin widening when Kite does a double take. "Wow," he breathes, appreciation flickering in his gaze as the basket of toiletries drops to his side. "You look…incredible."

"Thanks," I say. "It's nice to have clothes that fit again. I can't wait to tell Selkie thank you."

He waves a hand. "She's a sweetheart and happy to loan you anything you need. She wanted to be here to join the welcome committee, but she's on daycare duty until five. But you'll see her at the party tonight."

"Party?" I ask, excitement and anxiety fizzing inside me. I can't remember the last time I went to a party and wonder if I'll remember what to do.

"Of course." He scoffs. "You think I'd bring you home for the first time and not throw you a party? Besides, we're always up for an excuse to play music and dance until dawn. You'll learn once you've been around the shifter world a while—bears have a reputation."

"As party animals?" I tease.

"As connoisseurs of carnal pleasure," he says with a wink. "We like to drink good beer, eat good food, dance all night and take decadent, three hour naps the next day."

"Sounds nice," I say, my belly grumbling loud enough to echo off the tile walls of the bathroom, making us both laugh. "Especially the food part."

"Then let's get you a snack. My Aunt Nan is going to smoke an obscene amount of salmon for the feast tonight, but that doesn't mean we can't pre-game." He holds out the basket. "You want any of this stuff? I personally don't think you need it, but..."

I take the basket with a smile. "Probably the deodorant would be a good call, and I'm inclined to listen to people who tell me what to put in my hair. Left to my own devices, my signature look is rat's nest with a side of frizz."

"I like your hair," he says, adding with a happy gleam in his eyes, "And I like you. And I'm glad you're here." He leans in, pressing a kiss to my cheek that makes me feel warm all over. "Meet us in the kitchen when you're done. I'll have snacks ready."

I thank him and close the door, completing my primping rituals to the best of my ability, grateful for the lotion his sisters so thoughtfully provided. It's clearly homemade—something silky and light that smells of citrus and sea grass—and once it has soaked into my skin, a beautiful fresh scent rises around me every time I move.

I've never given a ton of thought to smelling good, aside from basic cleanliness, of course, but all of a sudden, I long to smell sweet, tempting, to give Kite a reason to bring his nose to my neck and inhale. I shiver at the thought, secretly hoping there will be time for us to be alone soon. So far I adore his family and friends, and I'm coming to care about all of the men on this mission with me, even Luke, though I know he probably won't be around for long.

But with Kite...

With Kite there's already something more, something so strong that when I slip into the kitchen to find the large table next to the stove surrounded by three gorgeous women I can only assume are his sisters, I can't help but feel a little letdown. I'm excited to get to know them: I'm just equally excited to keep getting to know their brother...

"There you are, welcome, welcome, baby girl!" The woman at the far side of the room rises from her seat at the head of the table and crosses to me with her arms outstretched. She's petite—no more than five three and a hundred pounds—but with well-defined muscles on the bare arms visible in her simple black shift dress and a powerful presence that surrounds me in warmth and welcome as she pulls me into a hug.

I blink in surprise at the sudden sense of familiarity, but then it hits me. "Mina?" I ask as I draw back from the embrace, gazing down into the human face of Kite's mother. Aside from the wrinkles around her eyes when she smiles, and the faint streaks of gray in her long black hair, she looks more like his big sister than a mother of seven.

She grins in acknowledgement. "Sorry I couldn't meet you like this before. I was out fishing all morning and ran out of time to change."

I laugh as I shake my head. "I'm sorry. It's just...I thought Kite was joking when he called you his sweet little mama before. Now I get it."

Mina grins. "That's confusing, isn't it? Growing up in a shifter community, you get used to the fact that human size doesn't have much to do with the size of your kin form. But I imagine a lot of this must be shocking for you. You've only known you were one of us a few days, is that right?"

"Not one of us," a woman wearing a heavy sweater that seems too much for the cozy kitchen pipes up from the table. "She's ancient lineage, mama."

"Best check yourself and respect herself," adds a younger woman with a red polka-dot bow in her hair and thick black liner on her upper lids. Their tones are good-natured, not judgmental or angry, but I can't help feeling like I've done something wrong.

"I'm still not sure what I am," I say, wanting to apologize, but not sure what to apologize for. "I know I'm supposed to have multiple forms, and I sort of...caught fire by accident once. But aside from that, I'm mostly a mess."

"A hot mess sounds like," Red Bow teases, rising from her chair. She holds out a hand. "I'm Lena. Also a hot mess, but for much less respectable reasons."

"Lena likes to go fast," Kite says from the sink where he's washing a bowl of cherries that look absolutely delicious. "In addition to being chief of our police—the cool cop, the one who never hands out speeding tickets —she's one of the top motocross racers in the northwest."

"Top crashers in the northwest in more like it." Mina tuts as she wraps her arm around her taller daughter's waist and hugs her close. "How many bones have your broken now, crazy girl?"

"Seven or eight." Lena grins. "But I'm hoping for an even dozen before I retire. What about you, Wren? What do you want to do with your one wild and wonderful life now that you've been sprung from the cult?"

My lips part, but Kite clears his throat before I can speak. I glance his way and he shakes his head, making it clear honesty isn't the best policy here. I guess our mission is secret even from trusted family.

Or maybe just most of the trusted family. The somber look that settles on his mother's face makes me think she knows more about the future holds for her son than she's told her daughters.

"I'm not sure," I answer, deciding it's close enough to the truth. I'm not sure what I'll want to do once our mission is over, or if that will even be my choice to make. If I'm in charge of creating harmony and balance in the world, will I have time for a career? Hobbies? A pet, even? "The past week's been a whirlwind."

"I can imagine," the sweater-snuggled woman at the table pipes up. "I'm Vera, by the way. I would come give you a hug, but I'm fighting off a summer cold and I don't want to risk infecting you. Since you just got off all those shifter suppression drugs, your immune system is probably still compromised."

"Vera is a doctor," Lena supplies, pressing her palms together in prayer position and lifting her gaze to the ceiling. "She's the good daughter, the angel to my devil."

Vera snorts. "Oh, please. I got into more trouble as a teen than you ever did. You were just too little to remember how many times Mom kicked my ass for sneaking out."

"I do not kick anyone's ass," Mina says primly. "I put my foot down. Firmly." She waves me closer. "Come sit down, Wren. Talk a load off, eat something. Kite's put out several options, but if there's something else you're craving, let me know, and I can send one of the grandbabies on a run to the market. They're out playing in the backyard, but I'm happy to put them to work."

I settled into a chair beside Mina's. "Oh, no, this is perfect. Amazing." I scan the plates. There are at least three kinds of cheese, an equal variety of crackers, a tray mounded with carrots and whisper-thin asparagus, a bowl of fruit, some pasta salad, other assorted Tupperware containers of leftovers, and Kite adds the bowl of cherries to the mix as he sits down on my other side.

"Just how much do you think I'm capable of eating in one sitting?" I ask beneath my breath, gazing up at him out of the corner of my eye.

"I don't know," he says, grinning. "But I look forward

to finding out. Nothing sexier than a woman with an appetite."

The words make me blush, but when I glance around the table, none of the other women seem fazed by the comment. Either they're used to Kite flirting with women, or he's already alerted them to the nature of our relationship. As I load my plate, I can't help but hope it's the latter.

The others join me in my snack, and the conversation turns to tribe business—how the oyster harvest is looking, who's in charge of the hillside gardens this year, and whether they can afford to buy new books for the Bookmobile that services all the various villages on the tribal lands.

"So this isn't the only settlement?" I ask, intrigued.

"This is the real settlement," Lena says, popping a cherry into her mouth and talking as she chews. "The casino village is a Disney version of tribal culture for the tourists, something for them to checkout in between losing their money. And the village by the highway is basically a military installation disguised as Main Street."

"We were attacked by Kin Born forces a few years back," Vera explains. "We lost a lot of people, so we learned to be more vigilant."

"And more heavily armed." Lena spits her cherry pit onto her plate with a sharp *thwup*. "Luckily the casino wasn't damaged in the raid, so we still have lots of money coming in to buy big, deadly toys."

"Let's leave that talk for the council," Mina says, pushing her plate away.

"Mom hates guns," Lena offers in sotto voce.

"I do not. I hate that we've drifted so far from our roots," Mina says. "There was a time when the shifter community had honor, even in times of war. For thousands of years we fought with only the gifts of our kin forms and nothing more. The day we started using mankind's weapons on each other was the day we signed away a sacred piece of our culture. Of our souls."

Silence falls, even Lena apparently having nothing sarcastic to offer in response. I twirl a cherry stem between my fingertips, wondering if Mina knows her gentle son is a crack shot, and if so, what she thinks about it.

"Now tell me about catching fire, baby girl." Mina pats my shoulder with an encouraging smile. "Let's see if some advice from an old timer can get you feeling a little more in control of these gifts you've been given."

"I would love some advice." I thread my fingers together into a single fist my lap. "Honestly, I'm scared to death it's going to happen again and I'm going to hurt someone by accident."

"That's your first step, then. Got to get rid of that fear." Mina rubs her palm up and down my back, sending soothing energy coursing through my muscles, making me feel instantly relaxed. "Fear takes you out of your head and your heart, both of which you need to control a shift. If you let fear call the shots in your body, it's going to force a shift, which is only going to make you feel more out of control and more afraid. It's a vicious cycle, yeah?"

I nod. "I learned that working with troubled kids at

the shelter I run. Fear is at the root of pretty much every behavior issue, even if it manifests as anger or bullying or drug abuse."

Mina nods. "Right. So you're a step ahead. You know how to spot fear, know where it likes to hide out and the disguises it puts on to trick you."

"It was anger when I caught fire," I say, the pieces begin to fall into place. "I was thinking about my sister, and I got so insanely angry, but..." I shake my head. "Beneath the anger, I was afraid."

"And what were you afraid of?" Mina asks.

I exhale. "I was afraid that... That I'm going to lose my parents. If they knew what they were doing, if they did it realizing that the meds were making us sick..." I meet Mina's compassionate gaze, throat going tight as tears prick at the backs of my eyes. "I can forgive them for hurting me, but not for killing her. If I find out they knew, then they're murderers, and I can't forgive them for that."

I feel Kite's hand on my knee beneath the table, and a second reassuring wave of comfort rushes through me, making me laugh softly even as I sniff back the tears trying to escape my eyes. "You guys are better than Valium and a puppy snuggle. I bet no one around here needs antidepressants, huh?"

Mina smiles. "We try to alleviate pain when we can, those of us who have a gift for it. But even bears get the blues."

"Though, bear snuggles are way better than puppy snuggles," Kite jokes, clearly trying to lighten the mood. "One look at Luke makes that obvious."

"Ugh, wolves," Lena says, rolling her eyes with a huff. "Why must they be so cranky and sexy and utterly irresistible?"

Kite scowls. "No more wolves for you. Especially that wolf. Stay away from him, Lena. I'm serious. He's an ex-con, and I don't trust him as far as I could throw him."

Kite pulls his hand from my knee, but not before I sense another emotion humming beneath his skin. He's afraid, too. I want to tell him that he doesn't have to fear Luke, but no matter how much a part of me is softening toward the wolf, the fact remains that he's killed people and feels zero remorse about it. At least six people, and maybe more—we didn't get into the specifics of how he became so skilled at assassinating people without getting caught in the first place.

"Focus, children," Mina says gently. "We're doing kin work right now, not human work." She brings her other hand to my back, until both palms are resting on my shoulder blades. "Can you take a deep breath for me, baby girl? Let's see if we can help get rid of some of this fear trying to take control."

I inhale, feeling a bit like I'm at the doctor's office, though no doctor has ever made me feel so instantly relaxed, grounded, or...whole.

I close my eyes, and Mina murmurs, "That's right. Focus on your breath and go deep inside. With every inhale you draw in light and with every exhale you cast out darkness."

My lungs expand, filling all the way and then stretching just a bit more before I part my lips and send the air out in a long, slow stream, visualizing black smoke streaming into the air, leaving my interior lighter, freer.

"Now imagine the world inside you lighting up as the shadows fade away," Mina continues. "And when you're ready, open your eyes and take a look around."

Sensing she means eyes other than the ones in my head, I imagine a smaller version of me cracking her lids somewhere in the tunnels inside my mind. But when Mini Me opens her eyes, I'm not in a dark warren or a crowded closet, I'm on a small boat in the middle of the ocean, brilliant blue and dazzling water all around me as far as I can see.

CHAPTER 27
WREN

A soft sound of surprise escapes my lips, echoing across the waves.

"What do you see?" Mina asks, farther away than she was before.

"Water," I say, my voice dreamy and distant. "The ocean. All around me. I'm on a small boat."

Mina hums thoughtfully, but when she speaks there's no judgment in her tone. "Interesting. What else can you see? Any islands? Land in the distance?"

Little Me lifts a hand, shielding her eyes from the glaring sun. I scan the horizon in one direction, finding nothing but more water. But when I turn, I spot land not far away. "There's an island," I say, squinting harder. "It's small and rocky, and there's something on it... At the top, but it's too cloudy to see clearly... Looks like there's a storm moving in."

"Inhale light and exhale shadow," Mina repeats.

"Inhale and exhale and see if you can clear those obstacles away."

I obey, and after only a few breaths, the clouds part. "A volcano," I say, the sight making sense in a deep, intuitive way I don't completely understand at first. But then it hits me, "Fire. That's my fire form! It lives on that island."

"Perfect!" The pride in Mina's voice reminds me of my mother, of Abby, and how utterly thrilled she was to see me hit each tiny new milestone on the road to growing up. The thought makes me sad, and a moment later the clouds are back, cloaking the island so thoroughly I can barely make it out against the horizon.

"It's okay," Mina says, seeming to sense that I've lost my clarity. "This is a great first look around. Before you come back to us, see if you can find anything that might be connecting your boat to that island. Maybe a rope or something? Could even be a brighter shade of blue beneath the waves or a warm vein running through cooler water."

I study the waves, but they're all the same crystalline blue, a color that brings to mind Greek islands and bleached white houses perched on cliffs bursting with bright pink bougainvillea. It's a Mediterranean ocean, which is strange, considering the only oceans I've ever seen in real life are the grayer waves off the coast of the Pacific Northwest. I reach down to trail fingers beneath the water, seeking signs of that warm vein Mina mentioned, but the ocean is all the same—almost too cool and getting colder the longer my fingers stay beneath the surface.

I'm about to tell Mina that I can't find anything, when I spot it, a long ribbon of seaweed about fifty feet down, waving gently in the current. But it only moves up and down, remaining otherwise in place as other pieces of seaweed pass it by.

"I think I've found it," I say. "There's a thick rope of seaweed leading from the boat to the island."

"Excellent," Mina says. "That's what you'll use to connect to your other form. Sometimes just laying your hand on it and focusing for a beat or two is enough to instigate a shift." She laughs as she hurries to add, "Though, don't do it now, if you don't mind. I'm pretty attached to these wooden chairs. Been in the family for three generations."

"I don't think I could reach it anyway," I assure her. "It's deep down there."

"But it's connected, right?" Mina asks.

"I think so…" I lean over, but I can't see far enough beneath the waves to make out exactly where it might be tethered. Maybe it's tied to the dropped anchor or something?

Do I have an anchor? I must since I don't appear to be moving.

I turn, glancing over my shoulder to look for signs of an anchor, only to find a staircase that I hadn't noticed before at the far end of the vessel. There are stairs leading down into the depths of my floating mental home. The realization is both exciting and scary —I'm not sure what lives down there, out of the sun, far beneath the waves, but my gut tells me it's something I'm not ready for just yet.

"I think you're ready to come out, aren't you, doll?" Mina asks, again sensing where I am mentally before I say the words aloud.

"Yes, please," I say, panic spiking as I realize how real this world has become—so real I'm not sure how to get myself out of it. As fear dumps into my bloodstream, the sky overhead begins to fill with clouds.

I look up, skin prickling as I scan the rapidly graying formations. There's no sign of a face in the clouds now, but I can feel someone watching me, someone who isn't thrilled to learn I've made it this far, to this ocean at the edge of the world where there are gods and monsters and it's often hard to tell the difference between one and the other.

"I want to come out, Mina." My voice trembles as my fingertips dig into the edge of the boat. "Mina? Can you hear me?"

But this time there's no reply, no sound except the rush of the wind as the storm clouds thicken, the lapping of the waves against the boat, and a larger splash behind me. I spin, heart surging up to lodge in my throat as I watch the tips of two giant tentacles swirl grotesquely through the air before disappearing beneath the surface.

My mind leaps to the obvious conclusions—calculating how large the rest of that creature must be if its tentacles stand seven feet out of the waves, and realizing how easy it will be for it to capsize my boat and devour me in a single bite. But before I can fully succumb to panic, more rippling, churning, squirming sounds come from my left.

And then my right…

And then from behind me…

I'm surrounded, encircled.

Trapped.

I whip my head around, catching glimpses of lichen-covered backs breaching the waves, more tentacles, the ominous dorsal fins of sharks, and finally the single golden eye of some ancient horror that emerges long enough to stare straight through me, it's soulless gaze assuring me there will be no mercy for puny human creatures on its watch.

I suck in a breath that emerges as a scream, but the splashing is too loud now for me to hear myself cry out over the sounds of the monsters roiling beneath the waves, working themselves into a frenzy of anticipation, preparing to feed.

Sweat breaking out on my upper lip and the back of my neck, I curl into a ball in the floor of the boat and cover my head with my hands. The jostle and bounce of the wood beneath me leaves no doubt that the danger is still real, present, and closing in with every passing second, but it's easier to think with my gaze fixed on the swirls in the plank in front of me instead of the ocean of horrors.

I stare into the eye of a knot in the wood, doing my best to think clearly.

What was it that Mina said? Fear is my enemy. Fear is trying to take control, but I can't let that happen. I have to use my head, my heart.

Closing my eyes, I concentrate on taking long, deep breaths, using the visualization Mina suggested. I draw in light and exhale shadow, forcing myself to stay with the mediation, even when something enormous rises beneath me, lifting the boat several feet into the air before abruptly diving, sending my tiny vessel splashing back into the waves.

Seawater rains down on me, and one of the monsters groans so loudly it makes the wood vibrate beneath my cheek. It's a primal call for food, for blood, and for a second it threatens to shatter my focus. But I fist my hands tight, fingernails digging into my palms. The sting distracts me from the chaos outside long enough to bring balance to the chaos within.

Slowly, breath by breath, the water calms and the sky clears, and Mina's voice is once again audible, a faint but comforting whisper on the wind.

"Come back to us, Wren. Focus on the beat of your heart and count backward from ten. Ten...nine...eight..."

I mouth the numbers with her.

By "five" the boat is less solid beneath my cheek, by "three" I can no longer smell the sea or feel the breeze, and on "one" I open my eyes to find myself sitting in a chair in Mina's kitchen, surrounded by four very worried looking pairs of brown eyes. Vera has gone pale beneath her golden skin and Leda has apparently been struck speechless with shock, something I'm guessing is pretty rare for her.

"Are you okay?" Kite's voice is calm, but his death grip on my hand makes it clear how not-okay the past few minutes have been for him.

They weren't great for me, either. "I'm not sure, I..."

I trail off, glancing from Kite to Mina, who looks even more spooked than her son or daughters. "That wasn't how that was supposed to go, was it?"

She shakes her head slightly.

"What did I do wrong?" I tighten my grip on Kite's fingers, needing something to cling to.

"You didn't do anything wrong, baby." Mina's lips press tight as she glances over to where Vera and Leda are still sitting speechless on the other side of the table. "Could you girls give us a moment? I have something I'd like to discuss with Wren and Kite in private."

"Of course." Vera nods toward the door on the other side of the kitchen. "Come on, Leda, let's go check on the kids."

"Yeah. Kids." Leda stands, starting to follow her sister across the room, but before she steps out into the cool evening, she pauses to pin me with a hard look. "Don't let her scare you, kid. You're stronger than you think. You can handle this shit and any other shit the world throws at you. I can see it. And I don't say that kind of mushy crap to everyone."

Before I can thank her, Leda vanishes into the night, the door slamming shut behind her with a sharp *thunk* that makes me flinch.

"You can trust her," Kite says with a quirk of his lips. "On that at least. Leda sees a person's truest self, their core being. It's her kin gift."

"But Leda doesn't know all the facts," Mina says softly. "Kite, our elders, and I are the only members of the tribe who know what you truly are, dear one. Leda can see your truth, but she can't see what you're facing. And not just here, but in your spirit realm, as well."

"Was that where I was?"

Mina nods. "The spirit realm can be a dangerous place, but for most of us the only monsters we face in that inner world are of our own creation. Which means we inherently have the power to destroy them. The spirit realm is where we go to fight the battles that decide if our truest self will shine forth, or if our truth will remain locked in the dark until it becomes a ravenous thing that eventually devours us—spirit, bones, and all."

I scoot closer to Kite. "So those monsters, the giant sea creatures and the sharks in the water—those were my personal demons or something?"

"No," Mina says, her voice flat. "You're not alone in your interior, baby girl. Another colonized that world long before you arrived. I felt him arrive not long after you slipped through the veil into your spirit realm. If I'd known, I would never have sent you there. That plane isn't safe for you, at least not yet."

"You're saying Atlas—"

Mina cuts Kite off with a hissing sound. "Don't say his name in this house. That monster doesn't deserve a name. He's a virus, a disease infecting this world, not a being worthy of being invoked."

Kite sighs. "All right, Ma, I'm sorry. But is that what you meant? That he's somehow...inside Wren? In her head?"

"His spirit world and hers overlap," Mina explains, laying one hand on top of the other on the table to illustrate her point. "Or maybe they were always one." She interlaces her fingers, mingling the two "worlds" she's created. "All the writings on the Fata Morgana's powers were destroyed in antiquity, but maybe that's why the Fata Morgana can take so many forms. Because they share a spirit world far older and more developed than that of shifters who have only one animal kin." Mina purses her lips. "Not that there's been much sharing on that plane in recent millennia, of course. That power-hungry monster has made sure of that."

"But it was a huge place. Why won't he share it?" But I realize it's a dumb question the second it's out of my mouth. I roll my eyes, answering myself before Mina has a chance, "Because he's a crazy, evil megalomaniac, and they don't like to share."

Mina's lips curve in a grim smile. "No, they don't."

I drop my chin to my chest but lift it almost immediately as another thought races through my head. "Is this why I saw him in my dream? Can he reach me while I'm sleeping, too?"

"He'll be able to reach you any time you get close to your spirit world," Mina confirms. "Dreams are right there on the border of this world and that, close enough for him to get a call through, but not close enough to reach out and truly touch someone. If that makes sense?"

I exhale sharply as I nod. "So I'm safe in my dreams."

"You are," Mina confirms.

I nibble my bottom lip. "But I can't learn to control my powers without going back to the boat, to the place I saw today in the spirit world. Right?"

Mina's brow furrows. "You can, but it will be like making your way through a maze in a blindfold or buttoning your coat with your mittens on—possible, but frustrating. Slow."

The hope I recaptured this afternoon falters. "So I'm going to have to kick him out of my spirit world and beat him in real life, too?"

The thought of learning to fight and facing down an army assembled by a madman was scary enough, but at least I have a basic understanding of how a person learns to fight. But how in the world do I go about growing my army of psychic sea monsters?

"But you won't be alone in this world." Kite wraps his arm around my waist. "I'll be here, and so will Dust and Creedence. That's what we're here for, to give you the strength you need to beat this piece of shit."

"The bonds you form with your mates will give you strength in the spirit world as well," Mina says, affection warm in her eyes as her gaze shifts to her son. "And not to mama-bear brag, but my son is a pretty incredible man to have on your side."

"I know." I cast a glance up at Kite, grateful for his strong, solid self next to me as the scope of the challenge I'm facing becomes more terrifyingly clear.

I never imagined any of this would be easy, but the knowledge that I'm so intimately connected to Atlas that he can reach me when we're thousands of miles apart is sobering. Sickening. It makes me feel like I'm diseased, infected with a darkness I have no idea how to begin to purge.

"And we'll work together, too." Mina pats my knee.

"I'll teach you some tricks to keep your psychic shields strong so he'll have a harder time reaching you while you're asleep. If you're going to be training hard every day, you'll need your rest at night."

"Whiskey helps, too," Kite says. "A shot right now sounds pretty good, in fact."

Mina shoots him a mock-stern look. "No whiskey before dinner. You give this girl whiskey on a mostly empty stomach and she'll be passed out before she can see what a terrible dancer you are."

"I am not a terrible dancer," Kite says, laughing. "And if I am, it's your fault for sending me to dance class in dresses for the first five years. How was I supposed to remember to learn the dances for boys when I was wearing pink every day?"

Mina's expression crinkles with delight as she reaches out to pinch Kite's cheek. "But you were so cute in pink!"

Kite growls, but he's clearly not upset, and the playful teasing does its job, for the time being.

We chat a little longer—Mina explains which dances the tribe will be performing after dinner, before the regular dancing begins, and Kite advises me on where to sit to get the best view of the show. By the time we push our chairs back, preparing to grab bags and brush teeth before we leave for the party, I'm back on steadier ground.

I've managed to banish the majority of my heebie-jeebies to the back of my mind, in fact, when Kite puts a gentle hand on my arm as I'm leaving the room and asks, "Do you want me to get you another shirt? I can run grab something from Selkie's room upstairs."

I cock my head, but before I can ask why I should change, Kite motions to my chest. I glance down, blinking dumbly as my brain struggles to make sense of the large blotches of water dampening the front of my shirt, turning the white fabric nearly transparent.

For a moment I'm too embarrassed by the realization that I sat and chatted to Kite's mother with my borrowed lace bra on clear view to think of anything else. But then the real take-home of this development hits hard enough to make my entire body tremble as I lift a shaking hand to touch the largest damp spot.

When I lift my fingers to my nose, I smell—"The ocean..." I glance up at Kite, eyes going wide. "The monsters splashed me while I was hiding at the bottom of the boat. I-I brought it back."

He nods darkly, holding my gaze as unspoken knowledge flows freely, frighteningly between us.

If I can bring back the ocean, then anything that happens on my spirit plane affects my body here, in the corporeal world. Which means, if I'd fallen overboard and drowned or been eaten by sea monsters in my spirit plane...

"If Atlas can kill me there," I whisper, "then he won't have to worry about meeting me on a battlefield."

"You won't go back there again, not until you're ready." Kite draws me into his arms, lending me his strength. "I won't let him hurt you, Wren. I won't let anyone hurt you."

Then he kisses me, a sizzling, searing, bone-melting

kiss that finishes the job the discovery of my damp T-shirt started. My knees go weak, and I sag against Kite, but he's there to catch me, scooping me into his arms and guiding my legs around his hips as he carries me down the hall to the guest room, his lips never leaving mine.

We kiss harder, deeper, until my blood is rushing hot and my bones start to feel solid again. The passion between us melts me, but the gentleness in his touch, the emotion I can feel rolling from him in waves every time his skin brushes mine, makes me strong.

It's the same way a hug from my sister when I was little and suffering from a relapse always made me feel better. She couldn't take all the pain away, of course, but I could feel her love, and love has mystical, medicinal properties.

As Kite sets me down outside my door and promises, "To be continued, beautiful," my heart fills with hope once more, in spite of all the logical reasons I should be curled up in a ball rocking in a corner.

Because he loves me, this brave man ready to stand by my side no matter what, and I love him. And I'm ready to show him how much.

Maybe soon.

Maybe...tonight.

They say an elephant never forgets, but cats hold grudges like no other creature on God's green earth—don't let our laid-back exteriors fool you.

I never met a grudge I couldn't carry strapped to my back until the end of time, and the rest of my family is the same way. We'll laugh off an insult and shrug away betrayal, giving every impression of forgiving, forgetting, and moving on.

But secretly we're waiting.

Watching.

Planning and hoping and looking for that perfect opportunity to pounce and rip your throat out. And when you ask why, we'll remind you of the exact date, the exact hour, the precise minute when you set the wheels of karma in motion and revenge became a foregone conclusion.

At least in our feline minds.

So while the rest of my team is enjoying the feast—smoked salmon and sea salt roasted potatoes with fresh spring greens and more berries and cream for dessert than even these hearty eaters can devour, I've got my eye on Luke.

I'm sure I appear to be relaxed, laughing at the kids running wild under the high roof of the main lodge, teasing Wren about how pretty she looks in her new duds, and appreciating the decorations through lazy eyes, but I'm hyperalert.

I haven't forgotten that Luke was the reason we had to leave our last safe house, and though I don't blame him for neglecting to inform us of the tracking device on his ankle—he was delivered to us against his will, after all—I'm curious to see what he'll do now that he has the chance to slip away from our happy crew for the first time since our flight from the authorities.

He's ankle-bracelet free and could make a run for freedom—fuck saving the world—and I can't say I would blame him for it. Or he could sneak off to call the wolves who delivered him to our door and apprise them of our location, in which case I would be forced to do things to Luke that I would rather not do.

If the wolves are deliberately trying to sabotage our mission, and if Luke is in on it, then that shit has to be sussed out and shut down.

Fast.

There are enough variables working against us without having a traitor rotting us from the inside.

Activating my kin gift to access visions of the various futures co-existing in any given moment is brutally exhausting, and something I'm only able to do once or twice in a week. But the last time I checked, there was still some unpleasant mystery surrounding Luke in all variants of the possible soon-to-be.

I can't tell if he's friend or foe, only that he has big secrets he's determined to hide at any cost, even if it means betraying the promises he's made to Wren.

"Penny for your thoughts," Wren murmurs from the pillow beside me.

We're both sitting cross-legged, waiting for Kite and the men of the tribe to take the floor for their performance. She has a half pint of beer in her hand—her first drink *ever* she confessed to me earlier—and her cheeks are flushed a healthy pink. It looks like tribe life definitely agrees with her so far.

"Just thinking about bears," I lie, not wanting to make her suspicious of Luke unless I have to. But even as I focus on the raven-haired lovely next to me, I'm keeping tabs on that wolf out of the corner of my eye. "A pack of them are called a sloth."

Wren tilts her head as she considers this information. "That's kind of odd, isn't it? Bears aren't slow. I mean, unless they're hibernating, I guess."

"Some resources say it's actually a 'sleuth' of bears," I admit. "But I don't think of bears as an investigative lot, either. Unless they're tracking down clues to find out where the food's hidden."

Wren grins, casting a pointed look to the little girl in front of us, who is on at least her fourth or fifth serving of berries and cream. "You might have something there."

"Maybe, but until tonight I've never actually seen a

group of bears. Real bears are like lynx. Aside from mamas and their babies, they tend to live solitary lives."

"And what about you?" Wren nudges my shoulder. "Are you a solitary creature, Creedence? Or do you like company?"

My lips curve as I bat my lashes. "Why, are you flirting with me, Miss Wren?"

She blushes as anticipated—the girl is adorably easy to embarrass—but she doesn't cast her gaze to the floor the way she would have even a day ago. "Not this time, buddy. I really want answers. What were you doing with your life before all this? Did you have a roommate? Family you lived with?" She shrugs as she swirls her beer in a way I'm sure she means to be casual but isn't. "A girlfriend?"

I shake my head, my smile fading. "No girlfriend. Not for over a year."

"What happened?" Wren asks.

"She left when she realized I was always going to be an asshole."

Wren's forehead wrinkles. "You don't seem like an asshole."

"Wait until you get to know me better," I say, though I know I shouldn't. I should be giving her reasons to like me, helping to make this transition from friends to something more as easy for her as possible. But my people are contrary as fuck sometimes, too, so I add, "I'm completely emotionally unavailable. I had shitty role models who—aside from insisting I share fifty-fifty with an accomplice—taught me jack shit about how to be a good romantic partner. And I leave the toilet seat up."

"But will you take out the trash?" she asks in a serious voice. "That's what I'm really looking for in a relationship."

I grunt. "Oh yeah? That's all?"

Her nose wrinkles and a cute-as-hell grin splits her face. "No, I'm kidding. I actually have no idea what I'm looking for in a relationship. Except a guy who's not afraid to buy me tampons when I need them. My friend Carrie insists that's how you can tell a loser from a keeper." She breaks into giggles as she reaches out to squeeze my knee. "Sorry. I can't believe I said that. I think I'm drunk."

"Off a half pint of beer?" I ask, laughing with her.

"Yes!" She leans her head against my shoulder as she giggles harder. "I guess I'm a lightweight."

"A featherweight is more like it. Give me that," I say with faux sternness as I confiscate her glass. "You're setting a bad example for the children."

The little girl in front of us turns around, shooting us a berry-stained smile as she announces, "No she's not. All the grown-ups have too much beer on party night."

"Were you eavesdropping on us, you sneaky squirrel?" I ask with an over-the-top glare that earns the desired giggle from our third wheel.

"I'm not a squirrel, I'm a bear," she says. "What are you?"

"Wouldn't you like to know," I tease.

"My sister said you smell like candy, so you must be

a kitty cat," she offers, earning a sharp jab in the ribs from the older girl next to her. "Ow!"

"Shut up, Helena," the sister hisses, casting an embarrassed glance over her shoulder. "Sorry, she never knows when to keep her mouth shut."

"I do, too!" Helena protests.

"No worries," I assure them, not wanting to be the source of a sibling meltdown. "It's no big deal. And yes, I am a cat."

"A very pretty cat," Wren offers.

I glance over to see her watching the exchange with an affection that confuses me until she adds, "You're good with kids."

"I'm not a kid, I'm nine, and that's almost a pre-teen," Helena offers, earning an eye roll from her sister.

"My apologies," Wren says, patting my thigh as she amends, "you're good with pre-teens is what I meant."

"Never grew up myself. It helps," I say, uncomfortable with her praise.

If she only knew how I've failed the kids in my life, her eyes wouldn't be shining the way they are right now. I haven't seen my nieces or nephews in so long I'm sure they've forgotten they have an Uncle Cree.

But I never really learned how to do family. It's hard to commit to maintaining bonds when half your relatives are in jail and the other half are up to their ears in their present con or on the run from the last people they screwed over.

"Why do cats smell like candy?" Helena asks while her sister buries her face in her hands with a soft groan, her mortification apparently complete.

"I don't know about other cats," Wren says, hooking her arm through mine, "but Creedence smells like candy because he's so sweet."

I force a smile and bat my lashes dramatically, making Helena laugh again.

But this isn't fun anymore because I know the truth. I'm not sweet, and the fact that Wren has so readily accepted my charm at face value is troubling. Not because I'm planning to betray her, but because there are so many seemingly "sweet" people in the world who will—without missing a beat.

The thought sends my gaze sliding to the right to find the place where Luke was leaning against the wall empty. A quick scan of the room reveals no sign of the wolf. I dropped my guard for five minutes, and he slipped away. It's enough to make me think he knew I was watching him and exactly when to make his move to avoid detection.

As the lights dim and the show begins, I lean closer to Wren, whispering in her ear as the drums start to pound, "Gotta get up. Save my seat."

"Okay." She turns to face me, her breath catching as our noses brush. But I don't give her space the way I would have even yesterday. "Wh-where are you going?" she whispers, clearly flustered by the less than two inches between us.

"To see a man about a horse." I angle my head to the right, clearing the path to her lips. "And for future reference, I'm not sweet, Slim. Not even close." Before she can respond, I thread my fingers into her hair and guide her lips to mine, laying claim to her mouth the way I would the mouth of any woman who belongs to me, making no allowances for how inexperienced she is.

Her lips part with a soft sound of surprise, and I stroke between them. I go deep, fucking her mouth with my tongue, tasting the orange peel and hops of the beer she drank and a more complex flavor that is Wren alone. She's spice and wild honey, sea grass and a salt breeze, and so fucking delicious I know I'm going to crave another taste as soon as my mouth leaves hers.

Slowly her surprise gives way to curiosity—her tongue dancing with mine and her hands coming to clutch my shirt as I fist a hand in her hair—and I realize she isn't exactly what she appears to be, either.

Yes, she's sweet and innocent. But she's also hungry, aching, and desperate to make up for lost time. For years, drugs kept her weak and frail, trapped in limbo between the girl she was and the woman she longed to become.

But now she's out of her cage.

Running free and ready to see what the world has to offer.

It's going to show her pain, I have no doubt of that—that's the nature of the world, and her path is going to be darker and more dangerous than most. But there will also be pleasure along the way.

I'm going to make damned sure of it.

Finally, after the kiss has gone on far too long for polite company, I drag my mouth from hers and whisper against her warm lips, "I want you under me, Slim. Under me and begging me to take you. How's that for sweet?"

Her breath rushes out, and her lashes flutter. "I... I'm..." Her tongue sweeps across her lips as her gaze lifts to mine, her blue eyes focusing with an intensity that makes my heart beat faster. "I'm a virgin," she whispers too softly for anyone but me to hear.

"That's okay," I murmur, fingers playing in her hair. "I can take care of that for you anytime you like. Or you can get one of the others to take care of it and come see me when you're ready to color outside the lines."

"You don't mind sharing?" she asks, brow furrowing lightly. "You don't think it's...strange?"

"Sharing is part of what we're going to be to each other. I knew that from the beginning, Slim. But it doesn't bother me. You know why?" She shakes her head, and I add in a rough whisper, "Because when you're naked with me, you won't remember their names. If I do my job right, you won't even remember yours."

She bites down on her bottom lip, the sight of her white teeth on her swollen flesh enough to make the uncomfortable situation below my belt even more...pressing.

"I can't wait to make you come," I murmur, surprised by how hard it is to force my hand from her hair and lean away from her sweet mouth. "But first things first. My seat. Save it."

"Will do." Anxiety flickers across her face as I slip away, and she glances over her shoulder. But we're seated in the last row, and the people standing against the wall behind us are too focused on the dancers spinning in circles in the center of the room to care about two strangers making out in public.

And we aren't the only ones feeling the influence of too much drink and those pulsing drums. As I make my way to the exit, I see several other couples taking advantage of the near darkness.

Outside, the amorous mood continues. As I search for Luke, I interrupt not one, but four pairs of lovers seeking privacy from prying eyes.

I make my apologies and continue on my rounds, but Luke is nowhere to be found. The wolf has seemingly vanished off the face of the earth, and now I have to decide what to do about it—find Dust and sound the alarm, or trust that Luke just needed some "me time" and will be back once he's had his fill.

"Fuck that," I mutter, circling back to the longhouse to find Dust.

I wasn't inclined to take chances with Wren's safety before, but after that kiss, I'm finding strange and powerful protective instincts rising inside me. Cats are not known for their romantic nature, and nothing in my personal history would indicate a likelihood to fall for a sheltered virgin at first kiss.

And I'm not in love with Slim—I like her, and I want to fuck her way more than I anticipated before my lips met hers—but there is something new growing inside me. Respect and affection mixed with a meant-to-be feeling swelling so large it can't be denied, no matter how much my inner cynic insists fate is bullshit and forming a mate bond with Wren is something I'll have to make the best of, not something I'm going to enjoy.

Certainly not something I would choose of my own free will if that were still an option...

Right?

Honestly, I don't know, but I know I'm not going to let anyone hurt her. Especially not a rogue wolf without the sense to realize you don't bite the hand that's freed you.

CHAPTER 29
WREN

Kite is an incredible dancer—strong, powerful, and so passionately focused on the story he's helping tell with his body that I can't pull my eyes away from him. But even though my gaze is fixed on the first man to ever kiss me like he meant it, my thoughts keep drifting to the second one.

My lips are tingling from that unexpected kiss, and my panties are...wet.

Wet, from nothing but a kiss and few frank words from a man I barely know and who, until a few minutes ago, I'd considered just a friend.

But there was nothing friendly about the hunger that roared inside me as Creedence laid claim to my mouth. He wasn't gentle or careful like Kite is, and I know that he isn't in love with me or me with him. But in the moment, that didn't matter. I still wanted him, ached for him, and even now, with Kite fixed in my sights and my plan to ask him to come to my bed tonight at the front of my mind, I can't stop thinking about Creedence, too.

About the things I would like to do to him...

About the things I want him to do to me...

A vivid image of his golden head bent over my breast as he draws my nipple into his mouth while his fingers slip down the front of my panties flashes on my mental screen, intensifying the throbbing between my legs. With every passing day, every hour, the desire building inside of me grows more intense. I have so many more dire things to worry about, but more and more often my thoughts turn to one of the men in my company and what it might be like to have them in my bed. Either that, or I find myself replaying every second of my time in the grass with Kite until I'm swollen and dying for something to take the edge off.

Now I'll be replaying that kiss with Creedence, too, and know that I'll never look at him the same way again. He's funny and kind, yes, but he's also the sort of man who believes in taking what he wants—no apologies.

And he wants you.

I swallow hard. It's hard to believe a man as experienced as Creedence would be turned on by an almost complete newbie like me, but the hunger in his eyes had burned every bit as hot as the heat he summoned to life inside me. And his offer to "take care" of my virginity seemed sincere.

I've always thought of my virginity as something to be thoughtfully given to the right man—not a burden to bear until it could be "taken care" of—but the higher the flames of desire rise, the more my inexperienced state seems like a road block standing in the way of my purpose.

My purpose is to form strong mate bonds with these men, bonds that will strengthen and protect all of us. And though the lingering prudish voice inside me insists that intimacy is meant to be between one man and one woman—the voice that sounds like my Sunday school teacher from sixth grade, the year we were taught the bare bones info that passes for sex ed in the Church of Humanity movement—I know sex is going to be part of that bond. It has to be.

And I'm starting to think I *want* it to be.

That maybe I want that *a lot*.

Nearly a half hour later, after the dancing is over and Kite and I wander out on the longhouse deck over-looking the waves rolling into shore under the nearly full moon, I'm still buzzing, humming, longing for something more than his arm around my waist or the relatively chaste kiss he steals as soon as we're safe in the shadows.

I want his skin hot against mine and his hands everywhere and the part of him I can feel growing thick and hard against my belly pushing between my legs, banishing the horrible emptiness that's gnawing at me from the inside out.

"Can we go back to the house?" I whisper against his lips, nails digging into his shoulders. "Or somewhere we can be alone?"

"Are you sure?" he asks, seeming to sense that I want more than we shared the last time we were alone. That I want everything, all of him. "Once we're together like that, there's no going back on the mate bond, Wren. Even if you decide you hate me, I'll still be yours and you'll be mine, our kin forms tethered together until death do us part."

"I could never hate you." I pause, gathering the courage to confess, "I love you, Kite. I've loved you since your first week at the shelter, when you proved you were as patient and kind as you were beautiful to look at."

His breath rushes out as his hands skim down my back. "I love you, too, Bird Girl. Since the first time you hugged me goodbye on the walk home. I pulled you into my arms, and I never wanted to let you go."

"Me either," I slide my fingers into his hair. "That's why I want you to be my first."

"God, Wren, I want that so much. But we don't have to rush. Truly. We have time." His palms cup my ass, pulling me closer to where he's so hard it makes me dizzy with desire. Feeling how much he wants me, how electric it is just to be pressed against him through our clothes, makes me even more positive that this is right and that it's crazy to wait any longer.

"I don't want to wait." I press onto tiptoe, murmuring my next words against his lips. "I want you to make love to me, Kite. Now. Right now."

With a groan, he presses his lips to mine, kissing me with an abandon that makes it clear I'm going to get what I want, what I need. He kisses me until my body is singing then stinging then burning with the need to have more than his lips bare against mine. By the time he finally pulls away, taking my hand tight in his and pulling me toward the steps leading off the deck and into the dark, I don't hesitate to follow.

I run after him, beside him, racing him across the village to a place where we can finally be alone.

We tumble into the house and kiss our way down the hall and into my room, where the door slams shut, and our clothes start to fly, and soon I am wearing nothing but panties Kite drags off my legs as he guides me back onto the bed.

CHAPTER 30
KITE

I want to go slow, to savor every second of this first time with her, but she's so responsive, so wild and completely stunning, naked in the moonlight streaming through the window.

And then I feel how wet she is, her molten slickness coating my skin as I glide two fingers inside her, and I know taking my sweet time is a lost cause.

"We'll go slow during round two," I promise against her lips as I find her nipple and squeeze it lightly between my fingertips.

She moans and spreads her legs, granting my other hand easier access as I thrust my fingers deeper into her tight heat.

"I don't want to go slow," she says, kissing me between the words, her tongue dancing urgently with mine. "I want you inside me. I'm dying to feel you, Kite. Please."

Before I can respond, she reaches between us, taking

my cock in her hand, sending a rush of desire through me, so powerful that rational thought becomes impossible.

Nothing has ever felt as perfect as this moment, with Wren's hand wrapped around where I ache, and her body wet and ready beneath mine. I'm drowning in how overwhelmingly *right* it is to be seconds away from claiming my mate, this heart-stopping woman I knew was meant to be mine from the first time we touched.

She's beautiful in every sense of the word, from those sky-blue eyes that make my stomach flip to the gentle way she touches people in pain, with such complete generosity of spirit that I am humbled by her goodness.

I can't believe this gorgeous person is going to be mine, that she's looked into my heart and decided I'm worthy of her absolute fucking sweetness.

"You're sure?" I ask, even as I allow her to guide my cock to her entrance. "I don't want you to ever regret this, Wren."

"Are you going to regret it?" She holds my gaze in the soft glow filling the room, the love in her gaze making my throat squeeze tight.

I shake my head and whisper, "Never. Not a chance. Not today or tomorrow or a single second from now until the day I die."

Her eyes shining with emotion, she nods. "Me, too. It's so right. Can you feel it?"

"I can." I fight to maintain control as the tip of my cock presses against her slick folds. "Nothing has ever felt this perfect."

"Then make me yours, Kite," she says, wrapping her legs around my hips. "Make me yours."

Too overwhelmed to hold back another second, I give my girl what she wants. I push forward, sinking into her inch by gentle inch, pulse rocketing as her pussy grips me blissfully tight. It's by far the most amazing thing to happen to my body in my entire life—bar none—but I still force myself to pause the moment I feel resistance blocking my way.

She's a virgin. My first virgin, and I'm terrified of hurting her. I only want to make my sweet Wren, my mate, my love, feel beautiful things.

Not pain, never pain.

But fuck if I know of a way to avoid it. At least not completely.

"Don't stop." She holds my gaze as her fingernails dig deeper into my ass. "Don't stop. Please, I need more of you. I don't care if it hurts, please, I need you, Kite, I—"

Her words end in a soft cry as I grit my jaw and thrust forward, breaking through the thin barrier. Slowly, gently, I sink deeper, all the way to the end of her, until I'm fully seated in her sinfully tight pussy. And then I force myself to still, hopefully giving her time to adjust.

But the wince of pain has already faded from her expression, leaving nothing but love and desire behind.

She brings her hands to my face. "Yes. This is it. What I've been dying for. You."

"Me, too," I echo, fighting to hold still. My body is demanding I ride her, thrusting in and out until we both explode, but I need to know she's okay first. "The pain?"

She shakes her head. "Gone. There, but over so fast I barely felt it."

"You heal so fast." I bite my lip as I shift my hips back and then rock slowly into her again, loving the way her lashes flutter in response. "Your body is amazing."

"No your body is amazing," she says, the hunger in her voice making me smile even as the feel of her hands gripping my ass makes my head spin. "I want more of you, Kite." She pulls me deeper, making me groan. "More and more and more."

"Yes, ma'am," I growl as I begin to take her in earnest, riding her harder, faster, deeper, until we're both clinging to each other, every muscle straining as we writhe together, racing for the edge.

"God, Wren, yes," I groan as I feel her pussy tighten around me. "Come for me, baby, come for me."

She ignites, calling my name as her body clutches at my cock, triggering my own release. Shoving my hips forward, I come harder than I have in my entire life, so hard the walls melt and the room disappears and I lose all sense of time or place. I'm consumed, lost in bliss, in the magic I've found with Wren and the seamless way her soul entwines with mine as we ride out the final waves.

Afterward, it's immediately clear that things are different between us, but in the best way.

I can feel her spirit whispering inside of me like the first shot of the finest whiskey, warm and soothing, smoothing away all my ragged edges, while our kin forms curl together in complete harmony. I always knew she would begin to acquire my kin gift after we were joined, but I hadn't realized that I would feel more powerful, too. Though I'm not sure if I'm literally absorbing some of her strength or if this is just what it feels like to find the one who's meant for you.

I'd always assumed there was nothing better than coming home to the family who loves me, to this place where, for thousands of years, my ancestors have loved the land and the land has loved them in return and there has never been any doubt that I belong.

But this right now, right here, with Wren...

This is something deeper than familial love or the peace of being part of a sacred lineage of bear-human-earth-ocean-spirit.

This is home in a deeper way than I've understood it. This is the safety of being joined with the woman who was destined to be the dearest part of my heart. There will be no more going to sleep aching for that ineffable something I have always sensed was missing. There's no need to hold back or hide my feelings or be anything but a man completely in love with his woman, his one, his mate.

And it doesn't matter anymore that I won't be her one or only.

As I roll onto my back, pulling her with me to rest on my chest while we catch our breath, the last of my jealousy fades. My girl's heart is more than big enough for four men, and when she opens the door to another mate bond, it won't mean that she loves me any less.

What we have is special. Sacred. One of a kind, even

though someday soon I won't be the only man in her bed.

I'm about to tell her so—tell her that I'm here to support her in everything she does, even bonding with her other mates when she's ready. But before I can speak, my phone bleats urgently from the floor, where it's still tucked into my jeans.

It's the breach alarm, the one programmed to go off on every tribe member's phone if our perimeter is compromised and enemies have made it onto our land.

Guiding Wren to one side, I roll off the bed and scramble for my phone, jabbing Leda's contact number. She's on guard tonight. She'll know what's happening.

Or she'll be dead, a chilling voice in my head offers.

But thankfully, my sister answers before that terrible thought can take root. "We're taking fire," she shouts, "Humans in trucks built like tanks. They penned us in, and we weren't able to stop the things they sent through. They're headed your way. You've got to—"

"What did they send through?" I ask, already calculating the distance between here and the armory, where I can grab something capable of taking down a truck built like a tank.

"I have no fucking idea, Kite." The fear in Leda's usually rock-steady voice makes her next words even more chilling. "I've never seen anything like them. They're monsters, Kite. If they make it to the village, they'll tear our people apart. They're headed down the north road. You've got to stop them."

"On my way." I'm about to end the call when Leda

shouts, "Be careful, baby brother," over the sound of gunfire somewhere beyond her location. "I love you."

"I love you, too," I say, praying it won't be the last time I get to tell her.

Ending the call, I circle around the bed, telling Wren, "Get dressed and get to the longhouse. Tell everyone it's imperative they seek shelter in the bunkers as fast as they can. Deadly force incoming from the north road."

"What about you?" She swings her feet off the bed, reaching for her clothes. "You need help, Kite, you can't take this on alone."

"The second-string defense are all at the party, they'll know what to do." I lean down to press a quick, but urgent, kiss to her lips. "But you go to the bunkers. Keep yourself safe." I hesitate one more precious minute. "I love you, Wren. If this was my last night, it's been the best one."

As I pull away, I see tears filling her eyes and wish I could stay and give her comfort. But there's no time.

With one last, "I love you," I head for the window and throw up the glass.

CHAPTER 31
WREN

I've never thrown on clothes so fast, but by the time I shove my feet back into my borrowed sandals, Kite is already out the window.

I hurry across the room, only to freeze with my hands on the sill, my jaw dropping as I witness his shift for the first time.

As Kite tumbles to the ground and rolls down the short slope into the grass behind the house, his shoulders swell impossibly large and his arms lengthen and thicken. Dark brown hair flows across his frame like water gliding onshore, banishing every inch of smooth skin in less time than it takes for my sharp inhale to become an exhale.

By the time he lands on all fours near the raised garden beds, there's a massive grizzly where my boyfriend used to be, an intimidating predator with teeth that flash in the moonlight as he drops his head back and roars loud enough to rattle the frame beneath my fingers.

Vibrations shiver up my arms, a visceral reminder to snap out of it and get moving. I have to find Dust, Luke, and Creedence and warn them that we're under attack.

With one last look out the window, saying a quick prayer for Kite as he bounds across the yard toward the bend in the road, I turn and race through the quiet house. Bursting out the front door, I take the stairs two at a time down to the footpath winding through the village and hit the gravel at a sprint. I run faster than I have in my entire life, faster than I realized I was capable of moving until the man I love ran off to face our enemies alone.

Alone.

Unarmed aside from teeth and claws and his brave heart that I can't bear to imagine not beating.

It's going to be all right. He's going to be all right, I chant silently as my lungs burn and my calves howl with pain.

But I don't slow down. I push harder, flying across the ground, past quiet houses and boats drifting peacefully in the harbor, toward the warm glow of the longhouse.

Every light is blazing, but I can't hear the music. I can't hear anything except the pounding of my heart in my ears and the harsh suck and huff of my breath. I'm halfway up the stairs leading to the feast room when I hear the screams, and my blood goes cold.

Oh God, I'm too late.

How can I be too late?

Leda said the threat was coming down the road, and

no one passed me as I ran. I should have made it in time to warn Kite's people to take shelter. None of this should be happening!

But it *is* happening.

I burst through the doors to see chaos and blood.

Blood on the floor…

Blood on the walls…

On what's left of the sacred costumes that are now ripped and torn, feathers floating through the air as a creature straight out of hell rips a man in half right in front of me. I scream, but there isn't time to process the horror before two other nightmare monsters chase a group of children past the dead man, out onto the deck, and still another lunges at an enraged grizzly, who is clearly out to draw blood of her own.

But it only takes a glance around the room to realize the bears are outmatched. The things they're fighting are as big as a grizzly, but with the haunches of a giant cat, giant, reptilian-looking claws with opposable thumbs, and the fierce, powerful muzzles of dogs bred to kill.

They are fast and merciless, jabbing and slicing at the bear kin in a controlled frenzy that's unnatural. Nothing made of flesh and bone should be able to move that quickly or kill with such utter lack of passion or remorse.

But these monsters are managing it and quickly taking down bear after bear.

They have to run. We all do. Standing our ground to fight is only going to get more people killed.

Maybe if I can create a distraction, something to pull the monsters' attention away from the bears...

Maybe that will give them time to get away...

I'm scanning the room, mind racing as I look for something, anything, I can use to make a loud noise, set a fire—*something*—when a high-pitched cry to my left makes me spin. It's Helena, wedged into a corner behind a totem pole, while one of the nightmares does its best to drive claws into her hiding spot.

"Mama, help!" Helena sobs and cringes closer to the wall, tears streaming down her cheeks as the monster goes after her, teeth snapping inches from her red face. The wooden pole cracks—her safe space won't be safe for long. "Mama!" she wails, hiccupping in terror as the thing slams its forehead again and again into the obstacle keeping it from its prey. "Mama!"

I don't know where Helena's mother is, but there's no one else on this side of the room—the battle is spilling out onto the deck and onto the grounds below —and no one coming to help her. I'm her only chance.

Before I realize quite what I'm doing, I've grabbed a wooden chair from along the wall, lifted it over my head, and I'm charging at the nightmare. I don't have fur or muscles or claws, but maybe I can at least distract it long enough for Helena to get away.

As I run, the beast turns, fixing me with its cold black gaze, as flat and pitiless as a shark's. They are heartless, soulless eyes that promise no mercy for me or anyone else in this room.

I have a split second to realize the thing is about to

pounce, and then it's on me, knocking me flat, sending the chair flying.

"Run, Helena!" I scream as I instinctively reach for the beast's neck, digging my fingers into its thick, elephant-like hide as I lock my elbows, fighting to keep its teeth from my face or throat.

Pain and heat explode along my left ribs as claws slice through my shirt and into my skin. I barely have time to acknowledge the pain before it comes again and again—my thigh, my shoulder, my hip. I cry out in agony and panic as I realize I'm being shredded alive. My arms begin to tremble, and the next time the monster snaps its powerful jaws, its rancid breath— motor oil and week-old trash left out in the sun—blasts hot on my face, making me gag.

I'm going to die like this.

On the ground, pinned beneath a monster, retching and bleeding while all the things I should have done and could have done and would have done if I'd only had the chance to grow and get stronger are left unfinished.

"No!" I shout into the snarling face frothing above my head, refusing to let this be my ending. "No!" Not like this, not when I've just started to live, to love, to learn the truth of who I am and what I can do.

What you can do!

The thought flips a switch in my head. Focusing inward, I funnel all my anger and rage at the creature into the hollows of my bones, into the neurons firing in my cells, into the skin growing red hot beneath my clothes.

A beat later, I ignite with an audible *whoosh*, bursting into a column of flame.

The nightmare howls as it rears back, falling onto its side with a whimper as it limps away. But I'm already up, stalking it across the floor as my clothes burn away, leaving me wearing nothing but fire, writhing flames desperately in search of more fuel, more food.

As the creature rises unsteadily onto its singed hind legs, lifting its claws in a warning to stay back, I thrust my palms forward, willing the fire to jump, to surge, to soar across the space between us and burn.

And burn...

Burn...

The sound as the monster falls to the floor, writhing in agony as its flesh catches fire calls to something primal inside of me. If given the choice between being predator or prey, I will choose predator. I will hunt and kill and rip out throats with my bare hands if that's what I have to do to keep my people safe.

I step closer, ready to deliver the final blast—one final torrent of flame that will finish off the creature that made the mistake of crossing me—when the dark gray flesh seems to melt away, falling off of massive white bones. And then the bones are twisting and jerking, shattering and reforming in an almost mechanical-looking dance until there's a scrawny naked kid with a shaved head lying on the floor in front of me where the monster used to be.

He rolls over, brown eyes wide and terrified in his bright pink face as he lifts a trembling hand, "Please. Please, help me... I can't stop it. I can't stop..."

The words make me pause, but it's the tears that stream from his eyes as he begins to sob that still the flames on the tips of my fingers.

"They made us, and we can't control it," he says, his voice raw and hoarse. "They turn us and make us do terrible things and I... God, I just want it to stop. I'm so sorry. Please... Please, help us..." He reaches for me again, his hand drawing so close to my flame I realize he's going to burn himself.

The knowledge short-circuits my rage, replacing it with concern for a fellow creature in pain. My fire goes out, leaving me as naked and vulnerable as he is. When his fingers brush my leg, we are skin and skin, human to human, and I'm instantly, violently horrified by how close I came to cold-blooded murder.

The self-defense excuse ended when he fell off of me and tried to scramble away. My violence should have ended then, too.

But it didn't, and I'm so deeply ashamed that I'm consumed by it, so lost in my private misery that I don't hear the footsteps behind me, and the gunshot takes me completely by surprise.

I jump with a scream that becomes a gasp of horror as the man at my feet jerks backward, falling to my feet with his eyes wide and a hole in the center of his head. I start to reach for him but realize instantly that it's too late—he's dead.

I spin to see Luke standing behind me with his jean jacket in one hand and a gun in the other. Without wasting a second, he tosses the jacket to me and jerks his head to the door behind him. "We've got to go. Now. The others are outside."

"But, he wasn't trying to hurt me." Tears rise in my eyes as I shove my arms into the jacket and do up the buttons with shaking hands. "He was in trouble. He said he was being forced to do this, that—"

"People will say anything to stay alive. If you'd given him two more minutes, he would have been ripping your heart out." Luke grabs my upper arm and drags me toward the door. "Now, move, princess. None of us have the fucking time for this."

"No, we could have helped him, or learned from him, we—"

"People are dead," Luke cuts in, his voice harsh and low. "Kids are dead, lying in the dirt next to their fucking stuffed animals. That shit was fighting for the wrong side, and now he's dead, too. That's the way war works."

"It wasn't your choice to make." I force the words out through a tight jaw and the tears filling my eyes. I can't think about the kids or I'm not going to be able to make it to the truck without being sick. "I believed he was telling the truth, that he was forced into this attack against his will. And if that's the case, he was as innocent as any other victim who was killed tonight."

"And now he's dead." Luke releases my arm with a jerk. "But if you want to run back in there and cry for him, go ahead. I'll tell Kite you care more about the freak who killed his people than getting your chosen-one ass to safety."

I balk at his caustic words even as a sharp wave of

relief courses through my chest. "Kite's okay? You're sure?"

"He's in the fucking car," Luke says, turning to leave without another word.

I watch him go, anger and pain and sadness so deep my heart feels like it's been hollowed out by dynamite pulsing through me. And then I force my feet to move. I hurry barefoot across the blood-smeared planks, step over the brightly colored pillows where people sat to watch the dancing mere hours before, and race after Luke to a black Hummer idling at the base of the stairs.

I see Dust in the passenger's seat, Creedence behind the wheel, and Kite bursting out of the back to usher me inside—relief and grief mixing on his face—and don't know what to feel.

We're all here, the mission is still in motion, and the future is still something we might be able to save.

But at what cost?

Innocent people died tonight for the crime of offering us shelter and friendship. Kite lost family and friends. Mothers lost their children, husbands lost their wives, and the Samish nation will never be the same after tonight.

As Creedence speeds out of the village, I can't help but feel responsible, a sentiment echoed by Dust as he softly announces, "We don't ask for help again. From here on out, it's the five of us. That's it. No more lives at risk."

"We can't be sure they were after us," Creedence says, but he doesn't sound convinced. "It could have been a random Kin Born attack."

"Those things weren't Kin Born," Luke says, his deep voice vibrating with rage. "They were lab made, and they were absolutely here for us. I found this on the first one I killed." He holds up a scrap of pink fleece that I recognize immediately. "It smells exactly like her."

It's mine, a piece of the snuggly I've had for as long as I can remember, since before I came to live with Hank and Abby.

The monsters were sent for me. And they found me, along with dozens of innocent men, women, and children who died because I was too stupid to realize how much danger I was in.

Mind spinning in miserable circles, I brace my elbows on my knees and hang my head, fighting the urge to vomit as Creedence speeds down the back road leading off the reservation.

CHAPTER 32

WREN

We drive until morning and then onward through a gray day filled with oppressive clouds that refuse to give rain. The leashed potential energy presses down on us as we streak north toward places unknown except to Dust, who promises to explain when he's authorized to tell us more. Luke invites Dust to go fuck his authorization, Kite insists keeping us in the dark isn't protecting anyone, and Creedence casually asks for a show of hands to see how many people would like to kick Dust off the island.

"And maybe you, too, Luke," Creedence continues. "What the hell were you up to last night? I tried to find you when the dancing started, but you were MIA for hours, right up until the fighting started. Then suddenly, there you were, back in action. Almost like you knew something was about to go down."

Luke leans forward, bracing his arm on the back of

BELLA JACOBS

Dust's seat as he replies in a too quiet, too calm voice, "If you want to accuse me of something, then do it, cat. Otherwise, you can take your passive-aggressive, holier-than-thou shit and shove it up your ass."

"All right," Creedence says, his voice menacingly pleasant. "What are you hiding? Are you on our team or are you working for the enemy?"

"Where was I aiming my gun, you smug fuck?" Luke growls. "That ought to tell you something."

"Stop, both of you." Dust says.

"I don't know. I think Creedence has a valid question," Kite murmurs from my left, speaking up for the first time in hours. I glance over to see his dark eyes still puffy from the tears he shed on the way off his people's land. "Where were you?"

The muscle in Luke's jaw twitches as he shifts his gaze Kite's way. But after a moment he says in a soft voice, "I went for a run. All the happy family shit when the only family I'll ever have is dead..." He shakes his head. "It was painful. So I ran up the coast and did a little rock climbing to blow off some steam. That's when I saw the headlights coming in from the south, from that secret road you said only a few people are supposed to know about. I ran back as fast as I could and grabbed a gun from the armory, but by the time I got close to the longhouse, those freaks were already laying waste."

"You killed three of them. You saved a lot of lives getting there as fast as you did," Dust says, still trying to play the peacemaker, though he clearly feels awful.

312

We're all blaming ourselves, and as far as I can tell we're all right.

If we hadn't gone to the reservation, twenty-one people would still be alive, including Helena's big sister. Kite got a text from his mom about an hour ago. All his sisters are safe, but he lost an uncle and a cousin, and the tribe at large lost ten more men, six women, and five children. One night, one mistake, one act of kindness gone awry cost his people more than we can ever repay, even if our mission is successful.

Which is a big "if."

I'm not ready now, and I may never be. Sure I can heal insanely fast—I'm already back in decent shape after my first fight—but no place feels safe. We have no idea who we can trust or who betrayed our location, and even Dust, the man who is supposed to have the plan, is shaken. We stopped an hour ago for Creedence to run into a discount store to buy clothes, water, wet wipes, and first aid supplies to tend to our wounds. Dust took advantage of the break to call his contact, the one to be approached only in the case of a life-threatening emergency, but he or she didn't answer, and they still haven't called back.

Something is wrong.

Everything is wrong.

The world is upside down and inside out, and it seems absurd that so much of life continues as normal. We still have to stop and get gas another thirty minutes up the road, and Luke still insists that we find something to eat and force it down our throats, and I still have to use the bathroom because I've been drinking water nonstop since we got on the road.

Turns out turning into a pillar of flame makes a person really, *really* thirsty.

We drag out of the car and head toward a faded gas station with a sign advertising "live meal worms" taped in the window, which has obviously seen better days. Luke refuses to make direct eye contact as he asks, "Peanuts or almonds, princess, what do you want?" Dust offers to accompany me to the restroom, Kite insists he'll do it, and Creedence rolls his eyes and says, "She can take a piss by herself, Prince Charmings. The door to the bathroom is right by the coffee machine. Both of you can stand there and wait for her."

Grateful for a few minutes of privacy, I use the facilities and then stand in front of the sink in the sparse, but clean, ladies' and let the water run until its hot. Doing the best I can with hand soap and a few paper towels, I wash my face, arms, and hands and run damp fingers through my wild hair.

But when I'm done, I don't feel any cleaner.

I feel broken. Wrong. And for a split second I wonder if maybe the movement is right. Maybe shifter powers *should* be suppressed. If there weren't any shifters in the world, then maybe the people who lost their lives last night would still be alive.

"Unless a human monster with a gun decided to open fire in their church," I mutter to my reflection. "Or a movie theater. Or their school."

It's true—there are monsters loose in the world without a drop of supernatural blood in them, and they do just as much damage, if not more. The answer isn't taking magic and trust and hope away from the people who deserve it. The answer is pushing back against the darkness until it has no choice but to go underground.

But how, when evil is so powerful, so relentless?

When our enemies have no morals, no limits, no line they won't cross in order to achieve their desired end and all we have are full hearts and a longing to build a better world?

Destruction is easy. Creation and preservation take time, focus, passion, and hard work. And setting things on fire isn't going to help change the world.

It'll only help burn it down.

I lift my hands, staring at the tiny broken blood vessels beneath the skin on my palms, stomach knotting as I remember how close I came to taking a life. The most terrifying thing was how easy it was to give in to the bloodlust roaring inside of me. It was like kicking a ball downhill—one small choice and then momentum took over, carrying me away so fast there's no longer any question of whether I'm capable of violence.

Now it's just a matter of figuring out how to control my power and my rage, of finding a way to choose the kindest path forward even when showing mercy feels impossible. But that's what separates the light from the darkness—the ability to do impossible things.

Hate can wreak massive havoc, but only love can work miracles.

Love...

I close my eyes as a wave of love washes through me so intense it leaves me breathless. Lips parting in a silent cry, I press my fist to my chest as love and pain and regret slam into me again and again, until my ribs feel like seaside cliffs battered by an angry ocean. Fighting to pull in a deeper breath, I stagger toward the bathroom door, my vision so blurred with tears that it takes three attempts to turn the lock.

I tumble out into the gas station, head whipping to look around, but Dust and Kite aren't waiting by the coffee station the way they promised, and Creedence and Luke are nowhere to be seen. Bracing myself on the shelves as I hobble down the chip aisle, I call out mentally for Kite. I send waves of longing through the air, hoping the bond we solidified last night might help him sense my distress, but I can't be sure my message is getting through.

I'm too overwhelmed by the emotional onslaught rolling me over and over, sucking me under like a riptide and dragging me away from the shore of my Self. I don't know who these feelings belong to, but they aren't mine.

They're coming from somewhere else.

Some*one* else...

As I round the end of the aisle and the parking lot comes into view, I instantly know whose pain this is.

I also know who's responsible for alerting our enemies to our location, and that the blood of all those dead shifters, those innocent people and sweet children, is truly on my hands.

CHAPTER 33

WREN

If I hadn't broken the rules and texted Carrie Ann, none of this would have happened.

My friend betrayed me.

Betrayed all of us.

Outside, Carrie Ann stands in front of a white and brown-striped van with her hands held up in surrender, a nasty bruise blossoming on one side of her pale face, and tears streaming down her cheeks. Kite, Creedence, Dust, and Luke have her surrounded, but they aren't close enough to touch her, and I know instinctively that they aren't the one who hurt her.

She feels responsible for the bruises, like she earned them, like they are the least of what she deserves for aiding and abetting an evil man.

Pushing hard on the door, I emerge into the bright morning, the gentle kiss of the sun on my face an abomination that makes me flinch. There should be nothing good and sweet in this moment, in this world where people you've given your heart prove your love means nothing to them.

"I never meant for this to happen," Carrie Ann is hiccupping between sobs as I plod slowly across the gravel lot. "I swear to you. I never knew he was going to try to kill Wren or hurt so many people. He said he just wanted to bring her in for some tests, that he finally had everything he needed to help her get better."

"What's his name?" Dust demands. "How many people does he have working for him?"

"You can't trust her," Luke growls, slashing a hand through the air. "She betrayed Wren once, and she'll do it again. This could be a trick to slow us down long enough for her boss to catch up. We have to get rid of her and get out of here."

"Killing crying women in parking lots is a good way to get arrested," Creedence observes softly. "We're already causing a scene. The best thing we can do is take this discussion somewhere private."

"There's no time," Carrie Ann says, swiping the tears from her cheeks. "We cut the electricity at the house and stole the portable radar, but—" She breaks off, her eyes going wide as her gaze locks with mine. "Wren... Oh Wren, I'm so sorry." Her bottom lip trembles and her hands shake as she threads them together in silent supplication. "I know you can never forgive me, but I came to help you. I promise."

I rear back, swallowing hard and shaking my head as another wave of love-pain-regret slams into me with enough force to make my head spin. Almost instantly Kite is beside me, taking my hand.

The moment his skin kisses mine, the emotional onslaught fades, but only a little. It's still strong enough to make my bones vibrate, to make it difficult to focus as Kite explains, "It's our mate bond. You can channel my power on your own now, even when we're not touching. So you'll have to learn to control it on your own, too."

I swallow hard. "How?" I ask, praying it's something I can figure out fairly quickly. Facing Carrie Ann is hard enough without feeling her every emotion magnified inside me.

"Visualize a wall," Kite murmurs. "There's a wall made of glass between you and Carrie. You can still see what she's feeling but the wall blocks the energy, the same way real glass keeps out the wind and the rain."

My tongue slipping out to dampen my lips, I try to do as he's instructed, mentally erecting a large pane bracketed by a wooden frame, but my wall is thin and breakable, shivering under the weight of the agony flowing from my friend and from…the van.

"There's someone else in the van," I whisper to Kite, not wanting to alert Carrie Ann that we know she's not alone. If she's planning an ambush, we need to be one step ahead.

Kite nods and squeezes my hand. "Are you going to be okay by yourself while I check it out?"

"I'll have to be." I clench my jaw as his fingers slide from mine and he eases away to the right, presumably to circle around and approach the van from behind.

My glass wall shudders at the loss of support, threatening to break, but I force more attention into the visualization, firming it up as I tell Carrie Ann, "Answer the question. Who are you working for? What's his name and what does he want with me?"

Her face crumples, but after a moment Carrie Ann sniffs hard and words rush from her lips. "Dr. Martin Highborn. He runs the Elysium Institute."

Dust curses, and my blood goes cold.

"That's the doctor who's killing shifters," I murmur. "The one who was going to operate on me if Kite hadn't taken me first." I see Dust nod out of the corner of my eye, but I keep my focus on Carrie Ann, who's sobbing even harder now.

"I didn't know," she says. "I swear, I didn't."

"Then who exactly did you think he was?" I ask, voice hard.

Carrie Ann sniffs, making a visible effort to pull herself together. "I knew he was a scientist and researcher, but I thought he worked on Meltdown viruses, like he tells everyone else. I didn't even know shifters existed until a few days ago. I was part of the other things he does on the side. I think his father used to be in the military or special ops or something." She shakes her head. "I don't know, but he's got a lot of really sketchy friends. They're the ones who picked me up off the street years ago. I thought they were going to kill me, or sell me or something, but instead they brought me to Dr. Highborn. He took care of me, Wren. He was good to me. He helped me get healthy, and then he... He sent me to you. As a spy," she adds, guilt thick in her voice. "For the first year, all I did was send him monthly reports on your health, your mental state, things like that. I didn't see the harm in it. He's a doctor and he helps people. He helped me. He saved me, and I… I thought he was going to save you, too."

She rolls her shoulders back as she stands up straighter. "But the past year he's been different, manic and angry all the time. And then last night… I was supposed to stay in the guesthouse—I'd already gotten punched in the face by one of his goons for spying—but I crept across the lawn after dark anyway. I watched the monitors in his office while Highborn and his thugs did what they did to Kite's people…" She trails off with a shudder. "It was so horrible, Wren. So, so horrible. And that's not who I am. I refuse to be a part of that kind of senseless slaughter."

"We do, too." The trembling voice comes from the other side of the van, out of my line of sight, but I recognize it instantly.

"Mom," I croak, my knees going weak as Abby steps out from behind the vehicle, Hank close beside her and Kite not far behind.

CHAPTER 34

That's where the worst of it was coming from, I realize as I take in my mother's tear-streaked face and my father's equally ravaged expression.

They are the source of the fiercest waves of love-pain-regret. My glass wall shatters in the face of it, tinkling to the ground in slow motion, leaving deadly shards littered on the ground between me and these people who are the only family I've ever known.

My family killed Kite's family.

My parents and my friend led those monsters to Kite's people.

My parents must have given them the blanket the dogs used to track me down. I almost died because of them, and for a moment, I wish I had.

The guilt and despair are crushing.

"Why," I force out through my whip-tight throat,

backing away as my mother takes several swift steps toward me. I hold up a hand, shaking my head, willing her not to come any closer. "Why did you do this? Why!"

Fresh tears spill down her cheeks. "Oh honey, I'm so sorry. We didn't know. The doctor said he would help us find you. He said he had special tracking animals and money to fund a real search and…" She breaks off with a sob. "The police and the elders weren't helping us, Wren, and we just wanted you back. We wanted to find you and keep you safe."

"We just wanted to protect our baby girl," Pops adds, the quaver in his voice making my gaze shift his way. His eyes are shining with unshed tears that hit me like another punch to the gut. This is only the second time I've seen him cry.

The first was at my sister's memorial service.

"Protect me by poisoning me?" I ask, anger helping me piece my wall back together, thicker and stronger than before. "By poisoning Scarlett?"

"No, baby." Mom shakes her head so fast it sends a tear flying from her cheek into the air beside her. "Never! We were trying to help you, heal you. Give you a normal life."

"She was never sick or abnormal," Dust says, his tone simmering with barely controlled rage. "She didn't need to be healed. She needed to be rescued from the likes of psychotic fanatics like you."

Hank's forehead furrows miserably. "No, son. We saw what happened to the kids who were allowed to start shifting. They became savages, monsters that killed their sisters and brothers."

"Those are propaganda films, you fools," Dust shouts. "Lies produced by your own cult to keep their idiot minions drugging and killing innocent kids. Real shifter kids aren't any more prone to violence than human children."

"Like those babies you helped kill last night," I whisper, tears filling my eyes. "They were sweet, innocent souls, and you sent monsters in to slaughter them. I barely saved one little girl. She almost died crying for her mother like any baby would, and she'll spend the rest of her life without the big sister she loved. I wasn't in time to save her."

My mother's entire body trembles as she sobs. "We didn't know. I still don't know what's happening. I'm so confused, Wren. I just—"

"Then let me help clear up the confusion," I cut in as I step closer, wanting to be sure my parents can see the truth in my eyes. "You killed Scarlett. You destroyed my sister. As far as I'm concerned, her blood is on your hands."

Abby's knees buckle as she breaks down, and Hank steps in behind her, holding her up as he says in a tortured voice, "Please, Wren, don't do this. Please, baby, you know we love you. We love you so much. You and Scarlett were the best things that ever happened to us."

"And you were the worst to happen to her," Dust says, his voice so cold it makes me shiver.

But looking at my parents, seeing the devastation

writ large on their suffering faces, feeling the tortured waves of emotion rolling from their hunched bodies, I know it isn't true.

They aren't the worst things to happen to me.

They're victims, too.

Victims of lies and deceit and a cult that rationalized their hatred by decreeing shifters to be something less than human. It's the same thing the Nazi Party in Germany did, using cartoons, movies, even children's books to demonize and dehumanize the Jews, gradually making it "okay" to lock innocent people in concentration camps, torture them, and slaughter them in increasingly horrific ways.

Most people can't make the leap from resentment to hate to murder without some help, without more diabolically evil, wickedly intelligent people yanking their strings. And once most propaganda believers have been sucked into a web of lies, they never find their way free.

Humans don't like to be deeply wrong, especially about matters of good and evil and which side they fall on. It's terrifying, triggering a flight or fight response that mimics threat of imminent death. Rather than face that terror, most people will cling to their dogma.

Admitting they've been wrong opens the door to being forced to admit that they are complicit, if not outright guilty.

Guilty of discrimination, brutality...maybe even murder.

But my parents are standing in front of me devastated and confused, questioning and suffering, but still loving me. I can feel it—real, true, undeniable. The mate bond I've formed with Kite has enhanced my empathy until it truly has become more like telepathy.

I know beyond a shadow of a doubt that, in spite of all the lies, one thing is true.

Love. It was always there, it was always real, and it still is.

"I can't forgive you for Scarlett," I finally say, trembling. "The chance for that died when she did, but…"

I take a deep breath, meeting my mother's tortured gaze as she lifts shining eyes to meet mine. "But if you'll promise to leave the movement, to stop helping drug children, and to accept that shifters have as much of a right to life and freedom from persecution as you do, then maybe we can find a way to move forward as a family."

My mother sobs softly, clinging tighter to Dad's jacket as she says, "Yes. Oh, yes, baby, thank you. That's all I want."

Dad nods, and adds, "Anything it takes. We'll do anything."

"What the fuck?" Luke curses as Dust turns to me, his jaw slack with shock. Even Creedence looks skeptical—his brows lifting until they disappear beneath his tousled hair—but it's Kite I'm most worried about.

What will he think? Will he ever be able to forgive me?

But when I meet his gaze, he's smiling ever so slightly. Almost like he's…proud of me.

Then he silently mouths, "I love you," and my eyes fill with tears of gratitude.

Any shred of doubt that I might have jumped into this too fast with him vanishes in a wave of gratitude. He understands, this man I love, this ally of mine, this hero whose heart is so big there's room for forgiveness even now, only hours after he lost so much.

I turn back to Carrie Ann, answering the fearful hope in her eyes with a nod. "You, too. If you promise never to betray me again, we can try to move forward."

Fresh tears spill down her cheeks as she sucks in a deep breath. "You won't be sorry, Wren. I'm going to do everything I can to make this better, to make up for what I've done. Starting now." She motions to my side. "There's a tracking device in your arm. We have to get it out. That's how Dr. Highborn was able to find you."

Brows pulling tight, I turn to my parents.

"It was put there when you were taken in by the movement," Mom says, looking a little steadier on her feet. "The Seattle adoption center implants all the children they put up for adoption. But Dr. Highborn did something to yours. When we went to the elders for help, they couldn't find your signal anywhere."

"They said you were dead," Dad adds, his jaw clenching. "But we knew it wasn't true. We could feel you out there. We knew you were still alive."

"We think the doctor scrambled your signal or something," Carrie Ann says. "Recalibrated it so that only his devices can find you. Like I said, we cut power to his house before we left, and took the portable radar he was using to track you, but he'll be back online within a day. Maybe less. Which means we don't have much time to put our plan in motion."

"You don't get to decide anything, blondie," Luke snaps, pacing back across the parking lot, finger pointed at Carrie Ann's chest. "Wren may have decided to play Mother Theresa, but the rest of us have more fucking sense than that. I don't trust you, and I never will."

"I understand," Carrie Ann says before I can tell Luke that his attitude isn't helping, lifting her hands in surrender. "I wouldn't trust me, either. But our plan doesn't require trust."

"We thought we could take the tracking device," Mom pipes up as she watches Luke with anxious eyes. "Take it and drive in the opposite direction you're going, hopefully tricking the doctor and buying you more time to get away."

"You don't have to tell us where you're going," Carrie Ann adds. "Not even the general direction. Just tell us where you want us to lead the bad guys, and we're out of here."

"You'll be putting yourselves in danger," Dust says. "Don't assume you're safe because you're human. This man is used to working outside official channels and taking the law into his own hands."

"That's a risk we're willing to take," Dad says, hugging Mom closer to his side. "As long as you and your friends promise to keep Wren safe. To look out for her."

I shake my head. "I can't let you do this. It's too dangerous."

"Not if they drop the tracking device somewhere on

the way south," Creedence says, evidently having decided we should head in a different direction. "I'm assuming this thing is waterproof?"

Dad nods. "It should be."

Creedence shoots Dust a meaningful glance. "There are a fuck ton of rivers around here, Captain. All they would have to do is tape the implant to an inner tube, send it downstream, and get the hell out of Dodge."

Dust sighs, but I can tell he's wavering.

Kite offers, "Maple Falls isn't far from here. That would be a good place. I can draw up directions."

"And I'll grab the first aid kit." Creedence backs toward the Hummer as he thrusts a finger Luke's way. "You've got a knife on you, right, wolfie?"

Luke bristles. "Because I'm Latino? So I automatically carry a knife?"

"No, because you're an ex-gangbanger, asshole," Creedence says pleasantly. "Just whip out that knife I know you have stashed somewhere and get it sterilized. We need to get moving."

"What do you think about this?" I ask Dust, crossing to stand beside him as Luke pulls a pocketknife from his jean pocket and glances down at the selection of blades.

"We have nothing to lose by trusting them with the implant," Dust says softly. "And as far as I can tell, they're truly repentant and trying to help."

I press my lips together as I nod. "They are. I can feel it."

"But I don't like this. I don't trust them, and I..." He shakes his head, his gaze going flat as it shifts my parents' way. "I don't understand how you can let it all go so easily. All those years, your entire life compromised..."

"I haven't let it go," I say. "And this is anything but easy. But if we refuse to forgive, if we forget how to trust, and we stay walled away from each other out of fear and anger, then things are never going to get better." I rest a hand on his arm. "And then the bad guys win, Dust. They want us to be isolated and afraid. They want to keep us apart so we can never learn how alike we are, how much we have in common. How much we all just want to love and be loved."

He turns to me, pain and wonder mixing in his expression. "I've underestimated you, Snow."

"Yeah?" Tears prick at the backs of my eyes again.

"Yes," he whispers. "You're not soft or weak. You're... sweetly ferocious."

I smile, chest tightening as his fingers thread through mine. "I want to stay as kind as possible, Dust. I know there will be times when fighting is our only option, but I want to make sure we've explored every nonviolent one first. I want every choice we make to prove that we deserve to win this war. To prove that we're truly going to make the world a better place."

"All right," he says, respect blooming in his eyes. "It won't be easy. But it was never going to be easy, so..."

"And I need you to help me get everyone else on board," I whisper, casting a pointed glance at Luke, who is now holding a small knife over the flame from the lighter in his other hand. Apparently, he comes prepared for stabbing, shooting, *and* setting things on fire.

Dust squeezes my hand. "I'll do my best." His forehead wrinkles, and sadness tinges his voice as he adds, "But you have to tell them all goodbye for now. We can't risk contacting anyone with links to our enemies. Not until our work is finished."

I nod. "I know."

I do know.

I also know that I might never see my parents or Carrie Ann again. We could be caught, captured, or killed before we make it to Atlas's doorstep, and the chances of triumphing over a supernatural being who has had thousands of years to amass power and arrange his defenses are slim.

So when I hug Mom and Dad goodbye, I linger longer than I usually would, focusing on the love, not the anger or regret.

"Please be safe," I whisper into Mom's hair. "Be safe and get out of the church and live a beautiful life filled with love and happiness."

"I'll try," she says, her breath hitching. "For you. But we'll be watching and waiting, baby. Any time you want to come home, our doors and our hearts are open."

"And we'll do what we can to help the others." Dad rests a warm hand on my back. "To get the other kids out and to people who can help them."

"I can give you some contacts," Kite says, appearing with a map he's drawn on part of the paper bag our clothes came in. "There are a few church members secretly working for the resistance. They can let you know how to help."

"Thank you," my father says, resting a gentle hand on Kite's shoulder. "And I'm so sorry, son. So very sorry."

"I believe you," Kite says. "And I'm glad to have you as an ally instead of an enemy."

"It's time." Carrie Ann steps into our circle with Luke close behind her. "We should get going, and so should you. Take care, Wren. And know that if there's anything I can ever do for you, all you have to do is ask."

"Keep an eye on them for me," I say, nodding toward my parents. "Maybe head over to help weed the gardens once in a while?"

"I'd like that," Carrie Ann says, smiling up at my parents as Mom adds, "So would we."

"So where is this thing?" Luke asks brusquely, clearly sickened by all of us.

"Just above her wrist." Mom points to my left arm, to the silvery scar I always assumed was sustained sometime before I came to live with Abby and Hank, in the dark time that I can't remember. "It should be just beneath the skin."

"All right. Arm up." Luke curls his fingers impatiently, and I place my wrist in his palm. He looks up with a baffled huff. "Just like that? You trust me that easily? A few days together, and you'll put your life in my hands?"

"All of our lives are partly in someone else's hands, Luke," I say, adding with a smile. "But I'm getting better with the fire thing, so try to be gentle okay?"

His lips quirk, up and down so fast I'm not quite sure it happened, but his tone is definitely more respectful as he says, "Will do, princess."

He draws the knife across my skin, using just enough pressure to pierce the puckered flesh at the center of my scar. I feel heat and then a flash of pain as he slips the tip of the knife into the incision he's made, but by the time it really begins to hurt, he's pulling out a tiny black dot no bigger than the tip of a ballpoint pen.

"That's it," Carrie Ann says, glancing down at what looks like a large black remote control in her hands. "Let's find something to carry it in and get ready to go."

"One step ahead of you." Dust trots back across the gravel from the convenience store, carrying a child's size inner tube already inflated.

It's shaped like a flamingo, reminding me of his sweet boxer gift, with a pearly pink finish and a long neck that bobs as we use the packing tape he's purchased to tape the implant onto one wing.

And then it's time to go.

Our entire encounter took no more than fifteen minutes from start to finish, but so much has happened, so much has changed.

I hug my parents and Carrie Ann one last time— saying goodbye to my old life. As we load into the car, bound east as my parents and Carrie Ann head west to a bridge near Maple Falls, high in the mountains, I'm no longer Wren Frame.

Wren Frame never had a choice.

About anything.

She was taken from her parents when she was so

young her babyhood memories were shredded and tossed to the wind, leaving nothing but fragments behind, tiny pieces too small to form a picture, too thin to build a girl upon. Wren Frame was poisoned before she had a chance to grow, shut down like a weed in a garden, kept so weak that each day was a battle for survival, leaving little energy for dreams or goals or becoming the person she was born to be.

But like a weed, I kept going, kept surviving until I found my way free of the dark garden and out into a wild, wonderful, terrifying world where I'm going to have to catch up fast.

I don't have years to make up for lost time. I have months, maybe weeks.

Maybe less.

It's time to seize the day, to seize every instant and squeeze every bit of life from it I can. Starting now.

"Dust, do you know my real last name?" I lean forward in my seat as we wind up a scenic byway into the mountains, keeping my voice low so as not to wake Luke or Kite, who have fallen asleep in the back seat on either side of me.

He glances over his shoulder. "Wander."

"Wren Wander." I touch my fingers lightly to my lips as I try the name on for size and find it good. Right.

Mine.

"But not all who wander are lost," Dust whispers, making me smile.

"No, they aren't," I agree, gazing up at the looming mountains and the glorious peak of Mount Baker, still snowcapped in early June.

sleep seconds falling into a dream of a
moonlit forest by a clear stream, where the red fox
waits for me again.

336

CHAPTER 35

WREN

But this time, she doesn't stay a fox, she rears onto her hind legs and throws back her head, lifting her nose to the sky as she transforms into a woman in a long red cloak, her silver-streaked raven hair the same color as mine.

Mama, my soul cries out, knowing her instantly.

It's my mother, my birth mother.

I know her as surely as if I'd spent my entire life looking into her kind eyes, seeing her smile that crooked grin, smelling the flowers and turpentine scent clinging to her clothes.

"Wrenny Roo." She reaches for me, her fingers giving off silver sparks as she moves.

"I remember," I say, the nickname bringing back smells of fresh baked cherry cobbler from our orchard and long afternoons in the sun and laughing with Mama and Daddy and Scarlett until I couldn't breathe.

I fall into her arms, hugging her close, tears filling my eyes as I feel how cold and thin she is beneath her cloak.

"Mama," I whisper, my throat tight. "Oh, Mama, I've missed you."

"I've missed you, too, love, but I've always been here. Waiting for you to be strong enough to see me." She smooths a gentle hand over my hair, making me feel like a little girl again even though I'm several inches taller than she is. "And I'll still be here, for as long as you need me. I'm not going anywhere until my girls are safe."

Pain shoots through my heart like a sliver of ice, shoved deep.

I pull back, tears falling as I tell her the terrible truth. "She's gone, Mama. Scarlett...she's dead. She died a long time ago, in a terrible accident."

Mama smiles, sparks dancing in her eyes now as she shakes her head. "No, love. She's alive."

I blink faster. "What?"

She lifts a hand, pointing to the sky where a crescent moon hangs low above the trees. "She's hidden far away, pretending to be something she's not to give you the chance to grow up. But her time is running short. She doesn't know that you're free. She doesn't know that it's time to stop hiding and start fighting."

I shake my head. "What do you mean?"

"She's been pretending, but he knows she's not the Fata Morgana now," Mama says, bringing her palm between us as she turns back to me. On it sits a tiny version of Scarlett made of moonlight. She sits in a tower high in the mountains, surrounded by a sea of clouds. "Atlas knows. And he will kill

her for it as surely as he will kill you for daring to lay claim to his throne."

"I don't want his throne," I say, panic clawing at my throat. "I just want to save our world and keep him from hurting anyone else. And to see Scarlett, to save her. Mama you have to tell me where she is."

"I can't find things in the human world, not anymore. But one of them can show you the way," Mama says, her entire body flashing with sparks now. Sparks that flare and fade, taking pieces of her away as they die. "One of your four has the answer locked inside of him. He doesn't remember, but it's there. You have to set the secret free."

"But how?" I reach for her, trying to catch the folds of her cloak, but my hands go straight through her. "Mama, don't go. Please. Stay. Help me."

"Wake up, Wren," she says, her voice going deeper. "Wake up."

"Mama, no! Mama!"

I wake with a start to find Luke's hands under my armpits and his face inches from mine as he urges me, "Wake up, Wren."

I shake my head, my thoughts still dream fogged.

I try to ask Luke what's wrong, but my lips won't cooperate, and my query as to why he needed me to wake me up so badly he decided to pick me up off my seat goes unspoken.

Pick me up…

I give my legs an experimental wiggle, but they aren't touching the seat or the floor of the Hummer. They're dangling in the air, and when I glance to my right, my clothes are lying in a puddle, as if some evil witch cast a spell and magicked the Wren right out of them.

I cock my head sharply as I glance back at Luke.

Much to my surprise he laughs beneath his breath. "Yeah, that was our response, too, princess. Never seen someone shift in her sleep before." He gives me an appraising glance up and down. "But you're cute like this. A lot less dangerous than when you're on fire."

I bare my teeth, and a soft growl emerges, but Luke only laughs again.

"You are cute," he insists. "See for yourself."

He shifts his grip beneath my front legs until he's turned me to face the driver's seat. He lifts me higher, and in the rearview mirror is the reflection of a gorgeous red fox with amber eyes and a fluffy white chin.

As I catch sight of it, I smile, and the fox's lips curve, too.

Thank you, Mama, I think, honored that my first animal form is like hers.

"Now we just have to figure out how to keep you from shifting in your sleep," Dust says, ever the practical one. "Or Kite might roll over in bed and crush you."

"Lies," Kite mumbles, his eyes still closed. "I know exactly where Wren is, whether I'm awake or asleep, whether she's a girl or fire or a fox or anything in between."

"A fire fox. Isn't that a search engine?" Creedence asks. "Can you turn into a search engine, Wren?"

I wrinkle my nose, and Dust rolls his eyes with a huff.

"I've been awake for almost two days straight. These are the jokes when I'm this tired, people." Creedence drives both hands through his wild hair, making me realize we've stopped on the side of the road. "So where to now? What have the people in charge finally decided? Please don't tell me we're headed in the wrong direction, or I may have to jump out and scream a little."

Dust holds up his phone, spinning the screen to face Creedence. "No, we're going the right way. See, the new safe house is up there, right on the Canadian border. When the times comes, we should be able to make the crossing at night in animal forms without getting caught." He casts a fond smile my way. "Especially now that Wren has a more...forest-friendly shape."

I grin as I flick my tail, tossing it in a wide arc as I squirm free of Luke's hands and drop lightly to the seat between him and Kite.

Still sleepy, I crawl onto Kite's lap and curl into a ball with my tail wrapped around me, eyes sliding closed in bliss as he begins to stroke my fur.

"Why do I feel like I'm watching something I shouldn't?" Luke grumbles, arching a brow as Kite's fingers dig deeper into my fur, hitting a sweet spot that causes a warm, whirring sound to hum from my chest.

I'm purring, I realize with a thrill. I didn't realize foxes purred, but it's a lovely feeling...purr-fect, if you will.

"Because they're rubbing it in," Creedence says.

"Shoving our faces in their happy, glowy new-mate bond."

"It's a good thing." Dust turns back to face the road ahead, his shoulders stiff. "The bond will make Wren stronger faster."

"That doesn't mean I can't be a little jealous." Creedence winks at me in the rearview mirror, and I flick my tail slowly back and forth in a way I hope he can tell means, "Play your cards right and maybe you won't have to be jealous for long."

Judging by the wicked grin that curves his full lips, he got the message loud and clear.

I have no idea which of my four men knows where Scarlett is, or how to "set the answer free" the way my mother said, but getting closer to each of them couldn't hurt.

And it's my destiny to form these bonds, not simply my fate.

Fate is something that happens to you no matter how hard you might try to stop it; destiny is something you fight for, no matter what stands in your way.

These men—strong, fierce, but oh-so-gentle Kite; serious and secretly tender-hearted Dust; dangerously sexy Creedence, and just plain dangerous Luke—they all belong to me.

I can feel it in my whiskers, a truth vibrating in the air between us, assuring me I'm exactly where I'm supposed to be, making it acceptable to snuggle in for a nap as Creedence pulls back onto the road, getting us closer to the safety with every passing mile.

To be continued in
Untamed
Dark Moon Shifters Book 2
Coming Autumn 2018.

Subscribe to Bella's newsletter to receive
an email when book two is released!
https://www.subscribepage.com/q9t2v1

SNEAK PEEK

UNTAMED releases autumn 2018

Once upon a time there was a very good girl, who followed all the rules.

That girl is dead.

I am no longer Wren Frame, the bird with the broken wing. I am Wren Wander, a rare shapeshifter determined to take back everything the cult stole from me— my health, my hope, and most importantly, my family.

My sister is still out there somewhere. **Alive.**

And with the help of the four brave, formidable, sexy-as-hell alphas destined to be my mates, I intend to keep her that way.

All I have to do is gain control of my unpredictable new powers, learn hand-to-hand combat, avoid capture by a mad scientist out to rid the world of shifters, and stay ten steps ahead of a Big Bad Evil hungry for my blood.

And that's not the worst of it.

In order to fully control my powers, I have to form bonds with all four of my mates.

But for a woman who's been betrayed by every person she's ever loved, trust doesn't come easy, no matter how much I'm coming to adore these incredible men.

Can I win this battle of the heart in time?

Or will the enemies closing in end our fight for the future before it even gets started?

UNTAMED is part two of the Dark Moon Shifters series, a red-hot reverse harem paranormal and urban fantasy romance. Expect pulse-pounding action, suspense, swoon-worthy romance, and four sexy shifter men who will make you wish you had a bear, wolf, lynx, and griffin of your own.

ABOUT THE AUTHOR

Bella Jacobs loves pulse-pounding action, fantasy, and supernaturally high stakes, mixed with swoon-worthy romance and unforgettable heroes. She's been a full time writer for over a decade and is deeply grateful for the chance to play pretend for a living.

She writes as Bella for her trips to the dark side and can't wait to take you on her next adventure.

Visit her at www.bellajacobsbooks.com

ALSO BY BELLA JACOBS

The Dark Moon Shifter Series

Unleashed

Untamed (Autumn 2018)

To be continued in early 2019…

BONUS CHAPTER

Please enjoy this bonus chapter
from NIGHT MAGIC by Bella's friends
L. Valente and S. King!

ABOUT THE BOOK

Mixing magic and street smarts, bounty hunter and P.I.
Aster Night always gets her man.

Except when it comes to...*literally* getting a man.

Thanks to a curse placed on the Chastity coven
centuries ago, she can't get busy with anyone until she
marries a man from the sanctimonious, boring, holier-
than-thou Koda coven.

Yeah, no thanks.

Instead, she finds a way out of the curse on her own, breaking it with such a bang that she ends up naked with one sexy as sin man and making some major emotional and physical connections with his two, oh-so-alpha clan brothers.

Her love life is looking up, until she's hired to track down a serial killer preying on witches, and learns her three new boyfriends were once romantically involved with one of the victims.

Now, she has to choose—her heart or her career.

Yes, Rake makes her laugh, Finn makes her knees weak, and Damon makes her feel safe in a way she never has before, but these men are too close to her case.

So close she's afraid one of them might become a killer's next victim…

This WHITE HOT reverse harem paranormal romance series is intended for readers 18 and over. This is a true reverse harem featuring one woman and her three fated mates.

CHAPTER ONE

Aster

"How bad you want to know?" Keller's voice was deep, radio DJ sexy and hoarse from too many late nights bouncing at The Bitch's Brew.

Despite being a scary looking motherfucker with borderline creepy tattoos, he had a killer smile, complete with a dimple, and baby blue eyes that had lured many a drunk college co-ed back to his double-wide trailer for fun of the horizontal variety.

Too bad his breath smelled worse than the monkey cage at the zoo or Aster might have enjoyed interrogating him.

"How bad? Real bad," she purred, tossing her long blond hair over her shoulder.

She placed a hand on the bricks behind Keller and leaned close enough for her breasts to brush against his arm. It was October in the Pacific Northwest and she wore only a black satin corset and a pair of skintight jeans. Her nipples were so hard Keller could probably feel them through his leather jacket.

"Real bad, huh?" the bouncer murmured, eyes glazed as his hand slid up her ribs, making a beeline for her chest.

Aster fought the urge to roll her eyes and faked an excited moan as Keller cupped her breast. She was

Chastity coven and Keller knew it—had known it since she started working the greater Savior City metropolitan area as a kid fresh out of high school.

Chastity didn't put out, *couldn't* even if they wanted to.

This entire seduction scene wasn't going to amount to anything but a major case of blue balls, but hope still glimmered in Keller's eyes. He was like every other man she'd ever worked for information with a little slap and tickle. They all thought they were going to be different, that they would be the man with a cock big and bad enough to break a centuries-old chastity spell.

Men.

They could be pains in the ass, but you had to admire their enduring, hard-on-inspired optimism.

"Keller, I don't know about you, but I'm ready to cut the crap." Aster arched into the hand working her breast, things low in her body tightening despite the stench of Keller's breath hot on her face. For the millionth time, she wondered if it was possible to die from sexual frustration. She didn't want to die at twenty-five. It'd be nice to at least make it to the ripe old age of thirty. "Let's get to the action."

"Baby, I'm ready for action anytime you are." Keller popped the top button on his jeans, preparing to release what looked to be an impressive package.

Keller was handsome *and* hung. If he'd break down and put up the cash for a halitosis spell, he'd be practically irresistible.

"You're amazing, honey, but I need that number before this goes any further," Aster said.

Even if it were possible for her to fuck him, she wouldn't get busy in The Bitch's Brew's back alley. The bar was one of the hottest entertainment venues in the city and tonight was an all-ages show. Getting caught *in flagrante delicto* by some fifteen-year-old kid with a contact high wasn't a turn-on, and the last thing her coven needed was another lawsuit.

"Business before pleasure, huh?"

"Always." Aster nipped his waist with her fingers, making him grin.

"He's staying in unit twenty-six. My old man rented it out to him last week."

Aster barely bit back a cheer. "Is he still there?"

"Should be. He paid a month's rent in cash."

A month, that was good. "What's he driving?"

"I don't know." Keller reached for her breast again.

"What's he driving, K?" Aster slapped his hand away and gave him her best glare. She was only five foot three, but growing up with two older brothers had taught her how to play tough and fight tougher.

Of course, being Chastity didn't hurt things either. People who got on the bad side of her gray-magic-practicing coven had a way of disappearing.

Forever.

Not such a good reputation to have when it came to dealing with human police, but great for encouraging a helpful attitude in almost everyone else. Chastity coven, a prim handle for a heartless group of witches—just went to show you shouldn't judge a book by its cover.

"It was a green Charger, spell-fueled 'cause there's no gas cap." Keller's hand slipped inside the top of her corset, his roughened fingers coming into direct contact with her tight nipple.

This time her moan was real. A bolt of electricity zapped between her legs, making her thighs tremble. Immediately her clit began to vibrate.

She was slick and aching in seconds, her breath coming faster and bright blue light flooding the alley as her magic gathered into a tight knot of power at her core. She wanted, she *burned*, lusting with all the pent-up frustration of years of denied satisfaction.

Before she knew what she was doing, her fingernails were clawing into Keller's strong shoulders as he spread her legs, hitching her up around his waist.

Her back hit the brick wall hard enough to bruise, but she hardly felt the impact. She was too busy grinding up and down the long, thick cock that Keller pressed against her. Even through their clothing she could feel the heat radiating from his arousal and was consumed with the need to get that heat pumping between her legs, shoving into her, filling every empty, aching inch.

"God, baby, you're so hot." Keller's lips were on her neck, his teeth dragging over her skin.

Aster shuddered.

"Keller, stop. We have to stop," she said, her voice a sexy whisper that did absolutely nothing to deter Keller from pulling at her corset until her breasts sprang free.

The cold night air hit her bare flesh, but it was Keller sucking her nipple into the heat of his mouth that made her gasp. The sensation was unlike anything she'd ever experienced.

A shockwave of desire stole her breath, making her womb hum and the force of her magic grow so thick and heavy she would have to cast soon or choke on the unreleased power. It was hard enough keeping magic in check the night of a full moon without the urgency thundering through her body making matters worse.

"I've wanted to do this since the first time you walked into the bar, Blondie," Keller said, his fingers tugging at the button on her jeans.

"Wait, no, you don't—"

Keller let out a sound halfway between a moan and a howl as his knees buckled. Aster, her legs still wrapped around his waist, went to the ground with him, hissing in pain as the bricks scratched her bare shoulders and did irreparable damage to the satin of her corset.

She cursed as her tailbone hit the pavement and a very heavy, very unconscious Keller slumped over her legs. He was out cold and likely to stay that way for the next five to ten hours, depending on how quickly his cells metabolized magic.

"Better than a chastity belt." Her cousin's voice drifted toward her from the shadows near the end of the alley.

Aster barely bit back a scream.

"Have you been there the whole time?" she asked, tugging up her corset while she glared in the general direction of Raven's voice.

Her little cousin was only nineteen years old, but she'd already mastered shadow-walking. Not even Gavyn, the head of their coven, could point her out in the darkness if she didn't want to be found.

"Not the whole time, but for all the good parts." Raven laughed as she emerged from the shadows, a naughty grin on her very wholesome-looking face. With strawberry blond hair and light blue eyes, Raven's looks were certainly not the reason her mother had chosen her name.

But who knew what her mother had been thinking? Aster couldn't remember much about Bridget.

Raven's mother had been Koda coven, and like most marriages between Chastity and Koda, her relationship with Raven's father hadn't lasted long. She'd abandoned her daughter when Raven was only three years old, heading back into the foothills of the Cascade mountain range, the brutal wilderness the "undefiled" coven called home.

Odd that such holier than thou witches would so regularly abandon their own children if they showed signs that their magic would develop Chastity rather than Koda. Even odder that the most powerful Chastity coven leader of the past two thousand years had cursed her people with an abstinence spell, which could only be broken after marriage to a Koda.

That ancient mage had probably thought she was doing something good for her coven, but that didn't stop Aster from hating her.

Fucking frigid witch.

"I think he gave you a hickey," Raven said with a snort. "Maybe two."

"Awesome." Aster turned her attention to Keller with a sigh, focusing on shoving the man off of her lap, avoiding looking Raven's way as a blush heated her cheeks.

Aster was six years older and had been working in the family bounty-hunting business since her cousin was a snot-nosed fifth grader with braces. She shouldn't let Raven get to her, but something about the girl had always given her the creeps. Finding out Ray was perverted enough to watch a relative getting felt up in an alley did nothing to ease the skin-crawling sensation her cousin inspired.

"Do you need help?"

"No thanks," Aster said, wiggling out from under Keller with a grunt.

"I meant with your shoulders." Raven's slim hand traced a figure eight through the air. "Those cuts look pretty nasty."

Aster closed her eyes and willed the knot of power within her into a healing spell, casting the energy out like a net that settled over her skin. The stinging scrapes on her back immediately vanished, as did the bruises on her tailbone. By the time she was finished, she didn't have so much as a hangnail.

Even her chapped lips felt smooth.

"Show off." Raven laughed as she skimmed her fingertips over the newly healed skin on Aster's shoulder, sending Aster's Skeeve Meter pinging off the charts.

Had the girl never heard of personal space?

"We all have our gifts," Aster stepped back until a good two or three feet separated her and Ms. Touchy-Feely. "Did you find out anything from the bartender?"

Raven sighed. "Not much. The perp hasn't been in here tonight or last night, but he left one of the cocktail waitresses a nice fat tip on Wednesday."

"What time on Wednesday?"

"I don't know," Raven said with a disinterested shrug.

"Did you ask?" Aster tried to keep the censure from her voice but failed.

What use was Raven ever going to be if she didn't try to learn from her mistakes? This was the third time this week she'd failed to ask the right questions. If Aster didn't know better, she would think her cousin didn't give a shit if they scored this bounty.

But the girl liked to eat as much as any Chastity, and there weren't any other jobs out there for members of their coven.

You either worked the family business or you became one of the many homeless witches who haunted the seedier streets of Savior City. Chastity looked human enough to pass, but sooner or later the telltale blue glow of a witch in power would start to shine at the wrong time. As soon as it did, that witch was out of a job, or an apartment.

Or a college class.

Aster had given up trying to earn her degree in criminology. The hassle of being kicked out of class after class as soon as the teacher realized that she was "one of them" wasn't worth the piece of paper. She'd learned everything she needed to know on the job, shadowing older coven members for the first few years as an apprentice.

Speaking of apprentices...

"Maybe you should follow Pierce around next week," Aster said. "I think he might be a better fit for you."

Raven's nose wrinkled. "I don't want to follow Pierce. He's an asshole."

"He's an asshole who knows how to get information. *All* the information," Aster said, tossing her waist-length hair over her shoulder where she hoped it would hide the damaged portion of her corset.

"Sorry to let you down." Raven didn't sound sorry at all, making Aster's teeth grind together.

"No big deal, I found out where the target's renting. I'll call the office and get a team out there to see if they can pick him up."

"Why don't we just head over there and do it ourselves?" Raven's eyes glittered. "I'm sure we can handle this guy. He's into identity theft, not murder, right? Let's nail his ass to the wall."

Aster stepped over Keller's prone body. "I have plans."

"Oh, hot date?" Raven laughed. It wasn't a pretty sound, though her twin dimples made her look like the poster child for wholesome, all-American good times.

"Keller's old man's trailer park is near the office. A team will be able to get there faster," Aster said, starting down the alley toward where she'd parked her car a few hours before.

Hopefully, it was still there. Even parking an old clunker like her Vesta in this part of the city was dangerous after dark. Despite the new mayor's promises to clean up the streets, automobile theft was at an all-time high, especially in witch-heavy neigh-borhoods.

"Hey, Aster," Raven called after her.

"What?"

"Didn't mean to piss you off."

"You didn't," Aster threw over her shoulder.

"I know what it's like you know," Raven said, her voice plaintive, vulnerable for once. "To *want* so bad."

Aster broke into a jog, her high-heeled boots clicking on the pavement, not bothering to validate her cousin's words with a response.

Give Raven six more years of "wanting" and maybe a month or two of the erotically torturous dreams that had made Aster dread sleep for the past year—then, *maybe*, they would talk.

Night Magic is available now!

Made in the USA
Middletown, DE
05 February 2019